ROAD RUNNER

MIKE BARON

WOLFPACK
PUBLISHING
— EST 2013 —

Published in the United States by Wolfpack Publishing, Las Vegas

Wolfpack Publishing
6032 Wheat Penny Avenue
Las Vegas, NV 89122

wolfpackpublishing.com

Paperback ISBN 978-1-64734-284-5
eBook ISBN 978-1-64734-283-8

ROAD RUNNER

CHAPTER 1

SCIPIO

At ten o'clock on a Friday night in early October, the TA Truck stop in DeForest gleamed—a hybrid of a gas station and a fast food joint. The red arch over the entrance read LODI TRAVEL CENTER, and a Starbucks and a Popeyes sat on the left. Karen Smallwood turned her nine-year-old Corolla off Highway 51 into the truck stop, where a dozen semis were lined up like sidelined railroad cars and the gasoline pumps were jumping with travelers.

Karen, who was seventeen and Ashley Calloway's best friend, had purple hair and pierced ears, but not the nose piercing she so desperately craved and her parents expressly forbade. Karen and Ashley both attended James Madison High on Madison's west side and were both due to graduate in the spring. They made an odd couple: Karen, petite and blond, and Ashley, tall, athletic, and black, her hair fixed in spring-like ringlets, wearing a black velvet jumpsuit with purple stripes and carrying a stuffed backpack.

Ashley threw her arms around Karen. "Thank you, I love you, you're my best friend. I'll call you."

"Are you sure?" Karen said, looking around.

"I have never been more sure in my life."

"But you've never met this guy!"

"I've been talking to him for six months. Face to face. I've probably talked more with him than I have with anyone else, ever, including you and my parents."

"Your father is going to go ballistic, you know that."

"Don't worry about my pops. I can handle him." "What if he's not here?"

"I'll call you in the morning and you can come get me."

"Are you sure you can take care of yourself?"

Ashley put up her hands in a kung fu pose. "I can kill with one blow! Don't worry about me. My dad's a cop. I know what to look for. I know all the signs. If Scipio were a psychopath, I would have known it by now."

"I wish somebody felt about me the way you feel about this guy."

"Oooh, somebody will! You're beautiful, smart, and funny. This is just something I have to do. I feel it in my bones."

Karen grimaced. She was going to catch holy hell when her role in Ashley's disappearance came out. She wondered how long before they zeroed in on her. She would not want Heinz Calloway as her father. Not that there was anything wrong with him. He was a great guy. But he was a cop. Imagine how hard that would be—having a cop as your father.

"Well, okay."

Ashley gave her one last squeeze. "Don't worry! I can take care of myself."

Then she was out of the car and into the truck stop. Karen took one last look around, put her car in reverse and headed back to the highway.

Wearing an overstuffed backpack and a leather bag around her shoulder, Ashley entered beneath the welcome sign and found herself in a great tiled room, off of which sprang the Starbucks, the Popeyes, a laundry room, showers and a convenience store selling everything from maps to condoms. Several dozen travelers milled about. Truckers sat in the laundry room poking at their phones. Families returning from vacation shepherded their young ones past the video arcade. Ashley ordered a meal from Popeyes and sat at a table by the big windows looking out on the parking lot wondering when he would arrive.

Online, Scipio was a movie star, handsome with high cheekbones, piercing blue eyes and black hair. His grandfather had been a Blackfoot shaman and had taught Scipio everything he knew. Ashley had learned about Scipio through a mutual Facebook friend, whom she had never met, but who had proclaimed Scipio the wisest man who ever lived and who had saved her from suicide.

A greaser with an untucked shirt and a duck's ass gave her the once-over.

"You looking for a ride, darlin'?"

"Just keep on moving, you Elvis-looking motherfucker. I'm not looking for anything you have."

The greaser put up his hands and smiled.

She checked her phone. Brent Forrester had texted her wanting to know where she was. She liked Brent, had dated him off and on through the school year, but Brent was just a boy. He didn't understand her the way Scipio did. She was afraid to check Facebook because her friends would see that she was online and try to contact her. Scipio insisted that she go dark on social media until they were at least out of the state.

She couldn't tweet, she couldn't Facebook, she couldn't Instagram, what was she supposed to do? Where was Scipio? She looked around. It was ten-thirty. He said he'd be there by ten. What if the whole thing was a prank?

No. It couldn't be. They'd spoken too often. They'd spoken to each other's hearts. Scipio sensed her frustration and yearning and promised her the life she craved, a life of adventure, the heart and the mind. Oh, this was maddening. Was it all an elaborate practical joke? Was there someone close by surreptitiously filming her discomfort? She looked around again.

When she turned back, a man stood at her table with his fingers splayed on the Formica.

"Hello, Ashley," he said in a low, seductive voice. She looked up.

He was smaller than she anticipated, wearing a fedora and sunglasses, but the high cheekbones were unmistakable. She looked up in wonder as he took off the shades and winked at her, igniting every synapse in her system. His teeth were perfect. He wore creased gray dockers and a white dress shirt beneath a navy blue jacket of rough cotton. He prodded the backpack at her feet with his toe.

"Is this all your stuff?"

"Yes."

He picked it up and slung it over his shoulder, held out his hand. "Let's go."

As if in a dream, she took his hand and followed him through the truck stop out the opposite entrance, into a parking lot half-filled with plain Jane sedans. He fingered something in his pocket and a shiny black Mercedes blipped and winked. He opened the trunk and put in her backpack. She still held the leather bag holding her phone and notepad looped over her shoulder.

He held the door for her. The interior smelled of leather and mahogany. He slid in beside her, smelling of sandalwood, and started the engine. He took off the hat and sunglasses, revealing a handsome face, black hair brushed straight back.

"You will never regret this decision," he said, putting the car in gear and heading out of the parking lot. "Your real life, the life that matters, begins here with me now."

"Where are we going?" she said breathlessly.

"Everywhere."

CHAPTER

2

GOOD GIRL

Ray McRaney clung to Josh on the sofa in the waiting room of the Veterinary Hospital on the UW Campus. It was nine pm. They'd brought Fig in the backseat of Josh's car, leaving the EMTs to deal with Josh's father, Duane. Screaming squad cars passed them going the other way.

Josh had bludgeoned Duane with Duane's pistol. Josh didn't care if Duane lived or died. All he cared about was Fig. Josh found Duane in Josh's garage trying to revive his piece of shit Camaro. After Josh told his father repeatedly that he never wanted to see him again, they got in a scuffle and Fig got shot. Josh took the gun and hammered his father's head.

Josh didn't think about Duane. He thought about Fig. He began to hyperventilate. Ray put her arms around him.

"Deep breaths, baby. Deep breaths."

He forced himself to do the four-count. Inhale for the

four-count. Hold for the four-count. Exhale for the four-count. Hold for the four-count.

Breath was the flywheel of life.

After what seemed like an eternity, a young man emerged from the back room dressed in hospital greens, a green paper cap, snapping off elastic gloves. His features were fine – porcelain skin and a hint of a five-o'clock shadow. Exuding confidence, he came to where Josh and Ray sat.

"It was just a graze. Cracked a rib. If you can convince her to take it easy for a couple weeks, she'll be good as new."

Ray squeezed Josh until his own ribs screamed, from when the running back Ryan Gehrke landed on him like a sack of rocks.

"Thank you, Lord!" Josh whooped, standing. He pumped the doctor's hand.

"What's your name, doc?"

"David Epstein."

"Doc, you're a fuckin' genius!"

Epstein smiled. "She's a sweet dog. She'll be fine. I'd like to keep her here overnight. We have her sedated and bandaged. She should be good to go in the morning."

"Can I see her?"

"You bet."

Four police entered the waiting room, two in MPD blue and two UWPD in darker blue. One of the MPD officers, a muscular woman named Slemons, walked up to Josh.

"Mr. Pratt, you know better than to leave a crime scene."

"I'm sorry, officer. I was concerned about my dog."

"How is the dog?"

"She'll be fine."

"Glad to hear it. We would like you to accompany us downtown for an interview. We'll bring you back so you can pick up your car. Or perhaps the young lady can drive it."

A line appeared at the corner of Ray's mouth. The unibrow that swooped above her eyes crinkled.

"Can't we do it here?"

Slemons' partner Martinez, a short man who looked like a ballet dancer, tapped her on the shoulder. They stepped away to confer. She glanced back at Josh. Martinez made points in his palm. She returned.

"All right."

Epstein left when he saw the cops. Slemons went to the desk where a middle-aged woman with cascading hair sat at a computer.

"Ma'am, do you have an empty conference room we could use?"

"Yes, there's a lounge just down the hall. Let me unlock it for you."

The woman came out from behind the counter with a key. The UW police were there as a courtesy. This had nothing to do with them.

Slemons motioned for Ray to stay seated. "Please remain here, ma'am."

Ray looked away and snorted.

Slemons, Josh and Martinez followed the clerk's staccato heels down a tile corridor lined with photographs of the original veterinary school, a two-story brick building framed by haunting oaks, black and white pictures of distinguished faculty changing to color in 1954, and photographs from the present hospital's construction. The clerk unlocked a mid-sized conference room with an oak table surrounded by eight chairs. There were no windows. A chalkboard hung on one side of the room, a flat screen on the other. At one end was an abstract painting that looked like cotton candy swirls. Slemons thanked the clerk and shut the door. She and Martinez sat on one side, Josh on the other.

"What happened?"

"My father broke into my garage to pick up his piece of shit Camaro. He pulled a gun on me. I was gonna turn him in for setting that fire in Creighton that killed the Gehrkes. We struggled over the gun and he shot my dog."

"Was it his Camaro?"

"No deed, no license registration, no insurance."

"You say he set fire to the Gehrke residence."

"I said it."

"What makes you think so?"

"My father worships at the Church of Payback. In fact, he's the grand wazoo. You think Arabs hold a grudge?"

"What was his beef with the Gehrkes?"

"It's a long story. He used to be Ryan Gehrke's coke dealer. Gehrke stiffed him, so my old man stole a painting. Only it wasn't just a painting. It was a historical artifact."

Josh made quote signs with his fingers.

"It's gonna be everywhere, trust me. Katy Varner's already phoned me three times."

Martinez stifled a smile.

"I only found out when he showed up. I have no desire to see him. Whatsoever."

"How did he sustain those injuries?"

"I hammered him with his gun. He'd just shot my dog. I think he's responsible for the deaths of a family of four in Rockford, August 19, too. At a motel. They died from carbon monoxide poisoning. Hang on."

Josh pulled out his smartphone and found the story in the *Rockford Courier*. He showed it to Slemons. She read it and handed it back.

"Would you email this to me please?"

"You bet. I found a hose and duct tape in his car. It's at my place."

"Had you been in touch with your father previously?"

"No. He abandoned me when I was fifteen. I hadn't heard from him until ten days ago when I came home and there he was. He broke into my house. He came in through the doggie door."

Josh brought them up to speed about Gehrke, the slab, Vegas.

"Can you tell us where to find the hose and duct tape?" Slemons said in a mannish voice.

"It's in my garage."

Fuck me, Josh thought. *What if they open my gun safe?*

"Where's Duane now?" he said.

"He's at University Hospital. You hurt him pretty bad."

"He shot my dog."

"Mr. Pratt isn't going anywhere. We're going to let you go now, but we'd like you to come down to the station later this week, when you have a chance, and answer a few questions."

Josh stood. "Thank you."

Martinez held the door for him. Josh returned to the waiting room. Ray sprang up like a ballerina. He hugged her.

"It's okay."

She hugged him back. "Okay. Listen. That pig, she just rubs me the wrong way."

"Huh?"

"The female officer who referred to me as a 'young lady,'" Ray said in a mannish voice.

"What's she supposed to call you?"

"A woman."

"Forget it. She's only trying to do her job."

"I can't help it. I'm just used to thinking of them as pigs."

"Yeah, okay. Listen. I have to see Fig and then we'll go."

"Of course."

He asked the clerk if he could see his dog. She motioned him and Ray down a corridor into a brightly lit room where Fig lay on her side, midriff shaved and bandaged, on a pet bed about a foot off the ground, tail thumping. Josh got down and put his arms around her.

"Who's a good girl? Who's a good girl?"

CHAPTER

3

BAD NEWS

Redd Kross' "Faith Healer" woke Josh from a sound sleep as Ray McRaney stirred next to him, reaching for her phone. She stood naked, a blue and gold butterfly on her ass, grabbed a terry cloth robe and walked out of the room.

"What's up, Kayla?" was the last thing she said before she shut the door.

Josh lay on his back, staring at the ceiling. Ray was pretty damn near perfect. She'd been there for him throughout the ordeal, but her attitude toward authority figures was disturbing. She was the only child of humanities professors, a red diaper baby. Her parents began taking her to demonstrations at age two. She showed him a picture of eight-year-old Ray holding an IMPEACH W sign.

Fig usually woke him by licking his face. Fig knew her rights. She was entitled to a meal every morning and then a run.

Josh sat up, stood, stretched, took a shower. When he came out, the bedroom door was still closed. He could hear Ray talking intensely from the living room. Josh put on sweatpants and socks, Adidas running shoes, and a Packers sweatshirt. Fall was in the air. The Packers had won their first game, against the Giants. It was getting nippy.

As he passed through the living room, Ray was still on the phone. She held up a finger, indicating she wanted him to wait.

"I know," she said. "It's awful. Maybe he can help. I'll ask him. I'll call you back."

She stood. "Wait a minute." She went into the bedroom and came out wearing blue jeans and one of Josh's T-shirts, set the phone on the coffee table, which held a Grateful Dead engine cover, the skull with the lightning bolt. A framed photo of a bikini babe draped across a chopper hung over the fireplace mantle, on which sat a Harley piston, some rocks, a drive chain and a copy of *Zen and the Art of Motorcycle Maintenance*.

"What?"

"You know my friend Kayla?"

"Yeah."

"She's been dating this creep and now he's taken her car. It's a classic 1968 Firebird her father left her. It's her only form of transportation."

"Why doesn't she call the cops?"

"She's afraid. Warren threatened to kill her cats. She's also got a couple of warrants out, for a DUI and passing bad checks."

Josh sighed. Kayla was one of Ray's projects, someone she'd met at her dance studio.

"What do you want me to do about it?"

"Would you talk to her, see what you can do?"

"All right."

Ray rose from the sofa and pasted herself to Josh, arms around his neck. "Thank you, oh mighty hunter. Thank you! I have to go but I'll see you tonight."

Josh kissed her. "Counting on it."

He left through the front door of his pale yellow ranch house, the cheapest house on Ptarmigan Road on Madison's far southwest side. Josh had bought the house years ago with money from an accident settlement. An old lady in a Buick ran a red light and struck him on his motorcycle. At the time, his was the only house on the road, but since then, splendid estates had sprung from the soil on all sides. A homeowners' association, including everyone but him, had built a clubhouse with tennis courts and a pool. The White Oaks Homeowners' Association had been trying to buy him out for years, but Josh hung on. He was there first.

He ran toward the city beneath a bower of oak, elm, and sycamore, hints of orange and yellow creeping in. Fall was in flower. Josh had met Kayla at Rise Up, Ray's studio on East Wilson Street, a converted warehouse with an Abdul Mati Klarwein mural of dancers covering the front.

Josh ran against traffic, waving to neighbors and service vans going the other way. Priscilla Bass passed him heading toward town in her Boxster, waving out the window.

"Hi, Josh!"

"Hi, Priscilla!"

Priscilla's husband, Phil, had founded the White Oaks Homeowners' Association. Phil had been trying to buy Josh out for years. Phil's offer was up to seven hundred and fifty thousand. Josh wasn't selling. He liked his neighbors, particularly the Lowrys, who lived across the street and had been the first to welcome Josh into their home. That's where he'd met Ray.

He'd met the Lowrys six months after they had moved in, when their twin schnauzers disappeared. Dave Lowry showed up on his stoop one night, a balding, middle-aged university administrator wearing a Badgers T-shirt and baggy shorts.

"Can I talk to you a minute?"

Lowry's two schnauzers, George and Gracie, had disappeared.

"Why me?"

"I heard you were someone who got things done."

"Where'd you hear that?"

"Daniel Bloom."

The lawyer who had secured Josh's pardon.

Josh suspected the dogs might have been picked up by a dogfighting ring. He was right. It was harrowing. Once Josh returned the dogs, the Lowrys couldn't do enough for him. Louise had been trying to fix him up for years. Ray was the first one that took.

Josh stopped to pick up somebody's doggie doo bag, neatly tied and left by the side of the road, and dropped it in a trash bin at the spanking new Stop'N'Go, on what had been farmland. The city was spreading.

He got home, showered, nuked a breakfast burrito in the microwave and went into his two-car garage. His ten-year-old Chrysler occupied one bay, four motorcycles the other. The cops had towed Duane's Camaro.

Duane was still in the hospital.

Josh was rebuilding an S&S 124 with a welded and trued crank, adjustable pushrods, 585 cams, and forged pistons. He didn't have a chassis yet, just the engine.

Josh hadn't held a regular job since NSA agent Roland Stoeckle had put him on the payroll. Once a month, a Bahamian bank deposited twelve thousand dollars into his checking account.

As Josh picked up a piston, his phone buzzed. Caller unknown. He swiped it open.

"Pratt."

"Roland Stoeckle. I have bad news."

"What is it?"

"I've been fired. You're off the payroll."

"What the fuck? What happened?"

"It's not a total surprise. Kaplan resigned last week and we've been waiting for the other shoe to drop. He had some beef with the President, who requested his resignation. Helen Ward's the Acting Deputy Director, and she's bringing in her own people. It's all politics, it's all bullshit, and there's nothing I can do about it."

Josh did a quick calculation. He was all right. His needs were simple. He had plenty in the bank. He could always sell out to Phil Bass when the offer reached a million. He'd just move farther out in the country and wait for the town to catch up to him.

"What are you going to do?"

"I'm joining Blackwater as a security analyst. There's a possibility of you working for us as a private contractor, if you're interested."

"Not really, but thanks for the offer."

"I just wanted you to hear it from me directly."

"I appreciate that, Roland."

"Your last check goes out next week. I told those fools that you were too valuable an asset to let slide, but they wouldn't listen. I wish them well. When I get a secure phone set up, I'll let you know."

"Thanks, Roland."

"Who knows, we might work together again one of these days."

Josh phoned David Epstein at UW Veterinary Hospital and left a message. Fifteen minutes later Epstein phoned back.

"You can pick her up. I'm including some Tramadol, a sedative and antibiotics. Make sure she takes it easy for at least two weeks. No running."

"Thanks, doc. I'm on my way."

CHAPTER 4

KAYLA

Tail wagging, Fig allowed herself to be carried into the house. She weighed seventy-two pounds.

Josh set her up with a doggie bed and water bowl on the back deck, two steps up from the lawn, and watched while she delicately negotiated the climb, squatted, tinkled, and climbed back up.

Ray phoned at two. "I'm bringing Kayla over at six. I'll bring dinner too."

"What are you bringing?"

"Never mind, buster. You'll eat it and you'll like it."

Josh got out his twenty-gallon Craftsman shop vacuum and did the living room carpet on his butt, working the narrow slot nozzle over every inch of the ugly beige carpet, which he should have replaced years ago. The Craftsman was the only way to deal with Fig's shedding. He pushed the sofa away from the wall and found three roaches, two of them smokable, and a pen. He did the dishes that had been sitting in his sink since Monday, putting them into his dishwasher and shutting the door, swept the kitchen with a broom, and went to work on the living and dining room windows with a roll of paper towels and some glass cleaner.

Having grown up in a gang, Josh didn't subscribe to *House Beautiful*. He got most of his clothes at Walmart or at thrift stores and owned one suit, which he'd purchased at the Men's Wearhouse for Charlotte Newton's funeral. Fig dozed contentedly in the afternoon light.

He rode to Woodman's and bought two bottles of Merlot, salad fixings, and a container of pesto. He'd learned to make his own salad dressing from Charlotte, his first serious girlfriend, serious as in thinking of getting married, serious as in my one true love, murdered by a spook called the Jesuit.

Charlotte called herself Fig. Josh named his dog after her.

He got home, took the groceries into the kitchen and put together a salad, using the lettuce spinner Ray had given him. Prior to that, he had courted death by eating his lettuce unwashed, straight from the supermarket.

He grabbed an apple from a bowl on the counter and ate it. He didn't wash it.

He turned on the little countertop flat screen, and there was Katy Varner, head reporter for WMAD TV, standing outside City Hall, a Soviet-style block on Martin Luther King Boulevard.

"Mayor Saul Brogden's new city budget contains no funds for additional police officers, despite Chief Emory's request. This comes a day after former police Chief Emmett Davis told WMAD that the city's lack of priority for public safety matters caused him to retire.

"When asked by WMAD about his decision, Chief Davis had this to say."

Cut to photogenic Katy standing one step below Chief Davis on the city hall steps. Chief Davis was a middle-aged black man wearing horn-rimmed glasses, a fringe of white hair encircling his artillery shell head.

"Frankly, we're getting ready to go through another budgetary process where I am completely frustrated in terms of what I believe are important priorities for this department that probably won't be met."

Josh mixed equal parts olive oil and balsamic vinegar in a plastic container, added a tablespoon of pesto, shook, and poured it over the salad, which he tossed with mismatched silverware and placed in the refrigerator.

A commercial for American Appliance promised a free bicycle with every purchase. Fig stumbled in through the doggie door and barked at the door. Josh turned off the television and opened the door to Ray, carrying a covered roasting pan, followed by Kayla, a wan twenty-something with ragged, dishwater hair, a tatted sleeve, and too much make-up, carrying a grocery bag.

Ray paused for a peck. "This is Kayla."

They shook hands.

"Thank you for seeing me," Kayla said, near tears, with the concave posture of a mistreated animal. She took one look at Fig, fell to her knees and wrapped her arms around the big dog's neck.

"Careful! She's recovering from surgery."

Kayla unwrapped. "I'm sorry."

"Lift her up on the sofa by her butt."

Ray went into the kitchen and set down the pan.

"Would you like some wine?" Josh said.

Ray pulled three glasses from the cupboard. "I think so."

Josh put his hand over the third glass. "I'm having beer."

Ray put her hands on her hips. "I might have known."

The pan emitted an enticing aroma. Josh lifted the lid and revealed a roast surrounded by potatoes, carrots, and onions. "Wow."

"I hope you like camel."

They went into the living room. Ray and Kayla sat on the sofa with Fig between them, getting petted on both sides. Josh sat in a chair facing them.

"Ray says your ex took your car."

"I need that car to get to work."

"Where do you work?"

"Merry Maids."

Josh had seen their cheap little sedans along Ptarmigan Road. He was the only homeowner who didn't use a cleaning service. They paid minimum wage, nine twenty-five an hour. A person couldn't survive on that.

"Where do you live?"

"The Shangri-La."

The Shangri-La was a three-story complex on the South

Beltline, inhabited mostly by blue-collar types, the desperate and penurious, drug dealers, those on the first rung on the ladder of success or on the last rung before homelessness. It had once been a hot market for singles, forty years ago, with a club, a tennis court, and a swimming pool. But the club was shuttered, the tennis court was a maze of heaves and cracks, and the pool hadn't been filled in years.

"Tell me about the ex."

"Perry's a disc jockey. I met him at the High Noon Saloon when I was waitressing. He seemed like a nice guy so we started dating. Turns out he was a coke dealer. I ain't gonna lie, I like a little bump now and then. He lost his gig at Club Pravda and moved in with me. He had a car at the time, but he lost it."

She paused to empty her glass, revealing a white throat marred by a couple of thumb-shaped bruises.

"Y'know, you never think your boyfriend is gonna start hitting you until he does. First time it happened, he swore it would never happen again. He begged me on his knees to take him back."

"Tell me about it."

"He got an eight ball and we hadn't slept in, like, two days. We'd been out at the clubs and when we got back, he ordered me to make him a bacon sandwich and I was, like, dude, you're not gonna eat it, you need to rest. He backhanded me so hard I fell down. I couldn't believe it."

"Why didn't you call the police?"

"Well duh, we had a pile of coke on the dining room

table."

Josh nodded. "So you took him back."

"Yeah. But then he started dealing coke to make money. We argued about that and he started slapping me around. One night his car died. It was some old piece of shit Chevy. He just took the license plate and left it in the parking lot at East Towne."

"They can trace it to him with the vehicle identification number."

"I thought of that, but they never did. I think maybe it was stolen."

"He raped her," Ray said.

Kayla stared into her glass. "That's not true."

"Well, what would you call it?"

Josh was losing his appetite. "What do you want me to do?"

"I just want my car back. I don't want any trouble."

"Do you want this guy to stop bothering you?"

"Well, yeah."

"Okay. What's his name and where can I find him?"

PERRY

Perry Lee had moved back in with his mother. The small, ranch-style house on Ferris Avenue in Monona had been part of the great post-World War II expansion, a planned community of one-story, one-bathroom homes for the blue collars who worked at Oscar Mayer, John Deere, and Gisholt Machine. Kayla's gleaming black and gold Firebird sat on the cracked concrete driveway in front of a one-car garage, next to a spotty front lawn overrun with crabgrass.

Leaving Kayla at Josh's house, Ray had driven Josh in her Prius, stopping a half block down. It was nine o'clock, and a half-moon was peeking through the trees. It was a clear cool night.

"Go on back to my place. I'll be along shortly."

"What if he gives you shit?" Ray said.

"What are you going to do? Go on back to my place. There will be no problem."

She looked at him dubiously, slowly blinking her brown eyes. Josh got out and carefully shut the door.

"Go on."

The Prius rolled silently away. Josh hung for a minute, shouldering a small backpack. Street lights cast a pale glow. There was no traffic, and most of the houses gleamed from within, residents settled in before their computers, phones, or flat screens, texting, playing, watching *The Masked Singer*. A dog barked down the street. Two more dogs joined in. They had a heated discussion. Planes flew overhead on their way to Milwaukee or Chicago. A couple of kids did board stunts up the block.

Manufacturing had thrown in the towel long ago. Now the game was government, university, and insurance. Epic, the medical software company, had built its own city in Verona and bused their young workforce into Madison.

In addition to a nine-hole golf course, a medical clinic, four restaurants and an Olympic swimming pool, the Moss campus contained a human-sized rabbit hole and an elevator to hell. It had its own nightclub. You never had to leave Moss, unless they fired you because you were burned out from the twelve-hour days.

The people who lived on Ferris Avenue flew their flags on Veterans Day, kept their lawns neat, went to church, and paid their taxes. They seldom went into downtown Madison, which they regarded as Sodom. They felt left behind.

Josh walked up to the Firebird and tried the driver's door. Locked. Kayla had epoxied a plastic gnome to the dash. He whipped a steel strip from the backpack and inserted it into the window frame just as the front door opened and Perry emerged in a muscle shirt, showing tatted sleeves. His skull was shaved and his waxed mustache pointed to the stars. Veins were popping from pumping iron, or 'roids.

"What the fuck?" he exclaimed, hot stepping toward the driveway.

Josh tossed his backpack to the ground and held his hands up in a placating manner.

"Hi, Perry!"

Perry came around the front of the car and confronted him, fists clenched, from six feet. "Who the fuck are you?"

"I'm Josh. Kayla asked me to get her car back."

"It's my car now, bitch."

"Can you show me the registration or bill of sale?"

"I don't got to show you shit. Get the fuck out of here before I kick your ass."

Josh turned as if to go and juked forward, kicking Perry's left calf with the point of his steel-toed right boot. With a howl, Perry fell to the concrete, clutching his leg.

"You motherfucker! You broke my leg!"

Josh shoved Perry's head back and dropped down, planting his knee on Perry's sternum. Perry collapsed like a deflated balloon. Josh rifled through his pockets, pulling out a cell phone, a gravity knife, a wallet, and the Firebird's keys attached to a vintage Firebird fob.

No one was watching. Crouching, Josh opened the wallet. Perry had three credit cards, all with different names. Twelve dollars in cash. Josh stuck the phone and gravity knife in his backpack.

"Are we gonna leave Kayla alone?"

Perry looked up, and for the first time, Josh saw a hint of fear. "Yeah, yeah. Who the fuck are you, man?"

"I'm Josh. I'm just going to hang onto this phone."

"Come on, man! I need that phone for my work!"

"The fuck you do. Come see me in a year. Maybe I'll give it back."

Josh used the key to unlock the door and slide in, kicking Perry away from the vehicle with the heel of his boot. He reached into the glove compartment and removed a manila envelope that contained the registration. Kayla Bissel, 4331 South Beltline Frontage Road, #214. It also contained an insurance card from Allstate that was four months out of date.

In his rearview, the lights went off in the house across the street. Josh started the car, backed out, and headed west toward Monona Drive, where he pulled into the parking lot of a KFC. He parked in a far corner of the lot and went through the glove compartment more methodically, finding three unpaid parking tickets, obsolete coupons for Vietnamese takeout, and a Dells Ho-Chunk Casino brochure highlighting their artificial dells, lavish accommodations, and world-class gaming.

He felt between the seat cushions and found seventy-five cents. He opened the trunk, which contained a faux leather shaving kit. Inside the kit was an ounce of primo blow, which he tasted on the tip of his finger. The rest of the trunk yielded nothing.

Josh went into the KFC men's room and flushed the blow. He got in the Firebird and drove clockwise around the lakes heading for his home on the far southwest side. He glanced left as he drove by the Shangri-La at sixty miles an hour, pulling off on South Gammon. In four miles he turned onto Ptarmigan Road. The new Stop'N'Go gleamed like an alien installation.

Josh drove with the windows open, elbow out the window. "East Bound and Down" bounced around in his skull. He checked the sound system. AM/FM with an eight-track. Lights gleamed from five-thousand-square-foot homes through the trees. Josh approached his house. He couldn't pull the Firebird into his driveway because Ray's Prius was parked there next to ann unmarked brown police car.

Josh parked on the street and was headed up the walk when Detective Heinz Calloway stepped out of the chocolate Taurus.

Calloway looked at the Firebird. "I ain't gonna ask."

"What's up, officer?"

"I need your help. Ashley has gone missing."

CHAPTER 6

MISSING PERSON

Ashley was Calloway's sixteen-year-old daughter, an honor student at West, already accepted at several universities, including Wisconsin and Yale.

"They told me you'd be back soon. I didn't want to impose so I waited in my car."

"Never an imposition, officer. Come on in."

"I'd rather not. Why don't you have a seat."

Josh slid in on the passenger side. A car freshener shaped like a pine tree hung from the rearview. "What's going on?"

"You know that she was infatuated with this online guru named Scipio, and we're afraid she's run away with him."

Heinz and Doreen had been concerned about Ashley's infatuation. She also wanted a motorcycle.

"How long has she been missing?"

"Three days."

"You notified the department?"

"We put out a nationwide alert and put in a request to the NSA to use face recognition software."

"I'll help you any way I can, but I don't know what I can do that a hundred thousand law enforcement officers can't."

"I reported her as a missing person yesterday, but this comes at the worst possible time. The department's under-staffed and I'm working too many cases. You have connections. Maybe you can use them to jump the waiting line on this face recognition bullshit."

"Okay, what about her laptop and her phone? That's where the pictures are."

"She took them both. I don't have the juice to do a real search, not unless there's evidence of a felony, and I pray to God there won't be."

The front door opened and Kayla rushed out of the house toward her car.

"You did it! You did it!"

Ray appeared in the doorway behind her holding Fig's collar. Fig grinned and wagged her tail.

Josh opened the door. "Give me a minute, Heinz."

He got out and pointed at Fig. "Stay."

He handed Kayla the keys. She hugged him. "Thank you! Thank you!"

"Can you stay with Ray tonight? I think Perry got the message but you never know. Come on back to the house."

They went inside.

"What's the cop want?" Ray said.

"It's a personal matter. Can Kayla stay with you tonight?"

"I guess," Ray said, clearly disappointed. Josh was disappointed too.

"What happened?"

"At first, Perry didn't want to give it up, but I managed to persuade him using Socratic dialogue."

Ray pursed her lips and looked around. She glared at Calloway. She was about to say something but didn't. Josh took her in his arms.

"I'll make it up to you."

"My show debuts on Friday. You'd better be there."

"I'll be there." The Madison Dance Company was producing *Kiss Me Kate*, and Ray was playing Lois. One night she made Josh watch the movie, and it had left him slack-jawed with admiration. He'd always thought musicals were for fags.

Ray and Kayla left in separate vehicles. Calloway sat in the living room, the only illumination coming from a table lamp. His left eye stared at the ceiling like a searchlight.

"Would you like a drink?"

"Yeah."

Josh poured a couple fingers of Glenmorangie into two glass tumblers, handed one to Calloway, and sat in the Barcalounger.

"We knew something was up when she never returned Friday night. Her friend Karen Smallwood gave her a ride to the DeForest truck stop. We got the videos and they show her leaving with some guy. Unfortunately, the parking lot video wasn't working and we didn't see the vehicle."

"Do you have those videos?"

"They're in your mailbox."

"Why didn't you phone?"

Calloway turned a palm up, forehead crinkling. "It's not something I care to discuss over the phone. I'm sorry. I'm a little distraught."

"All right. Did you talk to her friends? Who else knew about this?"

"We spoke with Karen, Brent Forrester, and Sharlene Young. Karen's parents took her car and cell phone away, but that's not going to bring Ashley back."

"I would suggest they give Karen her cell phone back, in case Ashley tries to contact her."

Calloway put a hand to his head. "Of course."

"Are the police trying to track her phone?"

"Once again, I have put in a request."

"Okay. I know a guy who can do that. What's her number?" Calloway took out a pen and wrote the number on a tablet on the table. "I don't know what else I can do."

"Did anybody interview people from the truck stop?"

"Right now it's not a police investigation, and like I said, we don't have any officers to spare. That's why I came to you. Everyone is under the gun. Everyone. Even me. We're under intense pressure from the chief to close cases to justify our existence. Over half the city council wants to disband the police, or forbid us from carrying weapons."

"Are they insane?"

"Yes. Madison's always been this way, but never this

bad. Every time officers respond to a call, some university professor shows up to heckle them."

Josh pulled out his phone and dialed Ashley's number.

"Hi! This is Ashley. You have phoned me. Tell me why."

"Ashley, it's Josh Pratt. Your family is having a meltdown over your disappearance. Call someone and let them know you're all right, why don't ya?"

Calloway grimaced.

"It's worth a shot. At least it's still activated. Let me see what I can do. Why don't you go home? There's nothing you can do here and Doreen must be worried sick."

"I know you don't work for free."

"Heinz, you're family. This takes top priority with me. I might want to talk to those kids you mentioned. Would that be a problem?"

"I'll speak to their parents. What are you going to do now?"

"I'm going to contact my IT guy and see if he can get a grip on her phone."

"I won't ask."

"He won't answer."

Calloway wearily got to his feet. Josh met him at the door and hugged him. "I'll find her. It's what I do."

"Thanks. Thanks, man. I knew I could count on you."

Josh watched Calloway get in his unmarked car that screamed police, back out of the driveway, and head back into town.

CHAPTER 7

WAFFLES

Josh phoned Ninja Preston, whom he'd met through Randall Kleiser. Kleiser had been Josh's first IT guy, but when Kleiser went off-grid, he hooked Josh up with Ninja.

"I'm sorry, this number is not in service at this time," said a patently phony voice.

A minute later, Ninja called him back from another number.

"What up, what up, what up?"

"You want to Skype?"

"Give me five."

Five minutes later they were face to face. Ninja was a slim black man with a fadehaircut, sparse mustache and tinted rectangular glasses, sitting in what looked like a sound studio with dark paneling, muted lighting, and a lone microphone standing behind him.

"What up?"

"Missing seventeen-year-old honor student Ashley Calloway. She disappeared Friday night when a friend dropped her off at a truck stop. She went to meet some guru she found online, name of Scipio. Her old man's one of my best friends. Need to find her ASAP, by whatever means necessary. Want you to track the phone, and dip into the NSA's facial recognition software to track her down."

"You don't want much, do you?"

"Cost is no object."

"Send me all her shit."

"You still in St. Louis?"

Ninja revealed a gold tooth with a sapphire. "I am at an undisclosed location. St. Louis became too bourgeoisie for me. I mean, can you imagine?"

"Okay. Sending you everything I got."

Ninja saluted. "Later."

Josh went through his emails from Calloway, including numerous pictures of Ashley. Stunning in a sapphire evening gown at her senior prom, with a lanky white boy. Brent Forrester. Ashley ahead by a foot in her James Madison tracksuit, flying above the ground, arms and legs pumping, about to cross the finish line. Ashley posing with a friend's dog. Her high school yearbook picture, confident and demure with a Josephine Baker bob.

Josh had only met Ninja online. Ninja sometimes posted raps to YouTube, but the last one was over a year old. Josh had tried using NSA resources to get a handle on the elusive hacker, but Ninja was too good. The NSA didn't hack him.

He hacked the NSA.

One of Calloway's emails said that Ashley had become infatuated with a faith group called God's Breath. A quick search produced an enigmatic home page showing an idyllic mountain meadow filled with wildflowers, and snow-capped peaks reflected in a mirror-like lake.

God's Breath is an ethereal and talismanic religious order dedicated to protecting our God-given habitat, promoting natural potential, and spreading peace, by any means necessary.

God's Breath has synthesized and extracted essential wisdom from all the great religions, and presents them in a metaphysical and transcendental form designed to promote our best selves. To learn more or make a donation, please contact us at godsbreath@godsbreath.org.

Josh forwarded the information to Ninja, who wrote back, "Check out my latest," with a link to a YouTube video. Broad daylight, an empty swimming pool, three stuntas swooping rim to rim on custom boards to a sinuous beat segued into Ninja rolling at the viewer, snapping and rapping.

"Pullin' like a platypus, playin' with my abacus, like that Roman Atticus, talkin' Greek to Oedipus, putting up an edifice, to house a homeless octopus.

"Rollin' like an ocelot, you know I know an awful lot, careful you don't lose the plot. My clothes are shiny, like Kim K's heinie. Ain't got no greasy spots, the kind you get from tater tots.

"Just confessin' while I'm stuntin', I'm Ninja Preston, always huntin'."

Josh guessed Ninja had used a drone and composed the music himself on a synthesizer. Ninja had his own YouTube channel featuring a dozen different raps. Josh admired the wordplay but he was more of a blues guy.

A search of God's Breath produced their website, articles denouncing them as a cult, articles about their struggle to obtain a religious exemption from Internal Revenue, and a website devoted to supporting those who had left, Godsbreathsurvivors.org.

Like other cults, God's Breath is relentless in harassing and pursuing apostates. They have an army of online trolls who will target any individual who dares to criticize the cult, and will employ multiple weapons, including ghost Facebook accounts, doxxing, and even swatting. Swatting is when someone falsely informs the police of a dangerous situation with the desired result that the police will send a SWAT squad to that person's residence. Swatting has resulted in numerous innocent deaths over the years, including that of Robert Terrence, a thirty-four-year-old God's Breath devotee who split from the Church when they tried to force his son William to work as a male escort. Robert Terrence is not his real name. Robert was forced to change his identity and relocate to escape the Church's wrath. They found him anyway.

Here is William Terrence's own testimony: I was eight when I entered the Byzantine embrace of God's Breath, with its never-ending lists of rules, rewards, and punishments. Prior to that I had a fairly normal life with my father in Pittsburgh. My father divorced my mother when I was seven, and embraced God's Breath soon after. I believe he was at a low point in his life, and desperate for some kind of direction. He had worked as the manager of a paint store, but harbored dreams of writing novels.

At the behest of God's Breath's director, David Scipio, we moved to Harrison, Colorado, a small town in the mountains near Salida. My father signed a contract committing himself to the order for a billion years, covering his future lives, as the church believes people are immortal. We settled into a compound with other families.

My father became a stranger to me. The Church put him to work as a carpenter and painter, working twelve-hour days to build habitats for new arrivals, and working on David Scipio's gated estate, which featured a fifteen-room main house, stables, and a tennis court.

We were required to join the Army of the Blessed, wear uniforms, and work up to twelve hours a day, often in harsh conditions. We were taught that if something bad happens to us, it was because we invited it in, or brought it on ourselves with negative thoughts. If people complained, they were labeled as troublemakers and assigned the worst jobs, such as cleaning the stables or digging ditches.

God's Breath believes in reincarnation. We were taught that when we die, we are born again, either higher up the Church's pecking order, or lower down. Those who had sinned egregiously were reborn as animals. Mostly snakes.

I was thirteen when I first caught Scipio's attention. Right in front of my father, he laid hands on me, told me I was a beautiful boy and that I could be of great service to the Church...

Josh stopped reading. He wrote Ninja.

"I need to contact God's Breath survivors. Needless to say, this group is under constant surveillance. Can you create for me a foolproof method of sending and receiving emails that can't be traced?"

Five minutes later, Ninja wrote back: "I gotta get out of town. Will arrive at your place in seventeen hours with all the necessary equipment. I will set up a delivery system that is impossible to trace. I like waffles."

CHAPTER 8

THE SMALLWOODS

Nancy and Keith Smallwood lived in a two-story colonial on Ozark Terrace on Madison's west side near Owen Park. They had three children. Karen was the eldest. The youngers, Bill, eleven, and Rita, nine, both attended Sojourner Truth Middle School.

The Smallwoods agreed to an interview with Detective Calloway and Josh at their home at five p.m. on Tuesday, following Ashley's disappearance. They had already spoken with the police, but not with Calloway. While Bill and Rita played video games in the basement family room, Calloway, Josh, Karen and her parents met in the living room looking out on their backyard with a view of brilliant orange, red, and yellow leaves falling from the trees, dappling the ground.

Keith Smallwood, a heavy-set man in his fifties, wearing suit pants and blue shirt with the sleeves rolled up, settled into a leather chair, while Nancy, a small, vivacious woman with gray hair, set down a platter with coffee, mugs, cream, and sugar.

"I also have agave if you prefer."

"This is Josh Pratt," Calloway said. "Josh is an old friend of mine and a private investigator. I hope you don't mind if he listens in."

Smallwood held up a hand. "Not a problem."

Karen wore elegantly-torn blue jeans and a gray Madison Memorial Spartans sweatshirt. Her knees were drawn up beneath her on the sofa, her smart phone on the table.

"Karen," her mother said, "do you have something to say to Detective Calloway?"

Karen looked down. "I should have told you about Ashley. I'm sorry."

Calloway pulled out a pen and pad. He wore gray slacks and a blue blazer over a white shirt. No badge was visible, but he looked like a cop with his shaved skull and no-nonsense demeanor. "That's all right, Karen. I know how it is among teenage girls, and I want to thank you for meeting with us now. I understand Ashley was enthralled with an online personality known as Scipio."

"Yeah. She's been talking to him for months over the internet. I have no idea how they got together, but she told me about him in July, but she never said anything about running away with him. Not until a couple weeks ago. She told me that Scipio was her soul mate, they were destined to be together, and that Scipio had promised they would get together."

"When did you know Scipio was coming?" Calloway said.

"Not until a week ago. She swore me to secrecy. I'm so sorry, you guys! I realize how crazy all this sounds, especially for Ashley. I mean, if anyone would be skeptical about some guy she met on the internet, it would be Ashley."

"Because her father is a cop?"

"Partly. Also because she's so real. She doesn't believe in lying or artifice. I don't know how she fell for his crap."

"Have you seen any of their communications?"

"She showed me a couple. It was all, like, you're so special, you're one in a million, you're destined for great things etcetera etcetera."

"Did you ever communicate with him?"

Karen put her hand to her chest. "No! I told her she was making a mistake. I told her that the odds of her meeting her soul mate on the internet was, like... You ever watch *The Bachelor*? And how two weeks after they declare their undying love for one another they break up? It's stupid! You have to get to know someone before you make that commitment."

"Did she mention where Scipio intended to take her?"

"No. Just away."

"They have a compound in Colorado," Josh said. "It's pretty remote. I imagine they patrol it too."

"The problem is," Calloway said, "in order to obtain a search warrant we would have to provide proof that they're together. I have gone over the video from the truck stop. It's not very high quality, and this man who picked her up was wearing a disguise designed to beat face recognition software. The license plate on his vehicle was registered in Oklahoma, but the state has no record of it."

Keith Smallwood poured coffee into a mug. "Why would a grown man drive for two days to pick up a teenage girl? I looked into this cult, and they have a lot of wealth. If this man seeks underage sex, he could find it in his compound. Why this fascination with your daughter?"

"I've been asking myself that. At first, I wondered if it was someone who held a grudge. God knows, I've locked up a lot of bad guys, made a few enemies. There aren't many pictures of this character, but there are a few. So why the disguise? I brought Josh here because he can devote himself to this one hundred percent. I can't take time off. The situation with the Madison police department is dire. We are severely understaffed and the City Council keeps cutting our budget. There are people on the school board who think we should disband the police altogether."

"That's crazy," Smallwood said.

"Not to them."

"Was Ashley using drugs?" Mr. Smallwood asked. Josh knew what he was really asking.

Karen twisted her hands together, her brow knitted in anxiety.

"Tell us the truth, Karen," Nancy Smallwood said. "We're not looking for recriminations."

"We'd smoke a little reefer from time to time, but that's all! I swear!"

"Where did you get the reefer?" her father asked.

"Oh, there are a thousand places to get it. Half the kids at school smoke reefer."

"But where did you get it?"

"What does that matter? Whoever gave her the reefer didn't take her!"

"Karen," her father said ominously.

"It was Brent, okay? He sells joints for five dollars."

"Brent Forrester?"

"Yeah."

"We'll have to talk to him," Josh said. "We don't care if he sold joints. This is about finding Ashley."

"What's his phone number?" Mr. Smallwood said.

Calloway handed her his notepad and she wrote it down. "And his parents' names and phone numbers, if you know them."

Karen wrote in the pad. She appeared smaller with every gesture.

"Anything else, anything at all you can think of that might point us in the right direction, please contact me."

He handed Mr. Smallwood his card. Josh handed him his card as well. Black on white: Josh Pratt. Private Investigator. His phone number and email account.

Calloway stood, thanked the Smallwoods, and he and Josh left. In the car, Calloway looked up the parents' address and phone number on the in-car computer.

"Mr. Forrester? This is Detective Heinz Calloway of the MPD. Do you have a minute?"

CHAPTER 9

THE FORRESTERS

They drove to the Forresters. Josh copied the phone numbers out of Calloway's notepad.

"Did it occur to you that Ashley may just be a means of getting to you?"

Calloway kept his hands on the wheel at ten and two. "Yes. I looked at this guy's pictures last night. He's not exactly camera shy. But nothing rings a bell. There's a surprising paucity on his personal life. No mention of his age, but he appears to be in his late thirties or early forties, which is already a fire alarm for anyone wanting to involve themselves with a teenager."

"Well let's start with the assumption that Scipio is not his real name. I got a tech guy maybe can find out. He'll be here tomorrow night, but I won't be free until late. Ray's putting on *Kiss Me Kate* at the dance studio and I gotta go."

"Is Ray the tall one?"

"Yeah. Met her at the Lowrys. What she sees in me I don't know."

"What can your tech guy do that mine can't?"

"He can tap into pretty much any data bank. Our government, the Russians, the Chinese, anything. He can trace untraceable shit. That's why I need him. If Ashley's still using her cell phone he'll find her. And he can tap into the NSA's face recognition software. SAFR, Rankone, you name it."

"I can send you more pictures."

"You sent plenty. Doreen loves that kid. You can see it in the photos. How's Terry doing?"

"Doin' well. Now he's working for Hot Wire. It's an ad company. They got the Pepsi account."

Terry was seven years older than Ashley.

"What's he do?"

"Account exec. They dream up ad campaigns, like the LIMU Emu."

"I hate that bird."

"I hate the gecko."

"Does Terry know?"

"I haven't told him. If she's still missing by the weekend, I'm gonna have to say something. I don't want Terry freaking out, quitting his job, and coming back here thinking he can do something. He's an action kind of guy."

"Marines'll do that to you."

The Forresters lived on Inner Drive off Mineral Point in a two-story red brick Williamsburg. Green shutters, mature elm, a carefully tended garden with the season's last burst:

daisies, lilies, chrysanthemums. A sign in the front yard said, *We Believe Black Lives Matter, Love Is Love, Feminism Is For Everyone, No Human Being Is Illegal, Science Is Real, Be Kind To Everyone.*

The outside lights were on, gleaming off a black Lexus SUV. There was a ten-speed bicycle on the porch, three steps up. The door opened before they could reach it. Sid Forrester was a balding, middle-aged insurance executive, wearing suspenders to hold up his suit pants. His glasses reflected the street light.

"Mr. Forrester, sorry to bother you like this."

"Come in. Very sorry to hear about your daughter. I pray they find her. Millie and I both think the world of her."

Brent and Millie stood in the living room as Josh and Calloway entered. Brent was a skinny boy with a pronounced Adam's apple, thick brown hair over shaved sides, wearing khakis and a knit cotton Packers shirt. Millie Forrester was a tiny, sparrow-like woman with an unhappy red face. A generic landscape hung over the brick fireplace. Pictures of Brent in his Memorial football uniform, water skiing, pictures of the whole family at some lakeside resort rested on the mantle. Brent's athletic trophies. Football. Track.

"Hello, sir," he said to Calloway as they shook hands.

"Would you like coffee?" Millie said.

Calloway flickered a smile. "I wouldn't mind."

"How do you take it?"

"All cops take it black."

"Cream and sugar," Josh said.

Millie went into the kitchen.

Forrester gestured to a sectional sofa upholstered in a blue floral pattern. Calloway and Josh sat on the sofa, and Forrester took the facing end chair. Brent sat opposite his father in a walnut and fabric Queen Ann chair.

Calloway took out his pad and pen. "Before I begin, is there anything you want to say to your parents, Brent?"

Brent clasped his hands and looked at the floor. "They know. I told them."

"He will be severely punished," Mr. Forrester said. "We took away his phone."

Millie returned with a walnut platter carrying a pot of coffee, half and half and packets of sugar in bowls. There were three mugs: Green Bay Packers, Wisconsin Physicians Service, and Isthmus.

"What do you know about Scipio?"

Brent looked up. "Only what Ashley told me. She told me she thought she was in love with him. And that she wanted to meet him."

"Did you know she planned to run away?"

"No! I hadn't talked to her in about a week. I would have told you!" Brent had little to add. Although he and Ashley were best friends, there was no romantic interest between them. Maybe not on her part, but Josh knew what teenage boys were like.

"Thank you, Brent," Calloway said. "Just one more question. Where'd you get the reefer?"

Brent agonized, twisting his hands. "Sir, I'll never have anything to do with that individual ever again! Is this necessary?"

"Yes, it is. Are you worried that he might come back at you?"

"Well yeah."

"I promise you he won't. But reefer's still illegal and I still gotta do my job."

"Adrian Green. He was going to Memorial but he dropped out. He lives with his mom over across from Elver Park, but he runs with this gang out of Milwaukee. The Kimbras."

"I know about the Kimbras. That's about it. What about blow, X, meth, anything else?"

"No! I wouldn't touch that stuff! I mean."

"Did Green offer it?"

Brent stared at the floor.

"Don't worry that this will come back to you. Green will never know. I know who Green is. We have enough on him already."

"If you think of something else, you know what to do." Forrester saw them out.

"You're not going to arrest Brent for dealing marijuana?"

"Nobody has to know about that, but he has to stop."

"Believe me, it's stopped. We're going to watch him like a hawk."

Calloway put a hand on Forrester's arm. "He's a good kid. I smoked reefer when I was kid."

"Half the town smokes reefer," Josh said.

"I went to West," Forrester said. "We didn't know what reefer was. I know he's a good kid. That's why this is so shocking. He's got a three-point-five grade point average. We're about to start applying to schools."

They shook hands again.

Calloway and Josh headed toward Ptarmigan.

"Adrian Green's on our radar. But we can't do anything about the Kimbras because we don't have enough men. And they just turned down the chief's request for new officers. I don't understand what's wrong with these people."

"Madison's always been like that. Four lakes, more flakes. The Committee City. Berkeley East."

There was a new Cherokee in Josh's driveway with Missouri plates. As Calloway parked on the street, a slim black man in a dark hoodie and jeans opened the back of the Jeep and grabbed two carbon-fiber cases. He stopped when Josh and Calloway got out of the car.

"Ninja! You need some help?"

Ninja set the cases down. When Josh stuck out his hand, Ninja pulled him into an embrace. "My brother from another mother."

"This is Heinz Calloway."

They shook hands. Ninja put his hands on his hips. "You a cop?"

"Heinz is a Madison detective. His daughter Ashley is missing."

"Well, help me get this shit inside. The sooner I set up, the sooner we can track her down."

Josh followed Ninja. The hacker didn't look like the face on the Skype calls, or in the videos. Similar, but different.

THE DOWNSTAIRS BEDROOM

They carried five cases into the living room where Fig lay on the sofa, still bandaged, wagging her tail. Thump thump thump. Josh sat down beside her and ruffled her ears.

"Who's a good girl? Who's a good girl?"

Ninja stood in the living room admiring the framed poster of a scantily clad babe draped over a chopper. "Where you want me to set up shop?"

"In the basement. Come on. Let's get this shit downstairs."

Josh led the way into his mostly finished basement, which featured a rec room containing a big flat screen and his gun safe, a small bedroom with a window looking out on the back yard, a half bath and the unfinished utilities room.

"Yeah, just set 'em down. It's gonna have to wait until tomorrow, boss. I been driving all day."

Heinz looked around. "Okay. I gotta go. Check with you tomorrow."

Josh and Ninja went upstairs. Josh got a couple brews from the fridge.

Ninja tilted back in the Barcalounger with his feet up, ripped off the cap and glugged.

"How was the drive?"

"It was a drive."

"You had to get out of town?"

"I have my fingers in many pies. Ain't nobody gonna find me. I'm a ninja. So, what about God's Breath?"

"Calloway's an old friend. Last week, his seventeen-year-old daughter met Scipio, head of God's Breath, and disappeared. Dad is understandably upset. The girl and Scipio had been chatting online for months. You think you can find 'em?"

Ninja shrugged. "I'll give it my best shot. Depends on how far off the grid they want to go. Shit only works if you're near a camera."

"I also need to get in touch with former God's Breathers. They're paranoid, and with good reason. The church goes after apostates with a vengeance. Doxxing, swatting, ruining their credit, draining their accounts. They got some serious hackers. I need a safe way to contact them over the internet so it won't come back on me or them. If I knew where to find them, I'd just go. But I don't. I hear about dark web hook-ups."

"No probs. Can I light up some reefer?"

"Go ahead."

Ninja pulled a fat doobie from the hoodie, lit it with a

yellow Bic, rotating the end. The smell of high-grade marijuana filled the room. He passed it to Josh, who took a drag. They sat there in silence looking at the smoke.

"Whatcha running from?"

Ninja exhaled a cloud and watched it disperse. "Johnny Torreo. I was seeing this girl Rhonda. She had a fifteen-year-old daughter. Brandywine. Greatest jailbait you ever saw. Johnny Torreo's kid Lyman picked her up at some club. Lyman's twenty-seven. They started seein' each other and Lyman got her hooked on crack. So, Brandywine moves in with Lyman in a renovated loft in St. Louis. You know St. Louis?"

"Nope."

"Funny city. One foot in Illinois. Anyway, Lyman had a loft in University City. Swanksville. One night he slips her a rufie and invites two of his friends to have a go. One of 'em gave her herpes and Lyman threw her out. All this time, Rhonda never said a word to me, but I could tell she was stressed. Finally she breaks down and asks me to find Brandywine. Took me a while, but I found her selling tricks in Richmond Heights. She'd lost a lot of weight. She looked like a drowned rat. I hadda wrestle her into the car. Rhonda freaked when I brought her back, and we got her into a drug treatment place in Boulder, but she ran away, hitchhiked back to Missouri and went to see Lyman. Lyman wasn't happy to see her. Beat the shit out of her and kicked her out."

His voice trailed away.

"Anyhow, Rhonda tells me if I love her, I got to do

something."

"Did you love her?"

"Who the fuck knows? I was used to her. I was never close with women, never had a relationship that lasted more than six months, but Rhonda is someone special. She works at a mortgage company. Met her at a Funkadelic concert. I don't know what she sees in me."

"Whadja do?"

"I froze Lyman's bank accounts. Now he had to pay cash for everything, only his landlord got suspicious, plus there were complaints from some of his neighbors. Loud parties, burnouts in the parking lot, unsavory characters. One day the cops stop him and the dog finds a key of blow in the trunk of his Audi. Up 'til then, Johnny Torreo wasn't involved, but when Lyman got charged, he got involved. He did a little digging and put Brandywine with Rhonda and Rhonda with me. Now I'm a criminal, dig? I try to stay off the radar. If I was smart, I would have moved out of the country years ago. Buy a crib in the Turks and Caicos. I could run scams outta there until I was old and gray.

"I don't deal drugs, I don't do rip-offs or strong arms, I make money off crypto-currency and shit like this here. I worked for some unsavory cats. They told me Johnny's comin' after me, that he blames me for all Lyman's problems, and bringing the heat. He used insecticides to kill some Dominicans who were dealing meth in his territory. Sealed them up in their warehouse and pumped in gas under the door."

"How you know that?"

"I read the autopsy reports. That was a while back. Now the feds are looking at Johnny, who lists himself as a liquor wholesaler. Sweet distribution system and good for money laundering. I had a loft in East St. Louis. No one gave me any shit. It was what you might call a blue-collar neighborhood. Or maybe a no-collar neighborhood. One night I'm working late I get a call. Get the hell out of Dodge. Then you called."

"Great."

"Not so great. He blew up the loft." Ninja held fingers up to indicate quote marks. "Gas explosion. Killed six people. There were four lofts in the building, me and three other parties. Family of four."

Josh felt a lead weight in his gut. "How bad was it?"

"Well, they only got into the ruins yesterday, it was so hot. They're sorting through the rubble, have recovered four bodies. Any luck, Johnny will think I'm one of them. But I ain't countin' on luck."

"You sure you weren't followed?"

"You'd teach your grandmother to suck eggs. I switched cars twice. I disinfect my shit daily. Didn't even bring a cell phone. I'll pick up some burners here. I am a black cat in the dark. That's why they call me Ninja."

"I tell you about Ashley?"

"Only that she's missing."

"She fell in love with an online personality. Scipio. Head of God's Breath Universal Life Church."

"Roman General during the Punic War. Fought in Spain."

"I did not know that."

"I looked it up. It might give us some insight into who he really is. Does he have another name?"

"Just Scipio."

"I hate those one-name motherfuckers."

"I gotta crash. You got the downstairs bedroom."

Ninja lifted a hand. "Later."

CHAPTER 11

KISS ME KATE

Wednesday, Josh rose at six, pulled on his sweats and running shoes, fed Fig a can of Purina Beef Lover's, ate a banana and a Nature Valley Sweet and Nutty bar, and headed to the front door. Fig whined and thumped her tail. She would normally accompany him on his five-mile run.

Josh sat with Fig and scruffed her up. "Not today, pal. We'll start with some walks this weekend."

It was a crisp fall morning, and Ptarmigan was a dazzling orange and red tunnel as Josh ran on the shoulder toward Madison against traffic. It was a broad, freshly black-topped two-way serving an upscale community. No sidewalks. Most houses hidden behind trees, many with gates. Every mailbox made a statement. Stone pillars, a wrought-iron dolphin, welded chain links. Traffic was moderate as people headed toward their jobs at the university, state government, insurance companies, Epic in Verona. The street was settled.

There were no more empty lots. The average lot size was between an acre and an acre and a half. Josh ran all the way to Gammon. As he was about to turn into his driveway, Phil Bass drove by and honked his horn. Bass abruptly braked and pulled onto the shoulder.

"Hey, Josh!" he called out the window.

Josh walked over, stood by the open passenger window. "What's up, Phil?"

"I'm thinking of getting a gun. What do you recommend?"

"You know, Phil, I'm not allowed to own any guns due to my felony convictions. But I would recommend a revolver. Why do you want a gun?"

"Thieves broke into Lou Bank's house over the weekend, made off with his wife's jewelry. The door was busted open when he got home. He called the police and they didn't send someone until two days later."

"So you want a gun for self-protection."

"Well, yeah. What kind of revolver?"

"A .38 special will take care of most of your home protection needs, but if you get one, I recommend taking a concealed carry course, which will help you qualify, and a general gun safety course."

"Thanks, Josh. Have you thought about my offer?"

Josh smiled. "I think about it all the time."

"Well okay! Thanks for the advice. See you around."

Josh watched Phil drive off in his Lexus SUV. Josh walked up his driveway to his house.

Fig barked. Josh walked her out the back door, carried

her down the steps to the fenced-in back lawn and watched her poop. When he reached to carry her back inside, she gave him a look over her shoulder and surely, if slowly, mounted the back steps, went inside and leaped back to her perch on the sofa.

Josh showered, put on blue jeans and a red and gray Badgers sweatshirt, and made some coffee. He heard Ninja moving around downstairs. Ninja had taken over a long fold up table on which he'd placed terminals, hard drives, and routers. Ninja wore black sweats, white Giuseppe Zanotti sneakers, and an untucked long-sleeved T with a printed dragon wrapping around the torso.

"Where'd you get that shirt?"

Ninja turned, looked down. "Ordered it online. Why?" Josh peeled off his sweatshirt revealing the dragon winding around his torso.

"Ho shit!" Ninja said. "We really are brothers!"

"What's going on here?"

Ninja pointed to the routers. "I run shit through a VPN server to Hungary, bounce it through a couple more VPNs owned by shell companies. It's all encrypted. It's all wrapped in so many layers no one has the resources to break through. The last server doesn't store logs. Even if they seize the server, there are no logs to examine. We'll be good to go this afternoon. What do you need?"

"I need to find people who left God's Breath. Survivor groups. GB has its own experts, so they have to be careful. I need to talk to these people to learn more about Scipio, and about their compound. He may end up taking her back there. Or he may not. It's a mystery to me why a guy like this, who's got his own harem, zeroes in on a seventeen-year-old honor student in Madison, Wisconsin."

"You said her father is a cop."

"Yeah, and don't think it hasn't occurred to me. But I wouldn't know where to start."

"What's his name?"

"You met him. You want coffee?"

"I'll come up."

Josh went into his office and found one of Calloway's cards. They went out on the deck. There was nothing much to see but the thick patch of woods between Josh's place and the five-thousand-square-foot McMansion behind him. Fig came out the doggie door and curled up at Josh's feet.

"You get any sleep?" Josh said.

"A little. I was wired."

"You got people?"

"A brother, trying to make it as a stuntman in Hollywood. Rhonda moved to Boulder to be close to Brandywine. I haven't talked to her in a while. I kinda keep tabs from a distance. She's working as a teller at a bank there. Had to be a comedown. She was an executive, know what I mean? What about you?"

"I've had bad luck with women. Seeing someone now. We couldn't be more different. She's a bleeding heart lib. Runs a dance studio. In fact, they're putting on *Kiss Me Kate* tonight, if you're interested."

"Fuck izzit?"

"It's a musical based on Shakespeare's *Taming of the Shrew*. That's all I know."

"Musicals are for fags."

"I wouldn't know. This is a first for me. Come on. You'll dig it. Lots of cute dancers."

"Lemme see how far I get today."

Kiss Me Kate was at seven. At five, Josh took Ninja to La Baguette on Mineral Point. Ninja brought along a leather backpack, which he called his purse. The inked hostess sat them at a booth looking out on the busy road. A gamin in lederhosen and Rosa Klebb shoes approached with menus.

"Good evening, gentlemen. May I start you off with something to drink?"

"I'll have a Stoly's martini on the rocks with an olive," Ninja said.

Josh ordered a Capital Autumnal Fire.

"Perfect," the waiter said and sailed away. A French Bakery, La Baguette looked like any modern delicatessen or sandwich shop with fake hardwood floors, dozens of pastries in a glass case, and pictures of the Eiffel Tower, Mont St. Michel, and the Riviera on the walls. The hard surfaces reflected sound and made talking difficult.

Ninja looked around. "I miss St. Louis already."

"You're kidding."

"Yeah. I don't miss that slag heap at all. There's nothing left. Ain't never coming back, either. Same thing happened there happened here. Rioters just trashed the place. Gave my favorite diner the torch. Looks like a war zone."

The waiter returned with their drinks. Josh ordered the Salad Nicoise.

"Can I get a hamburger?" Ninja said.

"Sorry. No hamburger. I recommend Le Parisien with ham, gruyere, cornichons and butter on a freshly baked baguette."

"Sure."

"Excellent."

They watched her whisk away. "What's a cornichon?" Josh said.

"Little pickles. Don't be jerkin my gherkin."

They arrived at the Rise Up dance studio on East Wilson at six-forty, parked a block up on the street and walked back. About a dozen East Siders hung out front drinking beer in paper cups and blowing reefer. The studio was a converted warehouse, with ivy climbing the brick walls. A marquee salvaged from a long-gone movie theater hung over the front door, which was a garage door that rolled up into the ceiling. There was a regular door next to it. It was a pleasant evening. Inside was a counter where a young man with a pink mohawk and eyebrows pierced like a shower curtain was selling tickets. He wore a shirt that said IMMANEN-TIZE THE ESCHATON.

"MISTER Pratt," he said. "You're good to go."

"Need one for Ninja."

"NINja."

Ninja smiled. "That's me."

"I can see you."

"I can't ninja all the time."

"Twelve fifty."

They went past the concession stand, which sold craft beers, beignets, and guerrilla cookies, into the theater in back, which seated one hundred and fifty. Josh found their seats up two steps in the back, which seated sixty in two rows. The room smelled of beer and marijuana.

In front of the stage, the band tuned up: guitar, bass, drums, keyboards. El Cignos was written in script on the bass drum. The keyboard player, wearing fifty-year-old bell-bottom trousers, suspenders, and a wide-brimmed hat, played a riff and the band hit "Why Can't You Behave."

The brochure showed a stylized graphic of the Globe Theater in Shakespeare's time, the people indiscernible from East Siders. They had the same floppy hats, voluminous sleeves and facial hair. The room quickly filled to near capacity. Only a handful of seats in the back row remained unclaimed. Pretty good turn-out for a hippy theater on the East Side.

When Ray blew in as Lois, the room swooned. "It's Too Darn Hot," she sang, dancing on a table. Ninja watched with his mouth open in a silly grin, and when it was over, was the first one on his feet. The actress who played Lili was a firecracker brunette speaking to the back row. The actor playing Fred Graham exaggerated his masculinity to the point of parody. There were two encores. Some of the actors sat on the edge of the stage afterward to talk to audience members. Stagehands started folding and racking chairs against the wall. Josh and Ninja joined them, opening up the parquet dance floor while El Cignos played "Whole

Lotta Shakin' Goin' On."

Josh and Ninja went up the side steps, backstage where the cast was getting drunk. Ray, still made up as Lois, opened her arms, planted a big kiss on Josh's face, and stepped back beaming.

"Ray, Ninja."

"Great. Just great," Ninja gushed. "I never knew I liked musicals!"

"Most people don't until they see one."

"Ninja's my IT guy. He's set up in the basement. He'll be staying over a few days."

Ray gave him a look.

"Hey baby. What's wrong with your place?"

She smiled. "That'll work."

Josh gave Ninja the keys to his Chrysler. "Can you find it?"

Ninja held up a black rectangle. "I got it, hoss. You need me to feed the dog?"

"Yeah. Give her a whole can of Purina in the morning."

"See you tomorrow."

Ray took Josh's hand. "How do you know him?"

"It's a long story."

"Well, let's go. I got time."

Ray's place was a fourth-floor condo in Monona with a view of The Capitol across the lake. As soon as they were inside, they clanged in a passionate embrace while Ray's cat Sid Vicious twined between their feet.

"Let me shower first," she breathed in his ear.

"No. I like you dirty. I like the greasepaint."

He picked her up, carried her down the hall to her bed-room and threw her on the old wood bed, which squeaked. They peeled off each other's clothes, Ray laughing as she hurled the wig across the room. She was already wet when he entered her. As they writhed and shivered, Sid Vicious leaped on the bed, onto Josh's back, digging his claws in.

"Ahhh!"

Laughing, Ray swept Sid Vicious aside.

They showered together. Ray took a California Kitchen Sicilian pizza from the freezer and put it in the oven. "I'm not much of a cook."

"I'm willing to overlook that."

She looked at her watch. "Damn it. I forgot to record Rachel Maddow."

Josh rolled onto his back and stared at the ceiling fan turning lazily. He hoped she wouldn't try to drag him to any demonstrations or vegan restaurants. She'd been with him the night they'd trashed State Street. Josh needed a woman in his life, and he was happy with Ray. But there were flags. The way she talked about cops. The way she talked about the President.

"You, of all people, should appreciate that the police perpetuate institutional racism."

Josh put his hands to his ears. "LA LA LA! I can't hear you!"

Josh had spent four years in prison. He went in with a bad attitude and came out with a good one, thanks to Chaplain Michael Dorgan who talked him into letting Christ into his life. He didn't talk about his faith. Most people wouldn't understand. He went to a small Baptist Church in Middleton when he could, and prayed at night. He tried to get Ray to pray with him, but she just laughed.

She jumped into a stance and threw some punches. "HOO! HA! HEY! I want you to teach me kung fu."

"Now? It's almost midnight."

"I want to do a kung fu musical. The Hung Gar Games. Is that right? Isn't there a kung fu called hung gar?"

"You should ask Nelson."

"It'll be great. I got a bunch of dancers who can do the moves."

"I can't teach you kung fu. I can show you some self-defense moves. But really, what you should do is get a concealed carry permit."

"As if. Didn't you tell me you were training with that kung fu guy out on East Wash?"

"Nelson? Sure. He can teach you kung fu. It takes years!"

"I don't want to be an expert. I just want to put on a good show."

"Is it written?"

"Is what written?"

"The kung fu musical."

"Well no. I just thought of it."

"Let me know when it's written and I'll help you with the choreography."

"You?" She laughed.

CHAPTER 12

RABBI FROM ANOTHER PLANET

Josh woke to the smell of fried eggs. He put on his pants and picked up his shirt. It smelled funny. He tossed it aside. As he entered the kitchen, Ray set a platter on the little table with two eggs and two strips of bacon.

"Sid Vicious pissed on my shirt."

Ray turned toward him, fists on hips. "He's a rotten little shit. I have some clean T-shirts."

Josh ate a piece of bacon. "This isn't bacon."

"It's turkey bacon. It's good for you."

Josh helped himself to coffee. The turkey bacon was flavorless. It was like so many other solutions to non-existent problems. Artificial sweeteners. Burger King's Impossible Burger. There was nothing wrong with bacon, sugar, or beef, but attitudes and egos gave rise to whole bullshit industries trying to convince you that up was down and black was white.

"How's breakfast?"

"Really good!"

Josh swilled mouthwash, kissed Ray and left, stopping at Woodman's to pick up some ground beef, dog food, canned pumpkin, apples, bananas, and strawberries. He got home at ten and parked next to Ninja's van in the driveway. Fig woofed him inside, tail wagging, still moving slowly. Gangsta rap drilled up from below.

Ninja sat at the table in front of a double-wide monitor making notes in a spiral pad while his printer churned out page after page. "God's Breath Survivors is holding a retreat next weekend at Manitowish Waters in Northern Wisconsin."

"You're shittin' me."

Ninja swiveled in the chair. "It took me three hours to find them on the Dark Web. Whoever administers their site knows what he's doing. I'm guessing they did the same thing for God's Breath before they left, 'cuz you know they're all over the internet tracking their apostates and critics. Dug up a lotta shit. I'm printing off some of the more damning stuff, orders to harass, lists of names and addresses, things like that."

Josh picked up a page.

Jerome Dickey is living at 1112 Franklin Blvd, #203, in Houston. His social security number is XXX XX XXXX. He is a traitor and deserter. He has a dog. Scipio wants the dog killed and left in his living room. You are to split the dog open and pull out its guts.

Monica Freivald is living at 409 RR #12 in Gurney, Nebraska. She is a traitor and deserter. She lives with her elderly father, Oswald Freivald. His phone number is XXX XXX XXXX. Scipio wants you to phone him and tell him that you have tapes of his daughter performing sex acts with barnyard animals, and to demand ten thousand dollars or you will release the tapes all over the internet.

Josh shook his head. "Holy shit."

"I got a million of 'em. These breathers are busy."

"Can you knock 'em out?"

Ninja leaned back. The chair squeaked. "Hmmm. They seem kinda diversified. Could I take down their web page? I might be able to do that, but what good would it do? He's got a dozen tech guys and thousands of phone numbers. They probably have websites waiting to go like airplanes lined up on a runway. Don't think it hasn't been tried before. These guys are like the Mafia. You hit 'em, you better take 'em out because they'll keep coming and coming."

Josh thought of Johnny Torreo.

"Yeah, well now I gotta get up there and talk to some people. Can you get me addresses and names?"

"I got some names. The exact location of their retreat I don't have. You're gonna have to ask around. They're understandably paranoid."

"You gotta stay here and take care of my dog. You need anything? You know how to get around?"

"I'm good. Anybody asks, I'll just say I'm watching the

place for a few days."

"Lemme ask you somethin'. You put up these You-Tube videos. Couldn't someone just use facial recognition software to locate you? I mean, your face is all over the internet!"

"I wish. And no, they can't. I avoid cameras. I'm familiar with most surveillance systems, commercial or otherwise. And on the few occasions I have to walk in front of a camera, I use face recognition foiling stuff. Here. Let me show you."

Ninja retrieved a valise from the floor, pulled out a mask that neatly covered his face. It was very lifelike with holes for the eyes, but covered the ears. "This alters the dimensions. FRS uses precise measurements as to eye width, ears, lips, etc."

"That's why you don't look like your videos."

"Exactamundo."

"Yeah, but you walk into a store with that on, somebody might think you're a robber."

Ninja put the mask on and smiled.

"Holy shit! How do you do that?"

"It's made from micromillimeter thin polymer that moves with your face. Wait. Check this out."

He pulled out a shirt covered with bizarre black squares, like a computer scan. "This looks like faces to the camera and distracts from the actual face. Then there are these things."

He pulled out a plastic box filled with geometrical beads attached to a skull cap and put it on. "Rabbi from another planet. The beads confuse FRS. They can't get a reading. And nobody gonna say shit, 'cuz who's to say I'm not just an eccentric rapper wearing odd jewelry? Now this pandemic makes it easy. Everybody's wearing a mask. Hell, all you got to do is wear sunglasses and a hat. What are they gonna do? Zero in on your nose?"

"Any luck finding our girl?"

"I tapped into the NSA database, and the top three commercial surveillance operations. Aside from that night she met the guy, nothing. They're staying away from cameras."

Josh regarded his guest. He'd worked with him before, long-distance. He didn't really know the man, and yet he'd opened his house to him. There was something about the young rapper that inspired confidence. But to live outside the law you must be honest. Things seemed to come to Ninja effortlessly. The way his hands flowed over his instruments like a concert pianist. The natural grace with which he moved. These qualities were also valuable to con men.

Bike or car? The car was good for weather, but when you showed up on a bike, people gave you respect and listened to what you had to say. He checked the weather. Scattered showers. Josh threw some clothes in a valise, threw that in his car, checked the tires. Forty pounds all around.

"Should I walk Fig?"

"Up to you. Start with short walks around the neighborhood. If she starts to limp, bring her home."

"Groovy, baby."

"Okay. I'm outta here. Call me if anything happens."

Ninja held up a hand. "Wait." He dug around in one of his plastic bins and pulled out three numbered burner phones, one through three. "Take these. Leave your regular phone. After we talk, drown the phone in water."

"I only get three calls?"

"Yup. Unless you can find a landline."

Josh put the phones in his backpack. "Great."

CHAPTER

13

RHINELANDERS

Josh gassed up at the Stop 'N' Go, forty-two bucks to fill the tank with premium. He swung around the capitol and headed north on Fifty-One, the state highway that ran the length of Wisconsin, north to south, beneath a slate-colored sky. Wooded hills rolled out on both sides, the color of Trix cereal. Josh slid a Butterfield disc into the in-dash player. Father Dorgan had turned him onto the blues harp player when he was in Waupun.

He stopped In Portage for a late lunch at Ellie's Diner, had an omelet with sourdough and two glasses of orange juice, was on the road forty-five minutes later. He passed trucks carrying produce to market. Josh had been to Manitowish Waters with the Bedouins before he was busted. It was beautiful country, covered with forest, dotted with sky blue lakes, rife with mosquitoes and black flies. He wondered what he was doing with his life. In prison, he'd accepted Jesus into his heart and soul. He knew he was not a good man, but he was better than he'd been before. That was progress. He didn't even have a private investigator's license, although he could get one. The governor had pardoned him, thanks to his lawyer Bloom, who'd been murdered by a sadistic meth dealer named Moon, who'd been killed by his own creation, the animal boy named Eric.

Josh liked helping people. He might have been a fireman or a paramedic, but he'd carved a unique role for himself as a court of last resort for people who couldn't get help anywhere else. It just happened. Most bikers thought of themselves as heroes except for one percent who were scumbags, and even then, some of those. He'd never expected to be where he was, a suburban homeowner with a two-car garage. He'd never looked past the gang, the next run, the next groupie, before he went to prison. Even that hadn't phased him. He'd internalized the ethic. Tough guy. Gang member. Thank God he stopped before he ruined his face like the Brotherhood or all those Dominicans. It was Father Mike Dorgan who turned him around.

A self-effacing former Ranger and Army chaplain, Dorgan exuded a quiet authority that commanded the respect of even the most hardened criminals. Josh never had much trouble in Waupun because there were four other Bedouins there. They never joined the Aryan Brotherhood. They didn't make prison jack or smuggle drugs. They hung together, kept their heads down, and did their time.

He pulled into Manitowish around four and took a

room at the Loon's Nest in Mercer, a few miles down the road. There were two other cars in the lot. He flopped on the bed and took a nap. It was dusk when he woke. He drove back to Manitowish, pausing for a pack of Canadian geese to cross the road, and parked at the Muskie Tavern, a one-story log building with a couple chops, some pick-ups, and a half dozen other vehicles parked out front and in the side lot. The interior was cool and dim and smelled of chili, with a dozen patrons seated at the tables or at the bar. All the men wore caps. Renk Seed. John Deere. Packers. Pool balls clacked at a table in the back. Josh sat at the bar, admiring the muskies, bobcat, deer head, and Canadian goose mounted on maple plaques above the mirror. The bartender, a squat, middle-aged man with salt and pepper hair and beard, came over.

"What'll you have?"

"What's on the menu?"

The bartender pointed to a chalkboard with the day's specials: buffalo chili, venison steak, hamburger, side salad.

"Not a wide selection, but it's all good."

Josh ordered a beer and a cheeseburger and watched the bar through the mirror. The two bikers sat in a corner staring at their cell phones. A family of four sat at a table, a pre-teen boy and girl playing their video games. The bartender set his cheeseburger down on a china plate with french fries. Josh peered under the hood. The lettuce was green, the tomato was fresh.

"What's with that stuffed goose?"

"It's a warning," the bartender said. "I hate the fuckers. Everybody hates 'em. They come down here, shit all over everything, block traffic, and they're federally protected. Should any Canadian goose make its way through these doors, it'll get the message."

Josh drew two fingers across his mouth. "My lips are sealed. Any Bible camps around here?"

The bartender leaned back and crossed his arms. "Plenty. Why? You lookin' to join?"

"Maybe."

"You don't look like a Bible thumper."

"What does a Bible thumper look like?"

"Joel Osteen. What kinda camp you looking for?"

Josh took a slug of beer, set the glass mug on the bar. "I'm a simple Christian. I'm a little bit Baptist, a little bit Episcopalian."

"Crescent Lake in Rhinelander, Lake Lundgren over in Pembine. Whatcha lookin' for?"

"I'm here to get baptized."

The bartender squinted. "You serious?"

"That's a joke. But I am serious about my faith."

The bartender stuck out his hand. "Russ Merritt."

"Josh Pratt."

"You look like you done time."

"You got a good eye."

"Hold on. Be right back."

The bartender walked over to the waitress, a twenty-something corn-fed All-American blonde, and took her orders. People entered and left. It was unlikely that God's Breath survivors would frequent such a place. They would be quiet, depressed, suffering from PTSD. They needed to belong to something bigger than themselves. They would reach out again.

Josh caught Merritt's eye and held up his mug. Merritt set a filled mug on the bar. "You oughta talk to Doug Mc-Graw over at King's Methodist. That's right down the street. Doug's a good man, been to most of these bible camps. They got some kinda program where all the ministers play musical chairs, so they don't get too doctrinaire."

"That's a good idea. King's Methodist, huh?"

"Ayup. You can't miss it. Red stone building with a bell tower."

Josh finished his burger with his elbows on the bar. The two guys playing pool were getting sloppy.

"That's my cue, asshole."

"Yeah, well fuck you!"

The cue flew, striking a red-faced man with a mullet in the chest. He shoved his assailant on his ass. The man on his ass, who wore a red plaid shirt, blue jeans, and black boots, charged, smashing the mullet up against the pool table, moving it an inch. Mullet seized a pool ball and used it to brain Plaid. Plaid staggered, picked up a cue, drew back, and the cue stopped. One of the bikers ripped it out of his hands. The other biker rounded on Mullet, finger in his face.

"Pay your tab and get out."

Anger, fear, caution rippled across Mullet's face. Without a word, he pulled out his wallet, threw a twenty on the pool table and stomped out. The biker turned on Plaid.

"Now you."

"The whole tab didn't come to twenty."

"Yeah, but you got to leave something for the owner, who put up with your shit."

With a scowl, Plaid threw a ten on the table and headed for the front door. The room erupted in applause. One biker smiled and waved. The other bowed at the waist.

Their colors said Rhinelanders.

CHAPTER 14

REB AND STAN

Josh took his beer and went over to the Rhinelanders' table. They looked up.

"Josh Pratt. I rode with the Bedouins."

The two bikers stared at him. One, a lean, pale man with a ponytail, had *Reb* inscribed on his denim vest along with the usual patches, POW/MIA, Realities For Children, Sturgis, Sergeant At Arms. The other, a bearded Dad Bod with amber aviators, fully tatted arms, bore *Stan* on his chest above an oval with the word *mouthpiece*.

"The Bedouins?" Reb said. "You don't look old enough to have ridden with the Bedouins."

"I was eighteen when I joined. I admire what you did there."

Reb shoved a wooden captain's chair out with his foot. Josh sat.

"Pratt," Stan said. "Pratt. Why do I know that name?"

Josh shrugged. Reb pulled out his smartphone and poked. Josh smiled. Ninja had created a program that erased Josh Pratt from the internet. "Says here you had something to do with the death of Ryan Gherke."

Fuck.

"I was there. I had nothing to do with his death."

"Wait a minute," Stan said. "Weren't you at Sturgis this year?"

"Yeah."

"You were at that guy's booth, with the crazy bike. The Hotchkiss Avenger!"

"Yeah, I know Hotchkiss."

"Man, that looked sweet. Did you ride it? What's it like?"

"It ain't like anything. The five cylinders rotate around the crankshaft like a revolver. Smooth and powerful. Beats electric, that's for sure."

Reb cranked up his middle finger. "Fuck that shit. Live-Wire my ass."

"They cost thirty thousand bucks," Stan said. "I picked up a used Victory with ten thousand miles for eight thousand bucks."

"Victory never stood a chance. Too much like Harleys," Reb said.

"Yeah," Stan said. "But look at Indian. Same company going like gangbusters. Go figure."

Reb reached for a cigarette over his ear, looked at it, put it back. "Yeah, but that's because it's got heritage. It's the real deal, unlike the half dozen fake Injuns been around forever."

"Well, what makes it the real deal? The fact that they bought the name?"

Reb folded his hands. "Here we go."

"What?"

"You're a Harley zombie. You're gonna ride Harleys 'til the day you die."

"I like what I like." Reb turned to Josh.

"Is there any other bike?"

Josh shrugged. "I'll ride anything. I have a 650 Hawk. I'd buy one of those Hotchkisses if they were for sale, but they're having trouble getting financing. This is a bad time for bikes. Kids are risk-averse. They don't even want to drive. They'd rather take an Uber, or something. They'd rather have some fucking Tesla that drives itself."

"Yeah, man. Remember in the nineties when they were still coming out with like a dozen new models every year?"

Josh waved the waitress over and ordered more beers. "I don't trust a bike I can't hear. Doesn't mean I'm gonna take out my baffles. I just don't trust a bike you can't hear."

"I hear ya. Our bikes are loud, but they ain't that loud."

"They're factory loud," Stan said. "Carefully calibrated."

"So, what do you guys do?"

"We're a fraternal order of like-minded gentlemen who enjoy cruising through this great land of ours on two wheels. I own a roofing company. Stan's a lawyer."

"You're shittin' me."

Stan reached into his vest and handed Josh a card.

STANLEY TURVILLE
ATTORNEY
MOTORCYCLE LAWYERS WHO RIDE

Josh tucked it in his vest. "Nice."

"What do you do, Pratt?"

Josh handed Reb one of his cards. Josh Pratt. Private investigator.

Reb rippled his hedgerow brows. "You workin'?"

"Yeah." He reached into his vest and pulled out a picture of Ashley. "Two days ago, this girl disappeared. Her name is Ashley Calloway."

Reb handed it to Stan. "Why you lookin' here?"

Josh leaned on his elbows and lowered his voice. "She left to join a cult. God's Breath. You hear of it?"

Reb and Stan looked at each other.

"Oh yeah," Reb said. "'Sposed to be a survivors' group up here. We keep it on the down-low."

"Why look here?" Stan said.

"She left with the head honcho. Scipio."

"That asshole," Stan said.

"You know him?"

"No. I just see him on TV, walking out of depositions. Lotta unhappy ex campers."

"I'm concerned that he may have taken Ashley back to their compound in the Rockies, and I want to talk to people who have been there before I make my next move."

Stan nodded.

"Know anybody?"

"How long you gonna be in town?" Stan said.

"As long as it takes."

"Let us ask around. We'll meet you here tomorrow night. Dinner's on you."

"Deal."

"What do you ride?"

"Modified Road King."

"Whadja do to it?"

Josh drew a deep breath. "Engine: 88 with oil cooler. Changed the cams to S&S gear drives with a .510 lift. Took out the fuel injection and replaced it with an S&S Super-E, Yost Power Tube, S&S manifold and Pingel High Flow petcock. S&S Teardrop air cleaner cover with a K&N filter. Screamin' Eagle Hi-Performance ignition unit with a 6200 rpm rev limiter. Accel SuperCoil, Firewire plug wires and spiral wound metal core wires. Accel Platinum tipped plugs. Five-speed tranny with Barnett kevlar clutch, self-adjusting hydraulic chain tensioner. Screamin' Eagle dualies. Progressive springs in front with higher viscosity, Progressives in back. Changed the rear swingarm bushings to "STA BOW" nylon high density. SBS semi-metallic disc brake pads and the brake lines are stainless steel braids. Went to tubeless wheels."

"You took out the fuel injection?"

"It was pissin' me off."

"Is it here?"

"Naw, man. Drove my box. It's gonna rain."

The Rhinelanders looked out the front window. It was almost dark.

"We should get going," Reb said.

They all stood. "I'll see you guys out."

They paused on the deck that ran the length of the building. Reb lit a cig and pointed to a fat-looking Harley with a rectangular headlight. "That's my Fat Bob."

The only other bike was a Victory with saddlebags. Both bikes had windscreens. Josh pointed to his 300. "That's what I'm drivin'. I woulda rode, but it looks like rain."

The first mist swept over the parking lot, blurring windshields and covering seats with moisture. Reb flicked his cigarette over the rail like a little comet.

CHAPTER

15

ON THE ROAD

The black Mercedes barreled west through Kansas on State Highway Ninety-six, between endless fields of corn and wheat. It was Saturday afternoon. Scipio had been driving straight for fourteen hours, swallowing little white pills from an amber plastic bottle, washing them down with cans of Red Bull. Ashley woke in the back seat and rubbed her eyes.

"I gotta go to the bathroom."

"Hang on," Scipio said. He sounded like Bing Crosby, whom Ashley knew from her father's annual *White Christmas* tradition. "There's a wayside up ahead, or do you want to hold it until we get to a town?"

"Now, please."

A green and yellow John Deere hauling a threshing machine passed them going east. Scipio and the farmer waved at each other. The wayside was a gravel rectangle surrounded by a wood fence enclosing a picnic table and a metal trash can with a smashed lid. They stepped out into crisp fall air. The sky was cornflower blue, and a hawk spiraled in the distance. Across the street, a herd of Guernsey lazed and nibbled. A plaque mounted on the fence said, "In Memory of Harold Groves, Loving Husband, Father, and Farmer, 1929-1991."

Grabbing her backpack, Ashley loped into the five-foot corn, found a corner, pulled down her panties and squatted, balancing herself between two stalks. When she finished, she pulled out a pack of tissues, wiped her bottom, stood and pulled up her pants. She put the tissues back in the pack and reached for her cellphone. She groped bottom. No cell phone. Frantically, she went through all the other pockets.

Returning to the wayside, she opened the rear door and felt around between the seat cushions, then did the same for the front. She turned to Scipio, who stood with his hands clasped behind him, staring west.

She walked up to him. "My cell phone is missing."

"I left it in a dumpster in Topeka."

Ashley couldn't speak.

"Why?" she said.

"They can track you that way. You're starting a new life. From now on, everything will be fresh. Your thoughts, your body, your friends, your work. Do you trust me?"

"Yes, of course."

"Then, believe me, I have your best interests at heart. Your father will command every resource to find you. He's a police officer. I understand the police mind. When the time is right, you will choose for yourself whether you want to talk to him."

He turned to face her, the boyish face, eyes that matched the sky. Paul Newman in *Cool Hand Luke*. John Stamos in *My Big Fat Greek Wedding*. "Do you understand?"

"Yes, of course. I just don't want him to worry."

"Why don't you write him a letter? Tell him that you have found your independence, you are in no danger, that you will be in touch, and that you love him. Show it to me when you're finished. I'll have it posted from New York. Or California. I do it all the time. When we get to the ranch, you can use our landline. It cannot be traced."

"You said that the human spirit is infinite, and that you believe in reincarnation."

Scipio pulled out a silver cigarette case, flipped it open, withdrew a Dunhill, and lit it with a gold Ronson. "God's Breath takes the best parts of Christianity, Buddhism, and Judaism, and intertwines them with Gaia, or love of Earth."

"Why did you come get me? Why drive all that way? I could have flown out."

"Do you remember the first conversation we had? On Facebook?"

"Not really."

"You said that people needed to believe in something greater than themselves to be truly happy. When you said that, I thought it was extraordinary. Most girls your age are consumed with what makeup to wear or getting an abortion. Our further conversations only confirmed what

I felt. You are one of the rare ones. You are one who can go all the way to the top."

"Top of what?"

"The mountain. Life. The spirit. You'll see. Let's go."

They turned south on Eighty-three, pulling into the Deerfield Truck Stop in Garden City. Scipio drove to the back of the parking lot and shut off the engine. Reaching over the seat, he pulled up a squarish black valise, opened it on the armrest, pulled out a wide-brimmed black hat, the brim encircled by tiny beaded chains.

"Want to go inside? Put this on."

Ashley put it on. "Takes up a lot of space!"

"You look smashing! Toreador!"

Ashley lowered the mirror, turned this way and that, smiling, tongue out, pouting.

"I love it."

Opening the door with her foot, she headed for the long low white building, blazing in the late afternoon sun. Scipio pulled up to the farthest island, pulled on nitrile gloves, put on a long-billed black cap and a pair of heavy-framed sunglasses, opened the gas lid, got out, shuffled through a deck of credit cards, choosing one belonging to Marcy Fensterman, a fictitious person created by his tech team.

Scipio zipped the card, placed the nozzle in the tank and filled the car with premium. Two thirty-seven a gallon. Gas prices were in the basement since Saudi Arabia and Kuwait got in a snit and began dumping petroleum. Scipio had seen it coming ten years back, when he'd invested in shale and natural gas. He turned his back to the station and crossed his arms while the tank filled. Pocketing the receipt, he returned the car to the back of the parking lot and headed for the truck stop.

Earl's Cafe flashed flamingo pink in the dirty window. Scipio stepped inside, repulsed by the odor of Pine-sol, rotating hot dogs, taco sauce, and gas. He tried the men's room door. Locked. He leaned against the wall, checking his cellphone.

Manny texted, "Clark broke arm in training. Viv fixed him up. He'll be all right."

Muriel texted, "Leader, what do you want me to do with all this rhubarb?"

The men's door opened and a heavy-set trucker exited, adjusting his belt buckle. Scipio went inside and closed the door. The stench would gag a dog off a gut wagon. Breathing carefully through his mouth, Scipio withdrew a book of matches and lit them serially, waving them around the room. Only then did he remove his gloves and throw them in the trash.

After relieving himself, he wiped his ass until it bled. He flushed. He pulled off a wad of toilet paper, dipped it in the water and wiped his ass again. He used more toilet paper to dab it dry, as one might powder one's cheeks.

He washed his hands over and over. He eyed the hot air dryer with contempt. More convenient his ass. All it did was spew germs. He pulled six sheets of paper towel from the machine, dried carefully, used the towel to open the door, and threw the towel in a trash can in the store. Ashley stood at the counter, framed by a cigarette display on her left and the state lottery on her right, as the cashier, a middle-aged woman with an unlikely blonde wave, counted out her change.

"Here ya go, honey. Love your hat."

Ashley put a hand to her mouth and smiled. "Oh thank you!"

Nothing Scipio could do about it. Chances are, no one would ever ask that cashier if she'd seen Ashley in her store. Scipio's license plate was designed, like his hats, to fool video software. The numbers, coloring, and state flickered and changed depending on the angle and the amount of light.

Scipio pushed the glass door open with his shoulder, held it for Ashley, who clutched a paper bag.

"Whadja get?"

"Some ice tea and salted almonds. I also had a hot dog."

Scipio looked at his Breitling. "If you can hang on for four hours, we'll hit Pueblo and I'll take you to a real restaurant."

"I'd love that."

More vehicles had arrived. When they reached the back row, a new Dodge Ram had pulled in so close to the Mercedes that Scipio couldn't open the door. He froze, staring at the shiny red truck, taking in every detail. The raised suspension, the cartoon skunk hanging from the rearview, the dirt and dust on the sides and windscreen. Deep within, a door opened releasing a hideous scream.

"Oh, what a jerk," Ashley said. "You'll have to crawl in on the passenger side."

Scipio turned and smiled. Ashley's face went blank and she stepped back. "What's wrong?"

"Nothing, my dear. One minute and we shall be on our way."

Scipio walked around back and crouched in the gravel at the edge of a fallow field, selecting a triangular rock. He walked up to the driver's side of the truck digging the point of the rock deeply into the dusty red finish. He walked around the front, dragging the rock across the hood like a tiny plow. Ashley stood frozen, clutching her bag.

Scipio tossed the rock over his shoulder, beeped open the Mercedes, crawled through the passenger door and sat behind the wheel. He looked up through the open door.

Ashley slid in beside him.

CHAPTER

16

STUART

Josh fell asleep to the loons on the marsh. He woke when sunlight slanted in through the gap in the curtains. He pulled on his sweats, white socks, and Nikes, pocketed his cellphone and keys and stretched, bracing himself against the dresser as he slanted forward, working his hams.

It was in the low fifties as he stepped outside to early morning traffic, mostly pick-ups and farm vehicles, trucks filled with corn, pulling cattle trailers, and four by fours. A yellow school bus passed, with *Herman County School District* on the side in black letters, filled with students, most looking down. At their phones. One kid with a cowlick waved. Josh waved back. He set off at an easy pace down the left shoulder, water running through a drainage ditch to his side. It was gray but the storm had moved on leaving the air fresh and fragrant. Soon Josh was on a dirt road that cut through swamp, rushes and cattails on either side. He passed turn-offs with locked gates and lonely mailboxes marked Rural Route. Sometimes a hand-carved sign. "The Hansens!" declared a cartoon crow.

A bald eagle floated down to its nest on an ash cantilevered over a lake.

Josh did about three miles and turned around. Back at the motel he showered and dressed in clean jeans and a fresh shirt, wondered if he should phone Ninja to see how Fig was doing. No. Ninja would have called him on one of the burners if anything was wrong. Josh sat at the little desk in his room beneath a landscape painting of a pristine lake surrounded by fir, and dialed the front desk.

"What's up, Mr. Pratt?"

"Can I make a local call through this phone?"

"Sure. Hang up, dial one, and then the number."

Josh pushed the button down and dialed Turville.

"Stan Turville."

"Josh Pratt, Stan. We on for the Muskie?"

"Sure. I don't have a whole lot going on. Five?"

"See you there."

Josh walked down the street to Erroll's Diner, sat at a breakfast bar with some fishermen, and ordered fried eggs and bacon. He walked down Main Street toward King's Methodist, a solid red stone church with a bell tower over the arched front entrance, a wrought-iron ringed cemetery in back, blanketed in orange, red, and yellow leaves. Fall came early in the north.

Josh entered through the double doors and stood in

the narthex, inhaling the scent of waxed oak. Rows of iron hooks protruded from the wall to hold parishioners' coats. A floor mat at the nave's entrance said, "Welcome." At the far end, a slight, gray-haired man in a tweed jacket with leather elbow patches swept the crossing. He looked up as Josh approached.

"Reverend McGraw?"

"That's right. What can I do for you?"

"Josh Pratt, Madison. I'm a private investigator."

They shook hands. "Well, this is a first. I hope Mrs. Hamilton hasn't accused me of stealing from the collection plate again."

Josh grinned. "No, sir. I'm trying to locate a missing girl. Her name is Ashley Calloway and her father is a police detective."

He showed McGraw the picture. McGraw took it and looked at it in silence for long seconds.

"A lovely child. Haven't seen her. We don't have many black parishioners."

"Sir, she left with a man called Scipio, who is the leader of a Colorado-based cult called God's Breath. I'm trying to locate a survivors' group around here. Do you know about that?"

"I know about God's Breath. I know they'll do anything to track down and destroy those who have left their group. They will use any subterfuge to advance their cause. I can't really discuss anything about them until I'm satisfied you are who you say you are, and that you're not secretly working for them. I'm very sorry to be so blunt, but God's Breath is almost satanic in their desire to control their people, and especially those who have left."

"Fair enough." Josh handed McGraw his card. "You can contact Detective Heinz Calloway of the Madison Police Department. I'll give you his number."

"Give me a couple hours," the pastor said.

Josh walked down Main Street. Jack's Hardware, Bob's Liquors, the Law Offices of Ben Henderson, Kyle Lonegan, Doctor of Veterinary Medicine, All American Karate, Belinda's Fashions. There wasn't a name brand or big box in sight. A couple blocks south he made out the Golden Arches across the street from the Arby's stetson. The street was lightly populated. Housewives shopping, skateboarders stuntin' on the steel handrail and steps leading to the Herman County Courthouse, a red brick Carnegie Library. Josh walked up the steps and read the plaque.

This Library is funded by the Andrew Carnegie Foundation. Andrew Carnegie was a Scots/American businessman and philanthropist who built over 2500 libraries between 1883 and 1929. The construction date was 1925.

There was a tiny park across the street, a rectangle of green surrounded by a wrought-iron fence, several inward-facing iron and wood benches, and a roofed dais in the center. An old man in conductor's coveralls and suspenders sat on a bench, feeding pigeons.

Josh read the bronze plaque.

Bremerton Park. In loving memory of Carl Bremerton,

beloved husband, father, horse fancier, and friend to the cranberry. Nick and Amy Bremerton, 1979.

"Carl Bremerton," the old man said. "Sumbitch knew how to drink."

Josh turned to the old man, who held a brown paper bag between his legs. "Excuse me?"

"Carl and me, we're old drinkin' buddies. It don't tell ya he drank himself to death on accounta what the bank did to him. No. They don't mention that."

"What did the bank do to him?"

"Called in its note, summer of '78. Worst plague we seen up here. Carl sold seed. Business was boomin'. So he borrowed a hundred grand to expand and then what happens. Flea beetles. Devastated the cranberry crop."

The man looked around, furtively brought his bagged bottle to his lips, swallowed, returned it to his thighs and placed a finger over his mouth. He winked.

"Public drinkin' is frowned upon in these waters. I don't know why."

"Sir, you know anything about God's Breath?"

The old man sobered up in a hurry. He withdrew in upon himself, like a turtle, eyes growing smaller, receding beneath an occipital brow.

"Fuck you want to know?"

"Sir, I'm a private detective looking for this girl."

He showed the man Ashley's picture.

"Pretty girl."

"Her father has reason to believe she joined God's Breath.

I would like to talk to someone who has been in God's Breath. The information could be helpful to her recovery."

"Any money involved?"

"No, sir. But the father would be grateful."

The old man mulled it over. He had a red face, a big nose, and fine white hair that hung down to his eyes. He offered Josh the bottle. Josh waved his hand.

"Can't. I'm working."

"Well, look here. I guess it's no secret. Young Lee Wipf was with them for two years 'til his old man up and hired some mercenaries to fetch him outta there. I think they called themselves the Black Morels or some such shit. You'd have to ask old Wipf."

"Where can I find him?"

"He runs the Wayward Inn on Lake Hermitage. It ain't far from here."

Josh handed the man his card. "Thank you. If you think of anything else, please call me. I'd be happy to buy you a drink, but I don't start drinking until five, at the earliest."

"Well, I admire a man who's got self-control. God knows, I never did have none. It's a fuckin' miracle I've lived this long. Stuart Federer."

"Josh Pratt."

They shook hands. Josh sat on the bench. "Those Rhinelanders a wild bunch?"

The old man spat. "Not hardly. Oh they're tough enough, but that comes from college wrestling. Not exactly the Hell's Angels. Upstanding citizens who like to ride.

I used to ride myself 'til I fell off my Harley goin' around a bend and hit a deer. If I hadn't hit that deer, it coulda been a lot worse."

"How'd you hit the deer?"

"Well, it was just the damnedest thing. I was coming around a tight corner on my Panhead, out by the Spackle Lakes, and I hit a patch of grease, like some goddamn bear paused in the middle of the road and took a shit, and slid toward the outside. I was certain I was a goner. Then this deer leaps out of the woods to cross the road and I hit it broadside. Knocked the fucker down. Me too. We both lay there a sec, and it looks at me, and I look at it, and then it gets up, shakes itself off, and limps off into the trees. Damnedest thing."

"That's just God lookin' out for you."

"Amen, brother. Well, I got to get going."

"You can catch me later at the Muskie, if you're serious about that drink."

CHAPTER 17

KING'S METHODIST

Josh returned to the church at three. An old Jeep and a Kia Seoul were parked in the parking lot. Inside, a young woman sat in the back row, her head resting on her folded hands on the back of the bench in front of her. McGraw sat in the front row, knee to knee with a stolid older woman wearing a dark blue wool suit and a narrow-brimmed felt hat. Josh sat in the bench opposite the young woman, plucked the Bible from the book rest in front.

He opened it to Matthew. Father Dorgan had been keen on Matthew, Luke, and John. "Till heaven and earth pass, one jot or one tittle shall in no wise pass from the law, till all be fulfilled." Daniel Bloom always said, "I don't have much use for the New Testament. Give me that old time religion. But I do gotta admit, Matthew may have been a lawyer."

Josh became so engrossed he wasn't aware McGraw was standing next to him until the pastor touched him on the shoulder. He jumped.

"Didn't mean to startle you. It's good to see a man such as yourself reading the Bible."

Josh replaced the Bible and slid out of the bench. "Can we talk?"

The pastor led the way back through the choir into a small office that might have belonged to a college professor, with a wall devoted to books, a framed Delacroix print of the Savior on the Cross, a rosewood cross, a framed Yellow Submarine movie poster, an Edwardian walnut desk, and a mounted globe. The multifaceted window behind the desk looked out on the cemetery where an old man in coveralls carried a broom from grave to grave sweeping off the leaves.

McGraw gestured toward a red leather chair. "Would you like some lemonade?"

"Sure, thanks."

McGraw knelt at a dormitory cube refrigerator crouching among the books and removed two bottles of Snapple lemonade. Josh twisted the lid off and drank half the bottle. "Yeah, baby."

"I talked to Detective Calloway. He told me quite a bit about you. Said you'd got religion in prison and named Father Michael Dorgan."

Josh nodded.

"I knew Father Dorgan from our Interfaith summer camps which we used to hold. Haven't had one in years, I'm afraid."

"Do you know how I can get in touch with Dorgan?"

"No, I'm afraid not. But I'll look into it. How can I

help you?"

"I'm looking for the God's Breath survival group."

"Yes, there is one. It's kind of informal for obvious reasons, but sometimes they meet out at the Wayward Inn on Lake Heritage."

"You know Horace Wipf?"

"I know he hosts the survivors' group."

"I heard he hired some mercs to spring his boy Lee."

"True. How do you know that, if you don't mind my asking? We're all pretty close-mouthed around here."

"Stuart Federer told me."

McGraw nodded. "Old Stu. Used to own a John Deere franchise in Rhinelander. Loved to ride his motorcycle, until he had an encounter with a deer. He rode that motorcycle drunk for years. God must have been watching over him. There's no other explanation. He was always a drinker. His old man was a drinker. Used to worship here every Sunday. Hasn't been in for ten years."

"How's he live?"

"He's got money. He sold that dealership right after he got divorced. Must have killed him to hang on. She was a real piece of work. Tried to take him for everything he had, but old Stu's a wily SOB. His lawyer hired a private investigator and got pics of the missus screwing the county tax assessor. It's our own little Harper Valley PTA."

"What do you know about the mercs?"

"You oughta ask Horace. I'll call him and tell him you're coming. Otherwise he might blow your head off."

"Appreciate it."

"Would you mind if I prayed for you?"

"Hell no."

McGraw came around the desk, sat next to Josh and took his hands.

"Dear Lord, please watch over this good man Joshua Pratt, and bless him on his journey. May he find this girl and return her unharmed to the bosom of her family. Thank you, Lord. Amen."

"Amen," Josh repeated.

"You go to church?"

"When I can. Not all the time. But most of the time."

"Where do you go?"

"I go to a little Baptist church in Middleton. Give me that old time religion."

"I fear Christianity is going the way of the newspaper. This used to be a Christian country. Don't get me wrong. We each worship God in our own way. I have nothing against other religions."

"I ain't too crazy about Islam," Josh said.

"Why is that?"

"Personal experience."

"Well, what does religion mean to you?"

"Preaching is one thing, but a true religion, to my thinking, is one that binds a group of people through use of laws and universal ideas to bring them together and give them a sense of belonging. Past that, you simply get the problems of religion as are the nature of humans. But is that worse than having a sense of fitting in and being part of a community?"

"To me," McGraw said, "religion is belief in a higher authority. A moral authority. I don't see how people can look at a butterfly or a lake and think this is all random. I was a profane little prick. I was into getting high, getting drunk, and partying all weekend. Then one day, I woke up in Milwaukee, glued to the floor in my own vomit, and some house I didn't remember entering. And I had a revelation. I won't bore you with my revelation, but it was enough for me to get straight and seek a life in service to Christ.

"This was after three years in college, mind you. Majoring in political science. We used to make fun of the Christians on campus, but they always seemed happy. Happier than us, at least. Once I sobered up, I attended St. Mark's Seminary School. I also visit the Bad River Indian Reservation and the L. Babcock Juvenile Offenders Camp."

"Do they have barbed wire and guard towers?"

McGraw laughed. "No, but there's only one road in and out, and it's surrounded by swamp. Most of those kids come from the big city, and when the guards start talkin' about the hodag, they get real nervous."

"No man is truly happy unless he believes in something greater than himself."

McGraw nodded. "Faith's a gift. You either have it, or you don't. Once you lose it, you can always get it back again, but it's hard. It's hard. Let me phone Horace while you're here."

Josh got up. "I'll meet you out front. Thank you for the lemonade."

CHAPTER

18

LEE

The Wayward Inn on Lake Hermitage was two stories tall beneath a steep Norwegian roof. It bore a hex sign below the eaves, a broad front porch with a dozen empty Adirondacks, a log cabin dining wing shooting off toward the left, and it was set before Lake Hermitage, which was as blue as a robin's egg, a relic of a bygone day. Josh's wheels crunched on the gravel road as he pulled into a parking lot surrounded by wood fencing, big enough for fifty, holding six, including Josh's Chrysler. An old Chevy pick-up, a Toyota 4X4, and an older cream Avalon, with Illinois plates. The other two were Wisconsin.

Josh tried not to memorize the plates. He was cursed with a near-perfect memory and worried that he might reach capacity someday and be unable to function. He would forget how to tie his shoes. It was a bright, crisp, cold morning, and there was a flotilla of Canadian honkers off the long wood pier. A chevron of geese flew overhead honking, heading south.

Josh went up wood steps to the porch, which was overhung with a slanted roof, and paused outside the front door to read the plaque.

Wayward Inn
State Historic Landmark, 1988.
Built in 1921 by Reginald Wipf, the Wayward Inn has been in the Wipf Family's hands continuously. Al Capone, Bugsy Siegel, John Dillinger, Machine Gun Kelly, and Baby Face Nelson all visited.

He opened the door. A bell tinkled overhead. The great room fronted the length of the building, sixty by forty, furnished in leather sofas with throw rugs on a hardwood floor and a stag horn chandelier on the ceiling. A wolf, a deer, and a bear looked down from their plaques over the front desk. To the left, a long wooden bar stretched before a huge map of Northern Wisconsin, skirted by row after row of liquor. It smelled of leather, sawdust, and history. Rows of framed black and white photos caught Josh's attention. Passing the broad steps going to the second floor, Josh got that *gee-whiz* feeling from looking into the past and thinking, Holy shit. Right here.

A smiling Al Capone with a beautiful chorine sat at one of

the dining room tables. The girl sported the flapper hairstyle and stood with one of her long, mesh-enclosed legs folded on the other. She was leaning back, mouth parted, holding a ten-inch cigarette holder, a cloud of vapor hovered at her lips. Capone was leaning back, smiling, hand to his brim.

Harry Truman was standing on the dock holding a fifteen-inch bass.

Tony Curtis and Janet Leigh in dazzling white, he with a captain's hat, she in a one-piece bathing suit, lounged in a magnificent wood-bodied Chris Craft. The lodge was in the background.

Elvis Costello wore a pork pie hat at the bar.

"I tell people Elvis slept here. I just don't tell 'em which Elvis."

Josh turned to find Horace Wipf, a tall, white-haired gentleman, with a nose like a conning tower, standing behind the front desk wearing a red and black plaid shirt.

"Good morning, sir. Josh Pratt."

"Understand you're looking for a missing girl."

Josh went over, slid his card across the desk and shook Wipf's hand. "Yes, sir. She went to meet a man named Scipio."

"Scipio." He said it like he was spitting a bad almond. "She must be very special to attract his attention. I will pray for her. Understand you want to talk to my boy."

"If I may. He lived at the compound in Colorado?"

"He was there for two years. Thought I'd never see him again. I went out there to bring him home, and they wouldn't let me on the property. Bunch of damn hippies with guns. That's when I decided I would have to take more precipitous action. Why do you want to talk to Lee?"

"Sir, it may be necessary for me to do what you did. I may have to go out there and get her myself, and if I do that, I want to know what it's like. Do they have a fence, do they have video, dogs, patrols, guns, a regimen."

"I had to hire some specialists. They done good. Happy to recommend them."

"Thank you, sir. I'm familiar with the Black Morels."

"You could ask them. They waited until a group from the ranch went into town for supplies. There were just two of them. They accosted the cult members as they were leaving the local supermarket. There were five of the God's Breath people, and two Black Morels. The Black Morels were able to convince the cultists to let Lee go. It ain't gonna be any easier."

"The Black Morels are in Richmond and I am here."

"Well, you got a point. Hope you don't mind if I sit in. Lee's twenty-six now, but he's still the same trusting fool. Only now he trusts in Jesus."

"So do I."

"All right. I'll go fetch him. You want anything to drink while you're waiting? You can help yourself to soft drinks. They're in that glass cabinet at the end of the bar."

Josh grabbed a bottled water and sat on one of the dark brown leather sofas beneath the chandelier. The rough-hewn table bore copies of *Field & Stream, Outdoor Life, Amer-*

ican Angler and hardbound *Readers Digests*. Josh picked one up. October 1969. *The Carpet Baggers*. *The Godfather*. *The Agony and the Ecstasy*.

Through the horizontal front window, he could see the pine forest receding, snatches of blue through the trees. Wipf returned with Lee, fresh-faced, blond bangs, wearing coveralls and smelling of dirt. Josh stood.

"Mr. Pratt? I'm Lee Wipf."

"Thank you for agreeing to see me, Lee."

Wipf headed for the bar. "Lee, you want a Pepsi?"

"Sure would, Dad. Thanks."

They sat on opposite sofas with the table between them. Josh pulled out a pen and pad. "Mind if I take a few notes?"

"No, I don't mind."

Wipf turned from the bar. "No recording."

"No recording," Josh said. "How'd you get mixed up with God's Breath?"

Lee leaned back, comfortable. "I hitchhiked out to Denver. I was a reckless and wayward child, didn't know what I wanted to do. Still don't. I ran out of money and was looking for a job when this girl comes up to me, starts talking about this wonderful ranch up in the mountains where people can just be themselves and learn to get along with nature and all that horse shit. I was young and stupid so I followed her up there.

"She introduced me to Scipio. He freaked me out. He put his hands on my head and told me that we had known each other in a past life, that it was fate we should meet, otherwise I was destined to wander, rootless, until I died from syphilis or AIDs or something like that. They sucked me in with free food and all the great looking girls, but the girls were strictly "look don't touch." Scipio saved them all for himself."

"Where's the ranch?"

"It's outside of Harrison, which is practically a ghost town, up near Gunnison. It's at eight thousand feet. There's only one road in and out, and it backs up against Mount Sagamore, which is thirteen thousand. It's about twenty acres in a little valley with a barn, and they keep about a dozen head of cattle, sheep, and a couple of horses. They're pretty much self-sufficient. They got solar and wind, grow shit all year round in a greenhouse. Once a week, some of them go into town for supplies."

"Tell him what happened when you tried to leave," the old man urged.

"Oh yeah. I'm kinda slow. Took me about three months to figure that it wasn't the life I wanted. Snowed three feet in November and I was trapped inside with a bunch of zombies. I mean, they had no idea what was going on in the real world. Scipio was their god. Whatever he said. I talked about maybe getting out of there and they clammed up on me. Treated me like a pariah. All of a sudden, I'm sleeping in the barn and eating slops, and Scipio's got me up the mountain every day, cutting down trees until I could barely move. So, one night I stole a pair of snowshoes."

"Show him the brand," Wipf said.

CHAPTER
19

FACILITATORS

Lee unfastened his shoulder straps and pulled up his shirt revealing a four-inch red welt on his left pectoral that appeared to be a stylized 'S' over a lightning bolt.

"They caught me sneaking out. Scipio's got this guy— they call him Gladiator. He's some kind of martial arts expert. He worked me over pretty good. Then, they held me down in the barn and heated up the branding iron. They've got a forge out there, make their own knives and shit. Hurt like a motherfucker. I couldn't believe it. They locked me in an unheated shed. I thought I'd freeze to death. I passed out. When I woke, it was just before dawn. Somebody had unlocked the door. I could barely move I hurt so bad, but I raided a box of clothes they keep in the barn, found another pair of snowshoes, and I didn't stop until I hit the highway, hitched a ride with a llama rancher."

"A llama rancher?"

"Yeah. Lotta llamas up there. They thrive in the altitude and their fur is worth a fortune. We go maybe two miles when they caught up with us. They were going into town anyway to get groceries so they decided to take me along. There was three of them, including Gladiator. They started telling me what all Scipio would do to me when we got back. They took me into the grocery store with them, had me carry the groceries out to the car. I come out with this box of groceries, and there are two men leaning against the car. You could tell they were military from the way they looked. Gladiator come out with the others. One of those strangers looks at a photo, looks at me. 'You Lee Wipf?' he says. 'Yes I am,' I replied. 'Your father sent us to bring you back.' And I knew right away it was true. So I said, 'let's go.' Gladiator started to follow, but one of the men turned around and held up his hand. And they let me go. Then, in their car going down the mountain, they said it was just dumb luck they saw me there. They were fixing to go on into the compound and get me."

"Tell me about Gladiator."

"A real tough son of a bitch. I've seen him break rocks with his bare hands. He might be an Indian. They have a kung fu school up there, or something like that. I wanted to train, but you've got to be there a year before they let you sign up. I watched them training in the yard, about a dozen of them, eight men, four women. They'd been at it for years. It looked like one of those kung fu movies at the Shaolin Temple where the old dude with a white beard leads fifty students in horse stance, throwing punches, shouting. Sometimes they screen kung fu movies. The dubbing is terrible. All the guards have training."

"Guards?"

"They call them God's Teeth. That's funny, isn't it? The only thing they facilitate is keeping anyone from leaving. They'll facilitate a black eye or a beat down. Sometimes, when two guys get in a tiff, they have to fight each other before the whole camp. Whether they've trained or not. I mean, they had these two guys, one was morbidly obese, and the other like a scarecrow. They had a slap fest, and then the Teeth stepped in and beat the shit out of both of them."

"Are you telling me God's Breath is not a peaceful religion?"

"Ha! You should hear Scipio go on. 'Jesus what a fighter! John 2:13. He didn't just chase those money lenders from the temple! He kicked their asses! He knew how to use a staff. And you know what the Bible means when it says money lenders! It means Jooooos!'" Lee drew it out with contempt.

"Any Jews up there?"

Lee lowered his shirt and slipped his arms through the shoulder straps. "Oh yeah. And they would tell you all about it, how they were breaking away from their oppressive religion now that they'd found the one true path."

"How long ago did you escape?"

"Next month will be a year."

"I wonder if you could write down for me the name of everybody at the camp you remember, and what they do."

Horace heaved himself to his feet, went behind the front desk and returned with a legal pad and a pen.

"Also, could you draw a map of the place?"

Lee picked up the pen and bent over the table. "I can do that. I'm pretty good. I'd like to draw comic books."

Josh thought about Polly Furst, the cartoonist who'd hired him to protect her. He thought about her every day.

"What about Google Earth?" Horace said. "Maybe you can get an aerial shot."

"That's a good idea. What's the address?"

Lee looked up. "Just the God's Breath Ranch, at the end of Sky Gulch Road."

Josh texted the address to Ninja on burner #1.

"Tell me about Scipio."

"I shoulda known that guy was bogus when I saw the women sneaking in and out of his house. He's got his own house set back against the cliff, above the main ranch. We got a lake, too. It's right up against the continental divide. It's a two-story Victorian house, looks brand new because he's got his crew working the trim, working the yard, whatever. He's got one of those kung fu wooden men on the front porch, and he would work it for about an hour each morning. You could hear him all over the valley. Thunk, thunk, thunk. He looked like he knew what he was doing."

"Are you telling me Scipio is a martial artist?"

"I guess. I wouldn't know hapkido from Kokomo Joe."

"Lee wrestled in college," Horace said.

"That's right, pops. I lettered too. I'm not afraid of any

man, my own size."

Josh made a finger gun. "You're a smart kid. Write down those names for me."

Lee looked at the legal pad. "This might take a while. This here's the garage. Scipio keeps his rods in here. We got a couple trucks and a beat-up old van for the ranch, but inside this here, he's got a Ferrari, a Cobra, a Jaguar, I don't know what else. I only saw a couple when he brought them out and drove them around. Then we'd have to wash and wax it. Every time."

"Scipio's a car nut?" Josh said.

"Big time."

Josh stood. "Take your time. I'll take a look around."

Horace stood. "Let me give you the tour."

They went out on the pier. The wind off the lake was cold and the water choppy. Another chevron of geese flew overhead. From the end of the pier, Josh looked across the broad lake to the opposite shore, mostly covered in fir, with a few big houses, each with its own pier and boat port. Aside from an aluminum skiff fishing in an inlet a mile away, there were no boats.

"How many are in the group?" Josh said.

"Five. These people are survivors and wary of outsiders. I let you talk to Lee because I know that girl needs help, and the reverend vouched for you. What assurances can you give me that nobody knows about your visit? These people are vindictive. I can't have any blowback. We're barely scraping by as it is."

"Nobody knows I'm here, and they won't. Any chance I can talk to some of the others?"

Wipf shook his head. "No chance. They're not as strong as Lee, and I doubt they have anything else to add."

"He your only child?"

Wipf paused at the end of the pier, hands in hip pockets, and gazed out over the choppy water. "My oldest, Rich, died in Afghanistan."

"Very sorry to hear it."

"Violet and I have learned to deal with it. McGraw helped. We have a daughter who's married and lives in Austin. She's expecting her second child."

"Congratulations, Gramps."

"I keep having nightmares. The Jonestown Massacre. Hale-Bopp. Branch Davidians."

"Talk to McGraw. If you would feel safer with someone else on the premises, let me know."

"Well, let's go back and see what he wrote."

CHAPTER 20

BIG AL'S CADILLAC

1. Scipio. You know about him.

2. Gladiator, about forty-five. Lean and mean. I've seen him break rocks with his hands. They call his enforcers God's Teeth.

3. Kristin Nunez. Late twenties, dark hair, a stunner, Scipio's main squeeze, although he's probably having relations with five or six at a time. I see them go to and from his house in back. She used to be in some game show, I think.

4. Scott Lazarus. His tech guy. Dude's got a set up in the main building, looks like a science fiction set. He's responsible for the websites, and all the shit they put on the dark web, and going after people who quit.

5. Lucy Rockpile. That's not her real name. We call her Frau Blucher. She's Scipio's other enforcer, always carries a clipboard. If she catches you goofing off, or doing something the wrong way, or if she thinks you're "smart talking" her, she makes a note and you have to go in for a lecture and

punishment, which includes hauling rocks, digging fence posts, or cleaning the bathrooms.

6. Bikers. I can tell they're bikers from the tattoos all over their bodies. They're mostly white, although there's one guy who looks Mayan and is built like a pyramid.

7. Movie stars. I'm not sure on the names because I don't go to the movies, but I think one guy was called Frank, short, dark hair, very handsome, liked to work out with Gladiator. I think he was in a movie called *Spaceship*. And a beautiful woman named Rose, very tall with long auburn hair. I think she won a Grammy or something.

"Anybody ever come around asking after Lee, or the others?"

Horace shook his head. "You're the first."

"Do they have guns?"

Lee scrunched. "I never saw any, but we heard gunshots from time to time. Upslope. They could only have come from someone who was either a member, or who passed through the ranch. And nobody passes through the ranch. Also, they serve a lot of fresh venison."

Josh took the pad. "Thanks very much, guys. May I phone you if I have any questions?"

Father and son looked at one another.

"You can phone me," Horace said, and gave Josh his phone number.

Josh went to his car and used one of the burners to phone Ninja.

"A cleaning service found Ashley's cell phone in a trash

can in a truck stop in Nebraska," Ninja said. "They over-nighted it to Calloway. He's going to drop it off."

"Okay. I got one more night here, then I'll be back. Any hits?"

"I'm having trouble hacking Facebook's face recognition vault. They must be getting paranoid. It's just a matter of time. I'm on it."

"Okay. Find out what you can about the Black Morels. They're a mercenary group. You find anything on that address?"

"Yes. Did you ditch the first phone I gave you? The one you used earlier today?"

Josh looked at the phone. "I'm still using the same phone."

"Get rid of it. Right now. Throw it in water. Damn fool."

"Okay. I'm outta here first thing tomorrow morning. Should be back by noon."

"Don't wake me."

Josh got out of his car, walked to the end of the pier, and hurled the burner as far as he could. A heron took off from some cattails, flapping its long white wings, skimming the surface like a seaplane.

Josh parked outside the Muskie at five. There were six other vehicles in the lot. He went inside and took a seat at the bar beneath the gaze of the stuffed animals. Josh liked sitting at the bar because he could watch the whole room in the mirror without being noticed. Stuart Federer wasn't there. The same bartender came over.

"You must crave my cookin'."

"I'll take whatever IPA you have on draft and a cheeseburger."

"Comin' right up."

Josh turned his attention to the television on the wall beneath the mounted deer. The Bucks were playing the Heat. BLACK LIVES MATTER was painted on the court. Bucks were up by six in the first quarter. Josh had just polished off his dinner when Stuart Federer came in wearing Oshkosh coveralls, a plaid shirt, and a John Deere hat. He sat next to Josh.

"Buy a feller a beer?"

Josh signaled to the bartender. "You know, I almost rode my bike up here."

"You a biker too, huh?"

"All my life."

"Ain't rid since I hit that deer. I figure that was my wake-up call. Now I owe God one." He drew a symbol in the air. "You find what you're lookin' for?"

"You were very helpful. I'm outta here tomorrow."

"Any luck with that girl?"

"Workin' on it. You were a John Deere guy."

Federer grabbed his hat. "Still got this hat."

"How long were you in business?"

"Just me? Or the Federer legacy? My old man started out selling Cadillacs, and ended up selling tractors. My grandfather started the first Cadillac dealership in Herman County. Sold Al Capone a Cadillac once. Paid cash."

"Did you see it?"

"No, I was in school at the time. Third grade. People

didn't talk about anything else for weeks. Nobody had a bad word to say about Capone. He was a generous tipper."

"That must have been something."

"My grandfather had a picture taken. Hung on the dealership wall for years, until my father switched over to tractors. Capone rode up in a new Caddy. My grandfather said, 'Mr. Capone, you got a new Caddy right there. Why do you want a new one?'

'Well, Marlon,' they were on a first-name basis at this time. 'That Cadillac is the wrong color. Now, who do you know around here who might appreciate a slightly used Cadillac? What archdiocese are we in?'

'Well sir, the nearest Catholic church is over in Rhinelander.'

"Well, who do you know who does good and would benefit from a slightly used Cadillac?'

"Marlon thought for a minute, and then he said, 'The Boy Scouts, I guess.' So Al left his Cadillac to Boy Scout Local Troop Nineteen. Signed the paper over and everything. We all wished he'd come back, but that was his last time up here. I never saw him."

The television showed a stock picture of Calloway. Josh signaled the bartender. "Can you turn that up?"

"...suspended with pay while the department investigates allegations of police brutality. Lieutenant Calloway is a seventeen-year veteran of the Madison Police Department. He is represented by Steven Fleiss who says his client will not comment."

"Hey!" a voice boomed. "What happened to the game?"

"Keep your pants on, Will!" the bartender sang back. "It's half time!"

Josh had one burner left. He paid for his meal and Federer's beer and went outside.

It rang twice and Calloway picked up. "Hello, Josh."

"What the fuck?"

"Elver Park. We got a report of gang activity. Peoples and Folks. When I gave the order to disperse, punk says to me he hopes my daughter's dead. I lost my temper."

"How would he know?"

"Katy Varner heard about it, tracked down the missing-persons report. Called me and I declined, but she ran a story anyway."

"Damn. I'm sorry, Heinz."

"Not your fault. Find anything?"

"I'm at Manitowish Waters. I'll be back tomorrow. I think I know where she's going and I'm gonna go get her."

"Where?"

"God's Breath. They got a compound in Colorado."

"I'll come with you."

"We'll talk about it."

Josh hung up. One was never far from water up here. He walked out behind the Muskie which had a broad deck looking out on Lake Nebagamon. Josh walked to the end of the pier and hurled his last burner into the water.

He went back to the motel, showered and went to bed.

He was on the road by eight.

CHAPTER

21

HANDICAPPED PARKING

The Mercedes sped west on Highway Fifty, with Bizet's *Carmen* playing through the eight Harman Kardon speakers. Ashley reclined her heated leather seat and drifted off, half-listening, half-dreaming. Scipio's phone chimed the Carmina Burana and he spoke via an Apple insert in his ear.

"Yes?"

He listened. "We should arrive by sundown. Don't do anything now. I will deal with them in the morning."

Beat.

"See if you can use the lasers. Ask Scott about the tracking system. That should be set up by now."

Beat.

"I want that root cellar completed by this weekend. It's going to be a bitch of a winter and we'll need the room. That's right. Thank you. See you when we get there."

Ashley stirred lazily. "I have to go to the bathroom."

"Hang on. We'll stop in La Junta."

They passed a sign that said LA JUNTA TWELVE MILES. Scipio pulled into a 7/11 on the east side of town, easing the Mercedes into a spot between two pick-ups that dwarfed it.

"Look," he said, pointing.

"What?"

"A boat-tail Riviera. I call 'em the Batcave."

"It looks kinda cool."

He handed Ashley the matador hat.

"If you would be so kind."

"Why certainly, good sir!" Ashley put on the hat.

Scipio put on a mask, a pair of thick-rimmed sunglasses and an Elmer Fudd hat that covered his ears. As they walked toward the store, a hot-rodded Subaru squealed into the parking lot straight into the handicapped spot blasting Dr. Dis.

"Omma plutocrat and a Pluto cat! I eat lean meat so I don't get fat! The chicks all dig me cuz I ain't no pygmy... my johnson's bigger than a rat-tat-tat!"

The music stopped and they piled out, heading into the store whooping. White boys with their pants clinging to their buttocks, one wearing a flat-brimmed cap. Scipio froze. Ashley was five feet ahead when she noticed.

"What's the matter?"

"Nothing's the matter. Go on and take care of business. I'll meet you out front."

When Ashley came out of the women's room, the three young men were shouting at one another across the aisles as they loaded up on Red Bulls, Pringles, beef jerky, and salted peanuts. They looked jockish, two of them in sweatshirts with the sleeves cut off, the third in a Bon Jovi T-shirt. Through the front window, Ashley saw Scipio leaning against the Subaru, arms crossed.

The tallest jock, with a fringe Mohawk like Chuck Liddell, did a double-take. "Dude. Some asshole's leaning on your ride."

The jock with the Bon Jovi T, the flat-brimmed cap and a tatted snake riding up his neck left his purchases on the counter and stormed out, followed by the other two. Ashley followed.

"Fuck you doin', man?" snake tat demanded.

"Dude!" Mohawk said. "It's Elmer Fudd!"

Scipio straightened up. "You gentlemen realize this is a handicapped spot, right?"

The three faced him in a semi-circle, puffing up, arms crossed.

"What the fuck, asshole," Bon Jovi said. "There's nobody here. Nobody gives a shit if we use the handicapped spot for five fucking minutes."

"I do. Civilization can't exist without mutual respect, not only for each other, but for common sense laws."

"Oh goody," Mohawk sneered. "A lecture."

Ashley stood in front of the car. "Come on, Scipio. Let's go."

The boys' heads swiveled like a gun turret.

"Holy shit. She's with you?"

The third jock, who went about two hundred pounds and whose torn sweatshirt said Loyola, said, "What's a fine piece of ass like you doing with a prissy little fuck like this?"

Scipio casually ripped the rearview mirror off the door. Mohawk lunged. Scipio ducked as Mohawk's fist slammed into the door frame and punched him in the groin. Mohawk bent over gasping. Scipio grabbed him behind the neck and threw him down onto his rising knee, which popped Mohawk back, dancing awkwardly like Martin Balsam falling backwards down the stairs in *Psycho*.

Loyola juked in with a kick. Scipio swept his left arm beneath the knee, heaved up, upending Loyola on the concrete. Bon Jovi threw a punch which Scipio ducked, throwing a fist into his sternum. Scipio lunged toward Loyola who skittered back on his ass like a crab.

"Boys," he said, "I can't tell you how important it is to be courteous of others." He pulled a balisong from his pocket, flipped it open and slashed the left front tire.

"Come on, Ashley. Let's go."

Heart in throat, Ashley followed Scipio back to the car and got in. She wondered how he always smelled so great. They'd been on the road straight for thirty-six hours and there wasn't a whiff of body odor. She wished she could say the same. She couldn't wait to take a shower. Scipio ditched the glasses and the Fudd hat. As he backed out and hit the highway, unobserved by the three combatants who were still licking their wounds and wondering what had happened, she tried to process what she'd seen.

They were all bigger, all pumped. Cocksure and arrogant in their strength and numbers. Any observer would have concluded the smaller Scipio didn't have a chance. It was like a Chuck Jones cartoon or a Bruce Lee movie. Biff! Pow! Sock! They drove past McDonald's, Burger King, Taco John, Taco Bell, Chick Fil A, KFC, Arby's. They drove past tire stores, a Habitat for Humanity store, a strip mall with a liquor store and a karate studio. Main Street was broad, lined with two-story red brick buildings. A bank with arched windows. An ice cream shop. Bent's Old Fort. The La Junta City Park.

"Why did you do that?"

"Civilization is only possible among people of goodwill. They chose to park in a handicapped parking spot. They could have parked in any of a dozen open spots but no, they chose that one. Why? Because they're arrogant. Because they're disrespectful. They were disrespectful toward you. Most people observe churlish behavior and choose not to get involved, telling themselves it's not their business. Or they're scared. John Donne said, 'No man is an island, entire of itself. Every man is a piece of the continent.' I believe that. I embrace the teachings of Jesus. I'm that random molecule who isn't afraid. All they had to do was say, 'You know, you're right, sir, that wasn't very nice of us, and we won't do it again.'

"But young men are full of arrogance and their own invincibility. I'm here to show them that there are consequences for bad behavior. I look on it as my duty."

For a while, Ashley didn't say anything.

"Aren't you worried they'll turn you in?"

"No."

"Was that some kind of kung fu or something?"

Without taking his eyes off the road, Scipio smiled. "You could say that. In addition to providing a loving environment conducive to personal growth, God's Breath has its own martial arts school. You may be interested in training with us."

"Yeah. That would be great."

CHAPTER

22

FIG'S JIG

Josh drove south on Fifty-one, the cruise control pegged at sixty-five, the speed limit. He passed a highway patrol cruiser in the median outside Tomahawk. Halfway to Merrill, a Challenger blew by him doing at least a hundred, followed seconds later by the highway patrol, lights flashing. Five minutes later, Josh passed the Challenger and the cruiser pulled over by the side of the road, the driver standing in the ditch leaning against his car while the trooper searched him.

Josh queued up Son Seals. *Midnight Sun.* All bikers loved the blues. He'd seen Seals once at Sturgis. He'd seen so many great bands at Sturgis. Stevie Ray Vaughan. Kenny Wayne Shepherd. Edgar Winter. Bob Dylan. He hadn't gone that year because of the virus. Only two hundred and fifty thousand bikers showed up, the lowest turnout in years. Antifa chartered a bus. They lasted just long enough to get their asses handed to them and had to be rescued by the town police. What they wanted wasn't clear. They had a list of demands, but they never got to the demands.

Josh stopped twice to relieve himself and fill up on drinks. He crested the highway and saw the lights of Madison in the distance. He arrived home at five. Fig launched a fusillade as soon as he pulled in. When he opened the front door, she jumped enthusiastically at him, and he knelt for kisses and hugs, examined her wound, and gave her a treat.

Ninja was still sleeping. Ninja was a night owl. Josh went into his office and checked his computer. Ninja had forwarded satellite photographs of the God's Breath ranch, which lay at the end of a winding mountain road, with buildings like tiny rectangles.

He phoned Calloway.

"What did you find?"

"I talked to a survivor who gave me a rundown of the camp and the personnel. It's pretty remote. What about Ashley's phone?"

"A maintenance worker found it emptying a trash can in a wayside in Nebraska. They overnighted it and I gave it to the crime lab, but so far, nada."

"I thought you were going to give it to Ninja."

"I can't do that, Josh. I have to follow the rules."

"Did they find anything?"

"Not yet. It occurs to me that this could be a dodge. Maybe they're not heading to Colorado at all. Maybe Scipio handed the phone off and had them dump it and they're going somewhere else."

"I got Ninja working on face recognition software. Any luck they'll show up somewhere."

"You trust this guy?"

"Yeah. I've dealt with him before. He's looking after Fig."

"'Cuz I did a search and I couldn't find diddly. Ninja Preston could be an alias."

"Could be."

"Well, ask him."

"He ain't up yet. I'll ask him as soon as he's up. If he'd found something, he would have notified me immediately."

"All right. Keep me posted."

Josh thought about going for a run, but Fig would only whine and beg to come along. He went through his emails. Someone named Nancy: "Hola."

And, "Hello i hope i don't offend you my name is zita wudu can i talk to you?"

And, "Hello dear. I could not stop staring at your profile on Facebook. You seem like a very kind and caring person and I would love to talk to you."

A woman named Lisa Dennis, whom he didn't know, wrote, "Hello, I am no longer on Facebook, please let's talk here."

And, "Am Jenny Ramirez, young loving lady from united states, who value friendship so much Please with due respect reply me back here immediately you recieve my message, i have something very important and urgent to discuss with you, and more explanation about me thanks warms greetings"

And, "Hello, I have been informed to contact you. The CIA has been doing intensive research for the past fifty years on what we call "so-called life." That information has been collected and presented for you here: https://bit.ly/3lqU-J3u. This has been the findings of seventeen years ago as of today. Now governments and other large organizations have developed technology around these concepts for their own deceptive uses. Soon you will be contacted by other means for countermeasures and the part that you play in all this. Please get this as soon as possible because there are powers that be to take down this information about this…"

Josh thought about forwarding that one to Stoeckle.

He went to Facebook. His profile showed a sober Josh wearing a ballcap and a Fool's Face T-shirt, seated, arms on knees, straight on. Josh Pratt. Private Investigator.

A message from Goose, his old buddy from the Bedouins. Goose had done his time in Illinois.

"Well Chainsaw, these old bones ain't gettin' any younger. I'm in a wheelchair now at the Cranston Retirement Home in Grinnel, Iowa. I'm on oxygen, too. How the hell are ya? What's your phone number? I just want to ramble. Your old brother Goose."

Josh wrote back. "Goose! Great to hear from you! I'm super busy for the next couple of days but I promise we'll talk." He gave his phone number.

An email from Katy Varner, of WMAD, wanting to know about his involvement in the Calloway missing persons case. Last week he had searched for do-it-yourself

Cobras and now his page was filled with kit cars.

Fig barked, a staccato spray fading into an agreeable grumble.

Josh found Ninja in the kitchen wearing black briefs, going through the refrigerator.

"I got frozen breakfast burritos. Nuke 'em for two minutes."

Ninja opened the freezer, pulled out one of the plastic-wrapped burritos, tore off the plastic, put it on a plate, and nuked it for two minutes in the microwave.

"Anything?"

Ninja made big eyes, went back to the fridge, pulled out a half-gallon carton of orange juice and glugged. Ninja's Adam's apple bobbed up and down like a dribbling basketball. Ninja held up a finger. The microwave beeped.

Ninja removed the plate, sat at the Formica table, pulled his phone out of his ass and set it down. He shook the burrito out of its sleeve and poked. He picked it up and dropped it, shaking his fingers.

"Nothin'. If there was somethin', I woulda told ya. But I ain't checked the shit this morning. If I get a hit, we'll know it."

"Can you check?"

Ninja leaned back, eyes wide. "A man's gotta eat."

Josh put some coffee on. "Yeah, you're right. I was just on the phone with her old man."

"If it can be done, it will be done."

Ninja broke the burrito in two and bit off a chunk. Fig

sat at his feet, gazing soulfully at the burrito.

"How's she doing?"

Ninja ruffled the dog's head. "Doin' great. We went for a little walk around the neighborhood last night. Everybody knew her. Everybody asked who I was."

"You tell 'em?"

"Fuck yeah! I smiled and smiled. Yassuh! Yas ma'am! I'ze just de hired help! I just told them I was a friend of yours watching Fig while you were out of town."

"You didn't scare 'em?"

"Fuck no! I'ze a lovable nigra. All right. Let's go see what we got."

Ninja led the way into the basement, which had taken on an electronic atmosphere, now filled with monitors, routers, hard drives, printers, the scent of ozone. Ninja sat before the big rig and poked. Josh hooked a chair on wheels and sat behind him, checking his own phone. The cell phone had revolutionized waiting. No longer did the hapless fool have to stand there shifting from foot to foot. Now you could check your bank balance, the Dow/Jones, Facebook, Twitter, Instagram, MeWe, the news, the weather, Peruvian porn.

He checked his mail. Vera Felicity had written, "How are you today, handsome?"

The picture showed a cute white girl.

Logged in using a phone number from Nigeria accompanied the message.

Lovely Salmara had written, "Hello dear, how are you

doing today? I hope fine. I found your email on Facebook and I have something to discuss with you, please reply me back as soon as possible. Thanks and take care."

Ninja stiffened. He sat up. His hands flew. A grainy video appeared on the monitor showing a fight in a parking lot.

"Dig this—Elmer Fudd takes out three jocks!" Posted by Gedda Life.

Ninja slowed it down. It had been shot from a security camera from about ten feet. The images were blurry and grainy. Ninja froze the image as a girl stepped into the picture, a tall thin black girl wearing a matador's hat. Only her hands showed her skin.

"I got a physical match. Plus, why else she wearin' that silly hat than to confuse facial recognition?"

"Where is this?"

Ninja poked and prodded. "I will have to contact Gedda Life and find out where they got it. That might take a while."

"Listen. I might have to go to Colorado to bring her home. I need drones."

"Drones ain't my thang."

"Know a drone guy?"

"Randall Kleiser."

"No shit. I haven't seen Randall since he went off the grid three years ago. You know how to get in touch with him?"

"He's in Denver. I'll call him right now."

CHAPTER

23

BLACK MORELS

Kleiser popped up on Facebook like a gopher coming out of hibernation, head framed by a wild furze of curly brown hair and a full beard.

"Randall!" Josh said. "You look like Jeremiah Johnson!"

"How the hell are ya, brother?" the hacker said.

"Randall, I have a situation in Colorado that requires drones. I can pay."

"Tell you what. Ask Ninja about an encrypted phone. When you get it, call me at the number I will send you via email. That email will contain a link to a page and will ask you for a password. That password is the name of the company for whom I worked plus my handle when you met me. One contiguous word."

Josh racked his brain. "Got it."

Black Widower. That's what Kleiser called himself, after his girlfriend died in a terrorist attack. A group of

Saudi nationals had boarded her plane and blown it up. The investigation revealed that TSA had elected not to search them because it would have been a violation of their religion. No one was fired.

He turned to Ninja, who had been watching over his shoulder. "Got any?"

"Yeah. I'll dig it out."

Ninja went outside, returned with a generic black flip phone the size of a pack of cigarettes.

"You coulda just given that to me when I went up north."

"Wouldn't have done you any good. I only got the one. You have to have one on both ends."

Josh phoned Kleiser. "Yo."

"What do you need?"

Josh told him. "Can you meet us when we arrive?"

"Who's us?"

"Me and the girl's father. Heinz Calloway."

"The cop?"

"So?"

"No prob."

Josh ate a banana and yogurt, grabbed a handful of doggie bags and an empty bag of charcoal briquettes and went into his fenced backyard to pick up dog shit. Somebody had to do it. That shit wasn't going to pick itself up. He deposited his load in a sunken compost heap.

He washed his hands, sat on the deck and phoned Calloway. It went straight to voice mail. "We may have a sighting. Will forward. Take a look and call me back."

He gazed over his yard. To rake or not to rake?

Fuck it. He decided to wash the car. As he was slathering the Chrysler with soap, he thought how often he had washed it. As he had with Fig Newton, who'd died at the hands of an insane killer, he knew every curve and contour. Every scratch and blemish. The overall shape was good, but there were hail and gravel dings. Someone had keyed the door, and Josh had worked it with Turtle Wax Scratch and Swirl Remover. He didn't care. He liked the car. He didn't love the car, like he loved his bikes. He didn't ride around in the car just for the hell of it. When he'd washed it, he rolled it into the garage and waxed it. By then, it was dark.

It was the best car he'd ever owned. He bought it used with fifty thousand miles. His phone beeped.

"We've been trying to reach you about your vehicle's extended warranty..."

It beeped with an unknown number.

"Pratt."

"Chainsaw! It's Goose!"

"Goose! How the hell are ya?"

"Like I said, I'm in a wheelchair. I'm hooked up to the oxygen. Gotta sneak outside if I want to smoke. I went to work for a security firm. I got a pension. It ain't so bad. I'm down here in Rockford. Say, I been readin' up on you. You're a private detective?"

Josh scoffed. "I wouldn't dignify it by calling it that. I help people out."

"I'll bet. Hey, you ever hear from Toad? That prick still

owes me two hundred dollars."

"Man, I haven't heard from Toad in years. I thought you and he were tight."

"I thought so too. Then I loaned him the two bills. Last I heard, he went off to join some hippie commune in the mountains."

"Too bad."

"That dude was the best wrench I know."

"Yeah. He could have got a job at any dealership. But he was psychotic."

"Remember that time he bashed that guy's head in with a plumbing wrench?"

"I forgot that until just now. Thanks a lot, Goose."

"What about Larry?"

"Larry wiped out. He's dead."

There was silence.

"Man. That's sad."

The screen flashed Calloway.

"Goose, I gotta take this call. I'll call you back."

"Good hearing from you, Saw."

"You too, man."

Calloway said, "You called?"

"We found a video that may possibly show Ashley in the parking lot of a convenience store. We're running it down now. It's possible they're headed to the God's Breath compound in Colorado."

"What's that about?"

"It's an isolated ranch in the mountains, perfect for

brainwashing. The boy I talked to up in Manitowish, his father got him out by hiring a group of mercenaries called Black Morels. They grabbed him while he was on an outing to the nearest town."

"You're not suggesting I do that. I'm a law enforcement officer. I can't turn to a band of mercenaries."

"No, of course not. I'm trying to get in touch with them to find out what they know. They could be very helpful. If I have to go out there."

"If you go out there, I'm going with you."

"Is that a good idea? What if we have to shoot our way out of there?"

"Fuck it. I've got my thirty years in. Let 'em try to fire me. I know shit."

"It's not the department I'm worried about," Josh said. "It's the press. You know what the press is like in Madison. You know what Madison is like. They hate the police. They'd like to disband the police. The last City Council Meeting wanted to release all prisoners and close the jails."

"Tell me about it. It gets harder every year. Gotta go. Call me as soon as you track down that video."

Josh walked around the car with a cotton rag, polishing stray wax wisps. The door to the kitchen opened.

"Got it," Preston said. "Came from a 7/11 in La Junta."

"They're heading for the compound."

"Looks like."

Josh contacted the Black Morels via their website.

"Dear Black Morels: I am a private investigator from

Madison, Wisconsin, working on a missing persons case. A seventeen-year-old girl named Ashley met Scipio at a truck stop near town. Her father is a police detective and a friend. We believe Scipio is taking her to his compound in Colorado. I would like to ask you about your experiences with God's Breath, if you are willing to talk. Time is of the essence. Yours sincerely..."

He took Fig for a walk. He carried a leash just in case, but Fig didn't need a leash. She was trained to walk just behind him on the left. As they walked southwest on Ptarmigan, he saw a young woman pushing a stroller with a cairn terrier on a leash. He put the leash on Fig, smiled, paused so the dogs could sniff each other's butts, and continued to the stone pillars at the entrance of White Oaks, Phil Bass' development. Fig squatted and did her business.

Josh dutifully pulled a plastic bag from his pocket. They headed back.

The Black Morels wrote back: "Dear Mr. Pratt: This is Ian Smith, President of the Black Morels. I would be happy to talk to you. I prefer Skype. My Skype handle is BlackMorel1. I am available now."

Ian Smith was a lean, grizzled man with a tight beard and deep-set eyes. He was wearing a blue shirt and sat in front of a wall holding an American flag, a framed Marine symbol, and a *Don't Tread On Me* flag.

"Good evening," Josh said. "Thanks for taking the time."

"You have an unusual background. You were a member of a motorcycle gang?"

"I was. I spent four years in prison before I was pardoned by the governor."

"How did you swing that?"

"My lawyer at the time, Danny Bloom. I don't know how he did it. I think they were close."

"Since then, you have been involved in a number of highly publicized cases and several shoot-outs."

"Sir, I don't seek confrontation, but I don't shy from it either. Since I welcomed Jesus into my heart and soul, I have tried my best to live up to His expectations. Thank you for your service to our country."

"Amen. What would you like to know?"

"We may have to go to Colorado to retrieve Ashley. What can you tell us about God's Breath?"

"They are highly disciplined and have a paramilitary security apparatus headed by an Army veteran named Hal Galper, who calls himself Gladiator. Mr. Galper is alleged to have studied kung fu at the Shaolin Temple in China. We're not clear how he hooked up with Scipio, but he's a true believer. In Iraq, he was in charge of base security and was accused of killing two insurgents in cold blood. The Army charged him and was going to court-martial him until an article appeared in the *Washington Post* citing two eyewitnesses who claimed Galper acted in self-defense. He was allowed to quietly resign.

"He worked as a contractor for the Albright Company providing security in Saudi Arabia, returned to the United States in 2015. Shortly after that, he became Scipio's right-hand man."

"Did you know he's teaching martial arts up there?"

"No, but I'm not surprised."

"Do you have any aerial footage of the site?"

"No. We arrived in Harrison prepared to retrieve Mr. Wipf. We brought a drone, but we wanted to hang out for a day and talk to the locals. We were very lucky to spot Mr. Wipf as he arrived with other cult members on a grocery run. Lee told us that he had been trying to escape when he was spotted by cult members, who took him along. They never expected an outside agency to interfere. He said sometimes cult members were allowed to go into town as a reward for good behavior. The flip side, of course, is that most people are held prisoner up there. I understand that they've tightened up their control after we brought the kid back, and only a handful of Breathers, as they call themselves, are permitted outside excursions. Has your client considered contacting us?"

"He's a police detective."

"Ah. Well, let me know if I can be of any further service, and please let me know the outcome of your mission."

"Thank you, sir."

CHAPTER
24

AMEN

As the car ascended the winding mountain road, Ashley hung her head out the open window like a dog, staring up at the snow-covered peaks.

"Look!" she cried. "Look!"

Scipio pulled over to the narrow shoulder so she could gaze at a nearly vertical cliff face with two long-horned sheep clinging to the side in defiance of gravity. An eagle circled overhead.

"You'll see a lot of animals at the ranch. Elk, moose, every now and then we see a bear, and one of our flock claims she saw a mountain lion while picking berries."

"Oh my god. A mountain lion. The only lions I've ever seen were at the zoo. I wouldn't know what to do if I saw a mountain lion in the wild."

"They don't normally attack people, but if they take an interest in you, don't run. Raise your arms, wave your shirt, do anything you can to try and look larger. All they see is mass, and if you look too big, they'll run away. Depends on how hungry they are."

They turned off on Sky Gulch Road and began the slow ascent over ruts and rocks, the chassis scraping on rocks.

"We're going to tackle this road in the spring. We'll grade it and pave it. I can't have my cars scraping off rocks."

"Why did you come and get me, Scipio?"

Without taking his eyes off the road, he said, "I knew there was something special about you the first time you reached out. I looked at your profile and I saw something extraordinary behind your eyes. I can only do that because I've achieved the highest level of enlightenment. I think you can too. What were you intending to study in college?"

"Sports medicine. I was on the Memorial track, gymnastics and basketball teams."

"Yes, I can see why you would be very good at that. You'll want to meet Vivian, our nurse practitioner. She can help guide you."

The underside scraped over a rock.

"Wow. I hope you don't hurt your car."

"I have lots of cars."

They came around a bend to find a herd of elk grazing in a high mountain menu. Scipio shut the engine off and they sat with the windows open, breathing the fresh mountain air, watching the elk. The elk moved on. Scipio started the car.

Twenty minutes later the road flattened out onto a high mountain meadow, and a wooden arch made of telephone pole timbers from which a wooden fence extended as far as the eye could see. Wrought-iron letters spelled out "God's Breath Ranch." A man in khakis, a rough rider hat, with a holstered pistol, sat on a bench next to the iron gate reading a book. Seeing the car, he got up and swung one half of the double gate inward. Scipio drove in and stopped. The man came around.

"Right on time, master!"

"Thanks, John. How're things?"

"One of the cows calved, and wolves somehow got into God's pasture and ate one of God's lambs." John stooped down to eyeball Ashley.

"John, this is Ashley. She's joining us."

"Welcome to God's Breath, Ashley! We're so happy to have you!"

"Thank you, John."

Scipio drove on, passing several pole barns and a longtwo-story log cabin with a stone fireplace.

"That's our dormitory, meeting and mess hall. Most everyone takes their meals in there except when we have picnic days."

They passed several barns and the road tilted up toward a grand, new-looking two-story Victorian on a shelf backed up against a cliff. No one wore a mask.

"Normally, you would be assigned a group leader and a barracks, but that can wait until tomorrow. You'll stay in the grand house tonight and tomorrow we'll get you sorted out."

He popped the trunk and grabbed his overnighter. Ashley pulled her backpack from the back seat and followed him up the steps to the veranda that stretched the length of the house. A swing bench hung from tractor chains along with five evenly spaced floral planters nearing the end of the season, and there were wood Adirondack chairs every couple of feet. Scipio opened the front door, with its etched oval window, into a hardwood foyer that smelled of wood polish, with a mahogany sideboard on which rested two houseplants. A wrought-iron coat rack screwed to the wall held some coats and an umbrella.

A sleek brunette came at them from the living room, gluing herself to Scipio in a lip-lock. Scipio disentangled himself with a hint of impatience. "Ashley, this is Kristin, my Girl Friday."

Kristin had a grip like a steelworker. Ashley squeezed back. They smiled.

"Kristin, show Ashley to one of the guest bedrooms."

"And how long will Ashley be staying with us?"

"Forever, I hope. But in this house, just the night. I'll assign her to her own group in the morning."

"How was your trip?"

Scipio grabbed his overnighter and walked into the living room, with broad windows looking out past the veranda and down the slope. They were surrounded by mountains covered with snow. Ashley could not stop looking. The living room was decorated with Victorian furniture, embroidered upholstery with armrest doilies, a floral-patterned chintz sofa facing a massive stone fireplace over which hung a framed oil painting of Jesus on the cross at Calvary. A Bible rested on the mantle next to *Principles of God's Breath* by Scipio, *Das Kapital*, *Atlas Shrugged*, *In Search of Being: The Fourth Way to Consciousness* by G.I. Gurdjieff, *How To Win Friends and Influence People* by Dale Carnegie, *The Secret Doctrine* by H.P. Blavatsky, and *The Book of the Law* by Aleister Crowley. Floor to ceiling bookshelves framed the fireplace, filled with books. Polished walnut end tables framed the sofa.

Ashley's room was on the second floor facing the cliff over a narrow strip of greensward. Douglas and bristlecone pine marched up the cliff face. Ashley could just see the top if she hunkered down and looked up. The bathroom was large and luxurious, with a claw-footed tub which she filled, and proceeded to luxuriate in the hot, soapy water. A half dozen hotel samplers sat on the counter: Mouthwash, toothpaste, shampoo, body conditioner.

She dried her hair with a hair dryer from beneath the sink, brushed it back, and secured it with an elastic. The closet was filled with women's clothes. She wondered if she dared to try them on, laughed and went through them, choosing cream-colored linen slacks and a shirt in a floral pattern.

Downstairs a bell dinged. She looked at her watch. It was six o'clock.

Downstairs, Scipio was seated at the head of a polished mahogany dining table beneath an antler chandelier, Kristin opposite. Where a wife would sit. To Scipio's right sat a hard-looking, dark-skinned man with an aquiline nose wearing khaki cargo pants and a green long-sleeved shirt. His dark hair swept back in a widow's peak and he had a five o'clock shadow. Next to him was a petite older woman with curly white hair wearing a dark blue cotton sweater. Scipio gestured to the chair on his left.

"Ashley, this is Lucy and Hal. Lucy is our den mother and Hal is in charge of security."

"Hello, Ashley," Lucy smiled.

Hal raised a hand. "Welcome."

Scipio indicated the chair to his right. "Sit here."

Ashley sat. The room featured white panel wainscoting above which burgundy painted walls were adorned like an art gallery. Exquisite watercolor landscapes of the Rockies, a mirror-like lake reflecting porcelain clouds, blue sky, jagged peaks in the background. Old photographs. Really old. Black and white, with that stiff attitude people adopted for the camera back then. The place settings were of the same china, with blue rims adorned with gold vines, heavy sterling silverware, white linen napkins. Two candle holders held burning tapers, two feet apart. It reminded Ashley of her grandparents' house in Chicago.

Scipio folded his hands together and bowed his head.

"Heavenly Father, from whom all blessings flow, please enlighten your humble servants on the best way to live, to help others, and to safeguard this Earth from those who would do it harm. "Amen."

"Amen," they all said.

CHAPTER

25

SQUIRREL COUNT

"I have to appear in court tomorrow. We can leave Thursday," Calloway said over the phone.

"I'm driving. I'll pick you up."

"No, we're not driving. We'll fly into Denver and rent a car. I'll pay."

"We might need guns."

"You're not allowed to have guns. I can check mine through. They might even let me keep it on my person."

"Okay. I have a contact out there. I'll talk to him and get back to you."

"Good idea."

Josh was sitting in his office when his Skype rang, an unknown caller, Rangatang. Josh had a hunch and answered. A face appeared. Not so much a face as a stacked concealment—a bandanna covered the nose and lower half, huge sunglasses designed to fit around regular glasses, and a knit cap pulled low. No skin showed.

"How are ya, Randall?" Josh said.

"Okay, talk to me. What do you need?"

"Why Skype? What about the encrypted phone?"

"Save it. We don't know who was eavesdropping."

"You're getting paranoid in your old age."

"I was born paranoid."

"Have you heard of God's Breath?"

"Oh yeah."

"I'm working a missing persons case. Daughter of a friend of mine. We think she's been seduced by Scipio and is living at his ranch out your way. We may need drones to scope the place."

"Is this a paying gig?"

"Within reason. She's the daughter of Heinz Calloway, Madison PD. He's coming out with me."

"A cop? A fucking cop?"

"So what?"

"A thousand a day."

Josh calculated. If Calloway couldn't swing it, he could. He'd been socking away money from his federal retainer and had over seven hundred and fifty thousand dollars in an interest-bearing account with First Wisconsin.

"No prob. We're coming out Thursday. Can you pick us up at DIA?"

"What time do you come in?"

"Don't know yet."

"When you find out, send me your itinerary to a number

I will text you Thursday morning. I will pick you up outside Door 14 on the Eastern concourse. I will be driving a gray Jeep Cherokee."

Kleiser broke the connection. Josh found Ninja on the back deck, smoking a bowl.

"I gotta go to Denver. Shouldn't be more than a couple days. Can you hang out and take care of Fig?"

Ninja passed Josh the pipe. "What else I got to do. We'll patrol the neighborhood."

"You know how much to feed her?"

"I'll figure it out looking at the can."

"Give her a Rimadyl every twelve hours, with food."

Josh sat in a nylon chair and inhaled, exploding in a paroxysm of coughing while Ninja clapped and pointed.

"What if I hook up with some chick? Can I bring her back here?"

"Long as you confine yourselves to the basement."

Josh phoned Ray. "What are you doing?"

"Nothing."

"Can I come over?"

"Why don't you pick up some Chinese on the way over."

"I don't like Chinese."

"You don't like Chinese?"

"No."

"How is that even possible?"

"Chinese food is like rap. I've been giving it one more chance for twenty years and I still don't like it."

"All right. Bring what you like."

Josh stopped at Monty's Blue Plate on Atwood and got two club sandwiches and two sides of slaw. Ray let him in and they went out on the balcony to watch the sun set over Lake Monona. Ray opened her club sandwich and inspected each level.

"It really doesn't require three pieces of toast, but they give you plenty of bacon."

Josh put on a hat and pulled the brim down to block out the setting sun. Ray's place was nice. Airy. Stacked on top of three floors, each with four units, sixteen units in all. He felt hemmed in. When he'd moved to Ptarmigan Road, his was the only house on the street. Madison spread like grip weed, rooting up nature, slapping down asphalt. Midtown was once a narrow country road that ran west past farmland and four oaks. Developers bought up the land. The country road became a four-lane thoroughfare. They ripped up the trees and named the upscale mini-mall Four Oaks. It contained a Baskin-Robbins, Flenz Jewelry, Mind and Body Gym, a Starbucks, and the Backfield Pub, a sports bar bedecked with stock athlete photos, all personalized.

"When I'm in Mad Town, I always hit the Backfield Pub. It's happenin', Jack!" —Donald "Cowboy" Cerrone.

"The Backfield's the best bar in Madison." —Aaron Rogers.

"If I ain't playin', I'm watching at the Backfield." — Khris Middleton

"My favorite bar, by far." —Reggie White, who died in 2004, ten years before the bar was built.

Ray joined him at the rail and put her arm around his

waist. He turned into her.

They lay in her bed. Sid Vicious eyed Josh's shirt.

"Is he gonna piss on my shirt?"

Ray sat up and threw a pillow. Sid Vicious squawked and vanished. "Put it in my closet and close the door."

"It's a sad commentary on our times that I can't come over here without your cat pissing on my shirt."

"He's jealous. He thinks you'll take me away from him."

"You should bring him over. See how he does with Fig."

"How is she?"

"Almost healed. I gotta watch her to make sure she doesn't take off after a rabbit and pull a muscle."

"Has Fig ever caught a rabbit?"

Josh held up three fingers. "This year. I remember one time, she was getting into the garbage, so I got a lidded container and shoved it under the table when I left. I was so happy when I got home and saw she'd left the garbage alone. Then I went in my bedroom. I look around. I see all these pieces of meat on the floor. And on my bed, the headless rabbit."

Ray stared. "You're making this up."

"Am not. One year she left a headless squirrel on my bed. She's sweet that way."

"How many squirrels?"

"Her squirrel count is seven. She paints little silhouettes on the side of her water bowl."

"That sweet dog!"

"She's a monster."

Ray regarded him coolly. "I can never tell when you're lying or not."

"Gotta go to Denver tomorrow. Don't know when I'll be back. Week at the outside."

"What?"

"Ashley Calloway."

She put her arms around him. "Is it dangerous?"

Josh shrugged, pulled her close, smelling her perfume, hard again. "I doubt it."

"I'm getting very attached to you."

Prior to Charlotte Newton, Josh had never had a real girlfriend. Just a string of one night stands. Sometimes a week. The longest was a month. His childhood held nothing to prepare him for life. He believed there was a secret book of rules on how to behave and everybody had a copy but him.

The Book of Life

If he could love a dog, he could love a woman. He gathered her in. "Me too."

What next? Would she sell her condo? Would he be responsible for her upkeep? How much money did she make? What if they had a kid? Responsibility was a bitch. How would parenthood affect him? Would it make him a better person? He knew a guy who shotgunned his wife and two kids and burned the house down. Then turned the gun on himself.

"Will you call me?"

"Yeah."

"Are you staying?"

"No."

CHAPTER

26

HACKER

Thursday morning, Ninja drove Josh in the Chrysler to pick up Calloway at his two-story Colonial in a leafy west side suburb. Calloway wore blue jeans, a blue work shirt, and a light blue cotton sports jacket, his badge fixed to his belt, gun in a pancake holster beneath his left arm.

Calloway slid in the back seat with his travel bag. They headed through town on University Avenue, turning north on East Johnson for the airport. The airport was under construction with sawhorses, orange cones, and police directing traffic through the maze.

"I remember when this was a quiet municipal airport," Calloway said. "I can't remember when it wasn't under construction."

Ninja dropped them at the curb. They put on their masks and stood in line at the Southwest Counter where Calloway showed his identification and checked his weapon through.

They went through security and boarded, sitting next to each other in the exit aisle. The seats didn't recline, but they had room for their legs. The flight was about two hours.

Once the plane took off, Calloway pulled out his laptop and read reports, unaware he was grimacing. Josh glanced over. The rows of tiny type and graphs gave him a headache.

Josh pulled out a Peter Brandvold Western. They were short and sweet. Every story was about revenge. He'd left his cell phone with Ninja, who'd given him a generic-looking encrypted flip phone.

"Use this call to Randy," Ninja told him. "Then throw it in the trash. Randy will give you new phones."

On the approach, the plane tilted and Josh looked down at the sere land, light brown soil, plum line straight irrigation ditches lined with green furze. The plane adjusted. Josh saw the Rockies. They seemed impossibly far away. The plane landed, taxied, and let them out on Concourse 3. They jostled along to the train that whisked them from concourse to concourse and finally to the main terminal, where they rose from the depths on escalators. Everyone wore a mask. Everyone broke for the nearest restroom.

While Calloway waited at the luggage kiosk, Josh called Kleiser.

"Ten minutes. Gray Jeep Cherokee."

They waited outside the designated door as vehicles oozed through the restricted corridor, dropping off and picking up. The socialite picking up her husband in a silver BMW. The college student dropping off her roommate in a battered Hyundai. A cop with a face mask stood in the corridor directing traffic. Josh spotted the Cherokee as it entered the covered area. Josh waved. Kleiser swooped in, bullying a Prius that had been waiting. Josh and Calloway stuck their stuff in the back and got in.

"Randall, Detective Calloway."

They bumped fists over the seat backs. "Hey, how are ya?" Kleiser said.

Josh and Calloway took their masks off and stuffed them in their pockets.

The cargo area was jammed to capacity with carbon fiber cases and cardboard boxes.

"Do you know where we're going?" Josh said.

Kleiser pointed to the screen on the dash, showing a big chunk of Colorado from Denver to the mountains. "That's Harrison. I've got everything we need. Drones, camping supplies, walkie-talkies, you name it."

"Did you bring guns?"

"Yeah. They're in the back."

Calloway put his hand on Josh's shoulder. "I don't want you using guns. I don't want you to get in trouble over this."

Josh grunted. The Cherokee swept by the blue mustang sculpture, sunlight causing its eyes to glow red.

"What the heck is that?" Calloway said.

Kleiser swung by without looking. "Blucifer. It fell on the sculptor who built it and killed him."

"Jesus Christ."

"I got some satellite pictures of the compound."

Josh pulled out his notes. "I interviewed a survivor who had to be rescued by a mercenary group. He gave me a list of key personnel and their characteristics. Here's a copy for you, Heinz."

Kleiser accelerated past a U-Haul truck. "Hal Galper was an Army Ranger with two tours of duty in Iraq. He was discharged in 2012 for killing two jihadis in cold blood. He barely escaped prosecution thanks to a congressman from his home state of Indiana, who intervened on his behalf. He worked as an independent contractor in Saudi Arabia before joining God's Breath. I don't know how they got together, probably over the internet, same as your daughter. But whatever it is Scipio had to offer, Galper went for it. He's been with them for five years, second in command only to Kristin Nunez, Scipio's main squeeze. You may remember her from that sitcom on NBC a couple years ago, *Where's Waldo?*"

"Who did he work for in Saudi Arabia?"

"Extrapolations, based in Dubai. Mostly ex-military, including Australian, English, and French Foreign Legion."

"French Foreign Legion?" Calloway said. "Is that for real?"

"You bet. Just ask Jean-Claude Van Damme."

A sign said, CASTLE ROCK TWELVE MILES.

"Anyone interested in lunch?" Kleiser said.

They pulled into an Arby's, put on their masks and went inside. They sat in a booth and took off their masks, Calloway poring over the notes Josh had given him. "What's Nunez's story?"

"She's hard to figure," Kleiser said between bouts. "Grew up in Fargo, class valedictorian, majored in drama at North Dakota State, moved to New York when she was twenty-two and began landing modeling and commercial work. Her big break came in 2012 when her agent got her a part on NCIS, which led to *Where's Waldo?*, which aired for three seasons beginning in 2013.

"In 2018, she met Scipio at a Woburn concert. Jake Woburn is one of God's Breath's more prominent members, eclipsed only by Sean Sheen and Rose Thurston."

"Huh," Calloway grunted. "I always liked Sheen. He was great in *The Male Factor*."

"Yeah, he's their biggest fish. He's one of those guys, got a clause in his contract that when he's on set, nobody is permitted to look him in the eye."

They returned to the car. Kleiser opened the rear hatch, rummaged around, handed Josh an old-fashioned leather shaving kit. It was heavy and clicked when he moved it. Inside were five burner phones and an Iridium Extreme Satellite Phone.

"You got any cash? I had to lay out four hundred bucks."

Josh pulled out his wallet, but Calloway stopped him. He reached inside his jacket for his wallet. "I got this. Imma need a receipt, though."

Kleiser laughed. "Where do you think I got this? Target?"

"No, a receipt from you," Calloway said slowly, opening his wallet.

"No way. I don't sign nothin'. In fact, I'm not even here."

There was a short showdown. Kleiser won. Calloway only had one eye on point. Calloway relaxed and got in the vehicle.

They hit the road. "Listen. We can stop for the night in Pueblo or somewhere, or we can drive straight through. It's gonna take eight hours. You can always sack out on the back seat."

"Straight through," Calloway said. "Josh, you want to switch places?"

Josh crawled over the center console. Calloway switched places with surprising agility. Josh figured he was in his fifties. The thrum of tires on concrete put Josh in a fugue state, not fully awake, but not asleep either.

"So what you do, Mr. Kleiser?" Calloway said.

"I'm a hacker. Call me Randall."

CHAPTER

27

THE TOUR

A young man with close-cropped black hair, who might have been Indian, placed a platter before Ashley. Roast beef, fresh steamed green beans, and mashed potatoes. Silver tureens of gravy circulated. Platters of homemade bread sat on both sides of the long table.

The man across from Ashley, mid-forties, lean, balding, bearded, said, "Welcome, sister. Call me Hal. It's very exciting to see new faces."

"How many new faces do you see?"

"Scipio only allows the most ardent and promising to live on the ranch. We have homes in Florida, Arizona, and California, but this is the center. We are at seven thousand feet, close to God. Once a month, weather permitting, I lead worshipers to the top of Mt. Cranston. We leave at two in the morning in order to summit before noon. After noon, there's constant danger of thunderstorms and lightning. Mt.

Cranston is among the most remote of the fourteeners, yet it has claimed twelve lives, of which we know."

"Why do you go up there?"

Walter grinned. "The closer to God, the better He hears our prayers. Also, because it's a blast. It's just so great to get out there on God's mountains, far away from the city, the traffic, the pollution. I hope you'll join us."

"Fersure," Ashley said.

People waited for Scipio. He dabbed at his mouth with a linen napkin and set it on the table. "My friends, tonight I wish to discuss the parables of Matthew."

"'The kingdom of heaven is like treasure hidden in a field. When a man found it, he hid it again, and then in his joy went and sold all he had and bought that field.' Years ago, when I first laid eyes on this high mountain meadow, I was confused as to which path to take. I had come out from Chicago with my best friend Darren. We'd worked hard all winter to save enough money to come out here, with our beat-up old Chevy and second-hand camping gear. I was supposed to attend Loyola that fall on a science scholarship. My father was a Bible salesman. He was a great guy, a friend to the downtrodden, someone who'd give you the shirt off his back. But you don't really get rich selling Bibles. I always had a job, ever since I was a teenager. I delivered newspapers. I bagged groceries. I mowed lawns."

"Anyhow. We come out here. We were in Colorado Springs. I had a job as a short order cook and Darren clerked in a grocery store. He'd heard about Harrison. He read about it an old book about Colorado cowboys. Harrison is where the posse chased Clay Dorman after he held up the Pueblo State Bank. Leading the posse was Gunther Luby, the last living Indian scout who had ridden with Kit Carson. Luby must have been in his seventies. In the shootout, Dorman killed Luby. But there was nowhere to run. They had him cornered up a canyon. They dragged him into town and hung him in front of the Tillerson Saloon. Darren heard there was a monument. He later went on to write Westerns.

"So, we came up here. This was over a quarter century ago, and sure enough, there was a monument to Gunther Luby in the little town cemetery. Most of you have seen it. 'Here lies Gunther Luby, Last of the Great Scouts, Killed by the Outlaw Clay Dorman, September 19, 1907.'

"But there was no monument to Dorman. We went into the Tillersoon Saloon and I asked the bartender if they had a mayor. No mayor. I asked if they had a sheriff. No sheriff. The closest they had to a mayor was the bartender, who owned the saloon and the hardware store next door. So I asked him why no monument to Dorman. After all, he was one of God's creatures. He'd ridden with Teddy Roosevelt and the Rough Riders. And he told me that Dorman was nothing to be proud of. They just wanted to forget. But Gunther Luby had been a great man and deserved to be remembered. But, I said, without Dorman, Luby would never have come to Harrison."

Scipio put a finger to his mouth, looked around and winked. Everybody laughed.

As acolytes cleared away dishes, Scipio laid two fingers on Ashley's wrist. "Let me show you around. Meet me on the veranda in ten minutes."

Kristen glanced at him and looked away.

Ashley went to her room and washed her face in the lavish bathroom, with marble counters and a shower with seven nozzles. She put on her sensible walking shoes and went out on the veranda. Loud words echoed from somewhere in the house, a man and a woman. Minutes later, Scipio came out wearing blue jeans, a Broncos ball cap, and a red and blue plaid shirt. They stood at the rail looking down the valley where the dirt road disappeared behind a boulder. It was a cool evening in the low fifties.

"Before we came, this was an abandoned ranch. There's also a mine where they tried to dig gold. You can see the fields. We have a short growing season but the greenhouse is active all year long. We grow lettuce, onions, tomatoes, squash, eggplant, and corn. We are mostly self-sufficient. We have a herd of twenty cattle, and butcher one a month. Through careful husbandry, we have been able to grow the herd incrementally. Some of these kids come from farms and ranches, so they know what they're doing."

He headed down the steps, Ashley close behind. They walked through the compound to the greenhouse, a long, low glass building with doors at both ends. Scipio held the door for her. The interior was humid and filled with the smell of growing things, including one she knew well.

"You grow marijuana?"

"It has many medicinal purposes."

"You ever smoke it?"

Scipio smiled, one corner of his mouth twisted up. "I used to. Some of the flock do. It's preferable to alcohol, don't you agree?"

"Oh absolutely."

"We use cattle droppings as fertilizer. There are also trout in the nearby stream and in the lake. We have our own fish hatchery."

Exiting at the far end, Scipio led her to a two-story chalet-style building built of weathered logs. "This is our main dormitory. It houses sixty people. Right now, we have about seventy-five acolytes. We teach the kids in the big meeting room which doubles as the mess hall. Our nutritionists plan out each meal in advance and post the coming week's menu on bulletin boards."

"Just like high school," Ashley said.

Scipio took her hand and led her toward the corrals. She was shocked and didn't know how to react. He was old enough to be her father.

"Here's our remuda. We have twelve horses and we encourage young people to work with them and learn how to ride. There are a lot of trails around here. Do you ride?"

"Nope. I want to get a motorcycle."

"A horse is not a motorcycle. A horse is a beautiful thing, a living creature, one of God's creations. Once I teach you to ride, you'll wonder how you ever got along without it."

The garage was a long steel building with eight retracting

doors. They entered through a side door. Scipio turned on the lights revealing eight gleaming vehicles. Ashley identified a Corvette and a Bentley, but the rest were unknown to her.

"This is my car collection. I've always been a motor head, but it's only recently I've been able to indulge my fantasies."

Who pays for all this? she wondered.

Scipio led her down the line. McLaren. Ferrari. Jaguar. The last car was a gleaming light blue antique with a cartoon road runner painted on the fender.

"Last, but not least, my '69 Roadrunner. Ain't she a beauty? It retailed for three thousand dollars. Hard to believe, isn't it? Comes with a three eighty-three cubic engines pumping out three hundred and thirty-five horses. Four speed transmission. Have you ever driven a manual?"

"Can't say that I have."

"I'll teach you."

"I'd better learn to ride first."

Scipio laughed. "That you will." He hovered awkwardly. Sensing he was about to embarrass them both, Ashley swept away.

"I'm really beat. Is it okay if I retire for the night?"

Scipio nodded sagely. "Of course you can. Of course."

CHAPTER
28

ALAMOSA

Josh dreamed he and Charlotte Newton were riding through Lafayette County, her hands wrapped tightly around his waist, leaning into the turns, blue birds hanging immobile in the air. They were headed for Lake Yellow-stone, an island of blue in a sea of green. The motorcycle shook. Kleiser shook him by the shoulder. Josh woke up, blinked. Kleiser looked like some rocker. It was the glasses, and the crazy hair.

Josh came up, rubbing his eyes. "Where are we?"

"Alamosa. We're stopping for the night. We don't want to find that place in the night."

Calloway was driving. "I gotta get my eight. Maybe make a courtesy call in the morning."

"Is that necessary?" Josh said. "Where we're going, the Alamosa police have no jurisdiction."

"Could be a valuable source of information."

"Randall, can you tap into the Alamosa PD and see if they have anything going on with God's Breath?"

"I don't have the hardware with me. I could call a guy, but it could take a while."

"Heinz, I think we should just handle this ourselves."

"Well, you would."

"Harrison's sixty miles from here. They don't even have a police department."

"Someone should know we're up there."

"Didn't you tell the MPD?"

"They know what I'm doing. But how're they gonna help?"

"If we can't do this ourselves, we can go to the Black Morels."

"If I have to go to a group of mercenaries, I might as well resign. I've been thinking of quitting. I've got my twenty. Madison doesn't want a police force anyway. They've made that clear"

"It's your call. She's your daughter. But I would advise not going to the police."

Calloway sighed. "It just seems wrong."

"They'll either go into a frenzy and tell you they'll handle it themselves, or warn you to back the fuck up."

"Fuck it. You're right. I'm her father. What are they going to say? I can't see her?"

"Whoa. We're not going to announce ourselves. We're going to look around first."

"How we gonna do that? There's only one way in or out."

"We'll come over the mountain from the back. Sneak up on 'em from behind. If we can catch Ashley alone, we can just grab her and take her with us. I think by now, maybe, she's having second thoughts. I mean, she's your daughter, and I don't know her that well, but she's too smart to fall for this guy's crap."

Calloway barked. "Yet here we are. She respects you. You're right. Let's try to get her alone and talk to her."

"They're not going to leave her alone," Kleiser said. "You know how cults work."

"We'll just have to create an opportunity."

It was dark out. Lights gleamed horizontally through the gloom. They shone at the Appaloosa Motel, a long, low, one-story structure that had seen better days. The fenced in pool was drained and covered. Calloway pulled into a spot at the far end of the lot, in shadow.

Kleiser pulled out a match book. "Who wants to go make the reservations? I would prefer not to. They might have cameras."

Calloway looked around. "I'll go. I'll put it on my card. You boys mind sharing a room? I'd just as soon keep expenses down."

"Fine by me," Josh said. "As long as you don't snore."

"As long as you don't fart."

Calloway headed for the office. Kleiser and Josh got out, wandered around the edge of the lot to the edge of a vast plain covered with dead grass. Lights gleamed on the slopes of the Sangre de Cristos. Josh and Kleiser spread out and peed in the grass. They returned to the car, opened the hatch and removed their bags.

"I brought you a gun," Kleiser said softly. "Beretta nine, if you want it."

"Man, I don't know. Heinz is a cop. I don't want to put him on the spot. Can you hang on to it? I don't want it unless we really need it."

"Yeah, well, that's the thing about guns. You never know when you're really gonna need it."

"I don't need it tonight."

Calloway returned, handed Josh an old fashioned metal key attached to a green plastic triangle with the outline of a horse and the room number.

"I'll see you boys in the morning. I gotta get my eight."

Taking his bag, Calloway unlocked his room and went in. Josh looked at his watch. It was nine o'clock. Plenty of time to get their eight. Across the street was Lupetia's Tavern, a long low log building, with six chops and a couple pick-ups in the gravel parking lot. "Against the Wind" issued faintly from its open windows.

Kleiser unlocked the door. Twin beds with olive-colored covers, a painting of wild horses before the mountains over the bed, a flat screen TV and a banged up dresser.

Kleiser threw his bag on the bed nearest the bathroom.

"Imma take a shower and sack out."

Josh took off his shoes and lay down on the bed with his hands behind his head staring at the cream-colored ceiling, spots discolored by water. He reached over and snagged a copy of *Alamosa Today* off the side stand.

Visit Great Sand Dunes!

Take the Rio Grande Scenic Railroad!

Alamosa National Wildlife Refuge!

The usual civic leaders jostling for attention.

His encrypted phone beeped. Ninja.

"Yeah."

"You alone?"

Josh heard the shower running. "Yeah."

"I ran computer simulations on Scipio. Three things you can't alter. Width of the eyes, height of the ears, shape of the skull. I found three thousand eight hundred and forty-five matches."

"Whoah."

"No. That's good. That's an extremely low number. Some of them were hidden behind firewalls which I ain't gone into. May not have to. I input everything I could find on Scipio, where he's from, where he went to school, what's his degree. It's all bullshit. He never attended Northwestern as he claimed, but he had false records implanted. They were good, but not good enough for the Ninja. I got a hit."

"Who is he?"

"Well, I ain't sayin' for sure, but I think he's Brian Pils, who served two and a half years for statutory rape in Joliet when he was twenty-six. He was also charged with aggravated assault and armed robbery in Berwyn and Midlothian. He got out in 2002. After that, nada. I'm trying to access his prison record but they just updated their system."

Josh grabbed the motel pen and pad. "Brian Pils?"

"Yeah."

"See what you can find out about him. And see if you can find out what Scipio's worth, and where he got it."

"I'm on it. I've been at it for twenty-four hours. Imma crash and then I'll hit it again."

"How's Fig?"

"Fig's fine. Fig loves oranges."

"Whoah."

"Here. Talk to Fig."

Josh switched to his Fig voice. "Figgy! Who's a good girl?" She barked excitedly.

"I'll be home as soon as I can. I love you. Now put Ninja back on."

"We good?"

"We're good. Is she sleeping with you?"

"Nah. Sleeps on your bed. Check with you tomorrow."

Josh called Ray. "Josh?" she answered.

"Hey baby."

"Where are you?"

"High on a mountain. I don't know exactly where. We're getting things done. Whatever happens, I'll be home in a couple days."

"I miss you, baby. My pussy aches for you."

"Don't tell me that. I'm literally on a mountain top. It's freezing up here!"

"Come home to me."

"I will."

CHAPTER 29

HOW TO BREATHE

Ashley threw herself on the king-sized hand-carved four-poster. The oak headboard depicted a herd of elk in the mountains, each Douglas fir lovingly delineated, jagged peaks on the horizon. She couldn't imagine what it cost. A painting of an Indian splashing into a river hung on the interior wall with a tiny spotlight and a brass plaque.

The Victor. By Jerry Bingham. She sat up and ran her fingers over the surface, feeling the whorls of the paint. An oak bookshelf held copies of the Bible, a coffee table book called *The Rockies*, several old *Reader's Digest* hard bounds. Allen Drury. Agatha Christie. Harold Robbins.

A slim hardbound volume, *God's Breath: a Working Philosophy* by Scipio.

> *Man is born alone and dies alone. Or so we are told. We are each trapped in this prison of flesh, our days*

numbered. *The clock starts ticking when the doctor slaps us on the bottom. But many do not hear that ticking until too late. The hedonist, the gambler, the drug addict devote themselves to trivial pursuits, scattering their seed, polluting their livers, blackening their lungs, and when the diagnosis finally appears, it's syphilis. It's AIDS. It's lung cancer or a drug addiction more demanding than any slave master.*

If only there were a way for each of us to realize our full potential when we're young enough to do something about it! In the past, institutions and disciplines inculcated the young in the mysteries of life. These institutions included military academies, the military, and to a lesser extent, the Boy and Girl Scouts, public school, the Church, and very occasionally, the family unit. Of all these, I have found the family unit to be the least satisfactory, consisting, as it does, of people bound solely by biology.

Biology lies! A wise man once said, "Families are institutions for the perpetuation of mental illness." Most families are Potempkin Villages created to fool the neighbors. They may look normal, and act normal, but inside the walls of their own homes, when no one is looking, they abuse each other emotionally and physically. The married librarian who claims she slipped and hit her head on the banister. The young girl with the hollow eyes who offers to stay behind and clean the classroom because she can't bear to go home.

Yet in the end, what else is there? It's only natural. It's only human to regard the self as the most important unit in the universe. If we don't love ourselves, who will? The circle expands outward. Next to the self, the family is the most important unit. In the Stone Age, each family was a tribe unto itself, solely reliant on each other for its survival. As man evolved, families sought out one another to form primitive tribes. They were of the same breeding stock. How could they not? Humans were few and far between in those days and you took what you could get. Inbreeding was common. As civilization advanced, as man developed skills, communities sprang up. They were tribal. It is only natural to want to stick with your own kind. This tendency, perfectly natural, perfectly human, has led to prejudices such as racism.

When man first crawled forth from the primordial muck, he had to compete with the elements, and with other men, for scarce resources. It was only natural for like-minded people of the same genetic stock to stick together. Life is tragic. Those of us who live in modern times, in civilized cities, take for granted the ease with which we drive to the corner supermarket and purchase fresh fruit and meat.

Fifty thousand years ago, man lived in caves and ate whatever they could kill. Throughout recorded history, the vast majority of humanity has lived on the brink, in desperate circumstances. Even today, while we in the west luxuriate in our security, behind locked gates, in air-conditioned castles, billions of fellow humans live in fear and poverty, subject to the will of tyrants, the vicissitudes of nature. Most of Africa. Most of Asia. Great portions of South America.

We take our wealth for granted, but it is only the past hundred years or so that has seen the emancipation of the middle class. It is the middle class that takes chances to open stores to create wealth. Occasionally you have a Henry Ford or Bill Gates who invents or promulgates some technological breakthrough that spreads like wildfire, increasing the reach and prospects of all who partake. But this is a recent development. We take our wealth for granted. There's an old saying. Bad times create strong men. Strong men create good times. Good times create weak men. We are seeing that now, in cities that give tacit blessing to riots, who venerate the lawless, who cloak greed and malice in high-sounding phrases such as "social justice," or "food justice," or "weather justice."

There is a certain breed of man that is glib, good with words, who does not work with his hands to create anything of value and provides no worthwhile services, but through his silver tongue convinces others that he has the wisdom to lead. The Founding Fathers never envisioned career politicians. This is not a plea for term limits, although that would be a good thing. This is a plea for understanding.

Human nature doesn't change. Technology chang-

es, and with the communication revolution, shallow, remorseless, glib men have, through trickery and lies, infiltrated every institution. But most especially, those institutions which masquerade as bastions of wisdom: Higher education. The media. Government. And always, their honeyed words and measured phrases are used to conceal what they're really all about. Power. And money. How many of our duly elected leaders could withstand serious scrutiny?

Unfortunately, we no longer have a free press. Today's so-called media is part and parcel of the ruling elite, dedicated to maintaining a false narrative that seeks to assign group blame to people solely on the basis of their skin color. We call this the Narrative.

The narrative is very simple. White=bad. All other races=good. Man=bad. All other sexual proclivities and permutations=good. America=bad. All other countries=good. This brings us to God's Breath.

God's Breath is a family I created for like-minded people to reach their full human potential through contemplation, honest work, and an appreciation of the natural order of things. Friends are the family you choose. Every member of God's Breath is blessed. Every member is chosen. Within the loose-knit family structure, you will learn to reach your full human potential. You will learn to breathe.

What's that? you say. You already know how to breathe? Most people do not know how to breathe

properly. *That's why "how to breathe" is among the first
lessons we teach...*

Exhausted, Ashley closed the book, set it on the nightstand, and went to sleep.

CHAPTER
30

ON THE ROAD

Josh woke at six, put on his sweats and running shoes, and went for a run down Main, took a right on Alamosa, a left on First, and found himself at Adams State University, a leafy oasis built around red brick buildings. He ran to their stadium, home of the Grizzlies, and ran around the track, then headed back. When he returned to his motel room, Kleiser was taking a shower. Josh went next door and knocked.

"Just a minute," Calloway responded, opening the door in his underwear.

"You want to get breakfast?"

"Yeah. Give me ten minutes and I'll meet you out front."

Josh jogged over to the office and asked the clerk about breakfast.

"Campus Cafe. You can't go wrong. Block and a half."

Josh returned to his motel room, showered while Kleiser

was dressing, and put on fresh underwear and the same jeans he'd been wearing for a week. Campus Breakfast was a cheery white block. Josh ordered a Denver omelet, coffee, and orange juice.

After Calloway had polished off his omelet, using a piece of sourdough bread to clean it up, Josh said, "I have to tell you something."

Calloway sat back, placid.

"Ninja thinks Scipio might be Brian Pils, a convicted rapist."

Calloway blinked. "How you spell that?"

Josh told him.

"Ahuh. Well, now it all ties together."

"You think Scipio targeted Ashley as some kind of revenge plot against you?"

"Makes as much sense as anything else. My father was a cop in Chicago. I remember the first time he shot a criminal. It was devastating for us. Very few police ever kill anyone in the line of duty. I would have to go through the records to learn the man's name."

"But you were just a kid when it happened."

"Josh, I don't have to tell you that understanding the criminal mind is a full-time job. It's as good a motive as any. I guess we'll find out."

They headed north on State Highway Seventeen, the Sangre de Christos gleaming to their right. The long straight road took them by ranches and high plains dotted with antelope; the Rockies loomed through the windshield.

Kleiser searched around until he found a jazz station out

of Denver doing a Sonny Criss marathon. Two hours later they reached Poncha Springs, gateway to the Ivy Leaguers: Mount Princeton, Mount Harvard, and Mount Yale, each a fourteener. Harrison lay at the feet of the Continental Divide, forty-five miles up a cracked two-lane highway. They stopped for coffee at a Starbucks.

"Harrison has a population of eight hundred. We'll stand out like sore thumbs," Kleiser said. "I recommend we proceed to Buena Vista, take Cotton Pass Road, park in a National Forest lot and hike in over the mountains. Come up behind them." He traced a route on page sixty of the *Colorado Atlas & Gazetteer*, which took up most of the table space.

"How long is that gonna take?" Calloway said.

"Six hours. You boys up for a little hike?"

Josh looked at Calloway. "You up for this, hoss?"

"Well, I've been hittin' the gym regularly, but I have to confess the altitude is giving me a little difficulty."

Kleiser closed the book. "We'll take it slow. You got hiking shoes and shit, right? I brought everything else. Ponchos, gloves, water bottles, tents. We ought to fill up here."

Calloway rubbed his temples. "You got any aspirin?"

"Yeah. It's in the car."

They hit the road, climbing Highway Two Eighty-Five. A few miles out of town, two cars with out-of-state plates were pulled over on the shoulder, families standing on the shoulder pointing and aiming cameras up. Kleiser pulled up behind them.

"This is the only way I ever see wildlife, when cars are stopped by the side of the road."

Calloway popped out of the rear seat and pulled his phone. "I gotta get a picture of that!"

Two longhorn sheep clung to an almost vertical granite face on the east side. The travelers snapped pictures. They exchanged pleasantries. The tourists got in their cars and continued.

"What's your story, chief?" Kleiser said. "You been a cop all your life?"

"Pretty much. My dad was a cop. We lived in Calumet City. I got a sister named Emma who lives in Nashville. She worked as a nurse for twenty years, and then one night, she takes her guitar and goes to a bar and starts singing. Now, she's got a record out. It's pretty good. If you like folk rock, you should check her out."

"*Folk* rock?" Kleiser said.

Calloway laughed. "My folks played Motown and the blues, but somewhere along the line, Sis fell in with Joni Mitchell and Melissa Ethridge. We keep askin' ourselves where we went wrong."

"That's not folk rock," Josh said. "That's rock rock."

"Joni Mitchell?"

"Why no Motown today?" Kleiser said. "Why is all the popular stuff rap and crap? Or if it is a song, it sounds like every other song with autotune and two chords."

"I don't know. We oughta ask Barry Gordy while he's still around. He was the voice of young America! 'Course the whole music industry doesn't know whether to shit or go blind. The Internet upended everything. Remember when bands used to put out albums? Now they stream a new video. I'm old fashioned. I got vinyl. Lots of it."

"Your folks still alive?"

"No. Pops died in the line of duty. Bank robbery. He got the call, wasn't wearing a vest, they shot him with an AK."

"I'm sorry to hear that! How old were you?"

"I was nineteen. I'd known I wanted to be a cop before, but that put a feather on it."

"That's funny. Being a cop got your father killed and made you want to be a cop?"

"It wasn't him getting killed, it was what he stood for. Law and order, all those good things. I got to admit, some days I ask myself why I bother. City does its best to make our jobs impossible. That's why I'm thinkin' of bailing."

"Do it, brother," Josh said from the back seat. "Start your own security company. You can count on me."

"What about your mother?"

"My sweet ma. Vera is her name, and she lives with my sister in Nashville. Vera played the piano in the church choir. If I hadn't gone into police work, I might have been a singer."

"Are you shittin' me?" Josh said. "Why haven't I heard you sing?"

Calloway broke into a flawless falsetto. "Now if there's a smile on my face, it's only there trying to fool the public. But when it comes down to fooling you, Now, honey, that's quite a different subject..."

Josh barked in disbelief. "Wow! Can you sing down low like you talk?"

Without missing a beat, Calloway segued into a Larry Graham bass. "'Tis your kind of music, that moves me that grooves me that soothes me deep in my soul..."

"Man, I wish I was musical," Josh said.

"Did your father ever kill anyone?" Kleiser said.

Calloway frowned. "Twice in his life he had to put someone down in the line of duty. First time, it was a meth freak comin' at him with a butcher knife. He told that motherfucker to drop the knife three times. Second time, domestic dispute. This here is what it's all about. They could hear the woman screaming so they went in, and here's this punk ass motherfucker holding this young girl around the neck, stabbing her with a hunting knife. I saw the pictures. There was blood all over the wall. My father had no choice but to put him down. Didn't hit the girl. She recovered, but she was never the same. Motherfucker was a serial rapist. Bernard Pils."

CHAPTER

31

HANNIBAL

Brian was ten when his father was killed. Even then, Brian understood their family wasn't like others. It wasn't until years later he learned the term *bi-polar*. There was only the three of them, his father Bernard, his mother Grace, and little Brian, moving from tenement to tenement, affordable housing to affordable housing, while Bernard eked out a living as a security guard, janitor, carpenter, and pizza delivery driver, a job he lost when he used his car to hold up a liquor store.

Bernard was lucky. His public defender convinced the court that Bernard was crazier than a shit house rat, and should be sent to the state mental hospital for a period of observation rather than incarcerated with hardened criminals who might prove a bad influence. The PD didn't know what Grace and Brian knew. Bernard routinely strong-armed drunks for money, which he would flash in bars drawing the attention of a certain breed of young woman. There was often no need to slip the lady a roofie. Sometimes he left twenty dollars on the nightstand.

A good drunk roll could yield a hundred bucks or more, enough to cover his bar tab and a cheap motel room. One night, a young woman with disheveled hair and smeared lipstick showed up on their doorstep with two police officers.

"You left your wallet behind, fucker! It had three bucks in it!"

Bernard denied any wrongdoing. The cops took one look at him, cuffed him, and threw him in the back of the cruiser. The woman's lipstick was on his shirt collar. Grace and Brian watched in cold silence. They'd seen it before.

The vic died of an overdose before the trial. Bernard walked. He did it again. And again. He was more careful. He'd choose a mark in a dive, drop the roofie while she was distracted, and then wait for her by the ladies' room, which was often in the back, near an exit.

There were good times too. Bernard would take Brian to the park, crabgrass with a half-assed baseball diamond, and they'd toss the old pill around. Brian could still summon the smell of his leather Wilson mitt. Bernard taught him to box down on his knees, holding up his palms for pads.

"That's it, Bri! Smack that sucker! Put your shoulder into it! Pivot off your rear leg!"

Brian could count those days on one hand. He knew Bernard was trying to do good. Trying to be a decent father. For Brian's seventh birthday, Bernard and Grace took him to the lake front downtown. They spread a blanket on the lawn, had a picnic, and waited for fireworks. Brian's birthday was the third of July, but they always celebrated on the fourth.

It was the last time he ever saw his mother smile. When they returned to the car, the police were waiting. Someone had spotted the '92 Explorer as stolen. He'd only had it a month. Said his boss had given it to him in lieu of payment for a carpentry job that lasted six months. Brian often wondered what his father had really been doing all that time.

Bernard snorted blow. Bernard was a gifted mimic. "I could have been a serious actor. I starred in our high school production of *Twelve Angry Men* and got great reviews! I would have gone Hollywood years ago if I hadn't hooked up with Grace here and had you."

Bernard encouraged Brian to read and brought home piles of books. The classics. Brian was a prodigious reader. Mark Twain, Charles Dickens, Turgenev. Julius Caesar, Clausewitz, Sun Tzu. Asimov, Heinlein, Herbert. Books were his friend.

After the cop shot Bernard, Grace fell apart and ended up on the street. Brian bounced from foster home to foster home, always an outsider, never loved. There was just something about him. With a father like that he never had a chance. His understanding of love was warped. He had a poor sense of self, and yet a firm belief in his own intelligence. He regarded everybody else as stupid and did poorly in school, excelling only at gymnastics, swimming, and computer skills. The schools he attended no longer taught English literature or anything resembling mathematics.

Brian dropped out in his junior year and began living on the street. He fell in with a scam artist named Tony, and together they worked the Midwest in Tony's van, which said Track Roofing on the side, claiming to be roofers. They'd show up after a tornado or hail storm, low-ball the competition, collect an advance, and move on to the next town.

That fell apart in Jacksonville, when a suspicious neighbor saw them talking up an elderly man in a sagging old wood house, and alerted the police. In the van the police found roofies, an ounce of cocaine, several ounces of weed, and fourteen stolen credit cards. Tony's real name was Anthony Perrone, and he was wanted for drug offenses in Illinois, Iowa, and Missouri. They busted Brian as an accomplice.

Once again, Brian found himself caught in the bowels of the justice system, only this time as an adult. Once again, he drew a public defender, a starry-eyed idealist named Turkel with a great blitz of curly hair that Brian called an Izro. In their talks, Turkel was quick to recognize Brian's intelligence. They had both read the same books. They both loved the classics. They agreed that *Dune* was the most perfect ecological parable ever.

"Brian, you're wasting your life. You're far too intelligent to be a petty criminal. You could be whatever you want to be. I'd like to help you. You can start with your high school equivalency degree."

Turkel was good enough to get Brian released for time served. Turkel had purchased a four-unit apartment building in Peoria, and offered room and board if Brian would live in the basement unit and help fix it up. Done deal.

Brian enjoyed working with tools, cutting the lumber, fitting the joists, pounding nails home straight and true with one bang. Turkel dragged him to Synagogue. They studied Torah together.

Brian was excited by the spiritual life while eyeing it for angles. He knew about Manson, Jim Jones, and Scientology. The lesson wasn't that these systems were scams; the lesson was that it was possible for a smart man to create followers who would do anything.

That summer, Brian decided to reinvent himself. There was no way he could explain his plans to Turkel. Turkel wouldn't understand. So, Brian left in the middle of the night, taking Turkel's car, cash, and credit cards, heading west. He ditched the car in Kansas City, stole another, and kept on going until he reached the Golden State, where he was now Scipio, after the general who defeated Hannibal. As soon as he landed in Los Angeles, he bought copies of The Bible and *How To Win Friends and Influence People* at a used book store.

CHAPTER 32

GOD NOD

LA in the nineties was wide open. Scipio found a street corner where non-union workers could pick up jobs. In his crisp blue work shirt with a leather tool belt, he impressed employers. He impressed them even more on the job. White guys were surprised to find a clean, well-spoken white guy. Latinos and blacks were surprised to find a clean, well-spoken white guy. They paid twelve bucks an hour under the table, picked him up and dropped him off.

Scipio had saved enough to rent a trailer in Rancho Cucamonga, from where he took the bus to wherever they were hiring. As he worked on housing developments in the valley, he tried out his powers of persuasion on his fellow workers, many of whom professed to be devout Christians.

"Jesus was a carpenter, you know."

He watched his language. He was polite and lavish with praise. He didn't expect these rough men to follow him, it was just practice. A perverse thrill ran through him when he found how easy it was to win their confidence. He picked up Spanish. There were often young people hanging around, smoking dope, riding boards, freestylin'.

Scipio saw them from the second and third floors, and during the lunch hour, he would often talk to them.

"Hi! I'm from outta town. We got any Christians here?"

This frequently led to mockery, but Scipio remained unshaken, cracked jokes, complimented them on their grace and wordplay, and in this manner, made friends. He stayed after work, in the parks, smoking dope and spinning his philosophy.

Within a couple weeks he had a coterie of seven kids who laughed at his jokes, hung on his words, and came to him for advice, and that was just one little park in Pomona, with a city skate park, a concrete bowl surrounded by ramps and banisters. The sign said USE AT YOUR OWN RISK.

"Bendix, you're a wizard on that thing. You ought to turn pro."

Bendix, a stick-thin black kid with a fade away and baggy shorts that hung to mid-calf, grinned with pleasure. "You really think so?"

"Absolutely. I see these kids on ESPN. You can run circles around them."

When darkness fell, he'd buy the beer. Nothing stronger. "Bad enough I'm buying you kids beer. You got to get your own reefer."

Summer of '98, there was one young white trash stunner, Amelia, in a ripped shirt and jeans, long blonde hair to her ass, swishing back and forth over a butterfly tat. It was the night he taught them how to breathe.

"You tellin' us we don't know how to breathe?" Bendix asked, incredulous.

"That's right. There's a technique to everything, from making love to landing on the moon. When you open your lungs to the bottom, you open your lungs to God."

"What if we don't believe in God?" asked a freckle-faced punk named Kevin.

"Then I feel sorry for you. No man is happy unless he believes in something greater than himself. For some it's Gaia. Nature. The Buddhists worship all life. Do they worship scorpions? Mosquitoes? Buddhism has much to teach us. I have incorporated its principles into my own life. The concept of reincarnation. No scorpions, though. Gotta draw the line somewhere. You ever think about it? Why would God create scorpions?"

"It's like you said, man," Bendix said. "God works in mysterious ways."

"Amen."

"Doesn't God say an eye for an eye?" Kevin said.

"That's a God nod. That's when you have the knowledge of God, but not the heart. No God, no peace. Know God, know peace."

"What do you mean you're gonna teach us how to breathe?" Amelia said. He wanted to jump her. That ass.

"Oh yeah. We call it square breathing. Let's sit in a circle." They sat. Five of them including Scipio, Indian style. Scipio touched his navel. "This is the bottom of the lungs. Most of us only use the top ten percent, but to get the full benefit of breathing, you have to draw it down all the way to the abdomen. When I say, inhale deeply through the nose and draw it down to your abdomen. Hold for the count of four. Release slowly through the nostrils to the count of four. Count to four. Repeat. Ready?"

Scipio pointed to Bendix's six-pack. "Don't suck it in. Let it out."

Silence, while they breathed. The sound of a lawnmower somewhere in the neighborhood, a barking dog, children playing, traffic on nearby Mason Street.

They looked up or down. All but Scipio, who watched. Their faces, so often animated by attitude, grew peaceful. When they opened their eyes, they smiled and nodded.

"Wow!" said Kevin.

"I know, right?" Bendix said.

"And here's something else. You can use this breathing to control pain, anxiety, or nausea. Exhale slowly, through the nose. Try it now. Be aware of your pulse. As you slowly exhale, notice how your heartbeat slows."

Kevin and Bendix put their thumbs on their wrists. Moments later, Bendix turned to him. "Holy shit!"

"I know, right? Guys, your thumb contains a vein. If you want to feel for a pulse, use your first and index finger."

A police car slowly cruised the park, which occupied a block in the baking suburbs.

"Fuckin' pig," Bendix snarled.

"Don't anybody do anything stupid," Scipio said. "Po-po got to do what po-po got to do. We're just sitting here talking."

"They busted Dartagnan for spitting on the sidewalk. Do you believe that bullshit?"

"That ain't Buddhist, Bendix. Is he out of jail?"

"Yeah, he out. Judge threw it out."

"A cop killed my father."

They stared at him.

"Are you shitting?"

"Nope. Shot him in cold blood. They thought he was another guy. I got no love for the po-po, but I respect them. Like you respect a wild dog. You kids have potential. Each and every one of you is one of God's children, and there's no limit to what you can do if you set your mind to it."

"Yeah yeah," Kevin said.

"I wish I'd known what I wanted to do when I was your age."

"What do you want to do?"

"I want to help people. I want to get rich enough to build a sanctuary, a place where people with no hope can go to get their hope back."

"How you gonna do that? You want to move some *mota*, I can hook you up."

Scipio waved his hand. "Thanks, but no thanks. It's going to be legal soon enough. I don't know exactly how I'm going to do it, but I know I will. God has spoken to me. I'm searching for my talent right now."

"Maybe God wants you to start your own construction firm," suggested Abby, a plump girl with purple hair and a unicorn on her arm.

"I have thought about that too. But I don't know shit about architecture. I'd have to learn a lot. I learn a little every day."

The police cruiser pulled away from the curb and disappeared.

"There he goes," Bendix said.

"We must have bored him. Well, it's getting dark. I gotta get home. Big day tomorrow. But listen. Let's get together again next week. Same bat time, same bat channel."

They nodded and got up. All except Amelia.

"Amelia, why don't you go home."

"I don't want to go home."

"Would you like to come with me?"

CHAPTER

33

MOOSE

The parking lot, delineated by thick logs and a green fifty-gallon trash can, lay at seven thousand feet off a National Forest access road off Cotton Pass Road. At eight-thirty in the morning, theirs was the only vehicle in it. They got out in heavy parkas, breath hanging like word balloons. Kleiser bungeed the carbon fiber drone case to the back of his backpack, like a boot in basic training.

Josh turned to Calloway. "Whaddaya think, boss? Should I bring a gun?"

Calloway's face twisted like a prune. "Better not. Randall, you packing?"

Kleiser patted a bulge on his left breast.

"Fuck it. I ain't gonna be the only one without a gun. Where is it?"

Kleiser moved bedding in the back of the vehicle uncovering a leather handgun case. "Sorry I don't have a holster."

Josh removed the Beretta, checked the slide, dropped the magazine and filled it from a box of Czech ammo. He'd brought a fishing vest which he wore over the parka. It had sixteen pockets. He dumped ammo into one pocket, his satellite phone in another, another held gloves, hand warmers. He clipped a quart canteen to his belt. A wood sign marked MOUNT SAGAMORE TRAIL.

Kleiser took lead, long legs moving at an even pace that would have been fast on level ground, his long brown hair tumbling out of the bottom of a knit cap he wore above the sagging, fur-lined hood. Calloway wore a burgundy quilted jacket and a green knit Packers cap pulled low over his eyes. Josh wore a kelly green hooded down-filled jacket. Within a few minutes, Kleiser and Calloway took off their knit caps and stuffed them in their pockets. They walked next to a rushing mountain rivulet, cold as ice.

"Is it okay to drink this water?" Calloway asked.

"I've done it," Kleiser said. "Not much above us. Only thing you'll get is maybe a little bobcat or longhorn sheep shit."

Calloway edged out on a flat rock and crouched, holding his cupped hands in the water, bringing it to his mouth. "Wheeee-*ooh!* That's *good!*"

Josh edged down next to him, got low over the water and scooped it up.

Kleiser lit a doobie. "Great. Now you're both gonna get the runs."

Kleiser exhaled a luxurious cloud and handed it to Josh,

who did likewise. He looked at Calloway.

Calloway waved his palm. "Let's get going."

The trail veered away from the stream and back again. Away and back. They passed through a pine forest. Calloway was a step behind Kleiser when twenty feet ahead a wall of fur glided from the right to the left.

"Holy shit!" Calloway said. "What the heck is that?"

"Moose."

"I never realized they were so big."

"You never saw a moose before?"

"Maybe in a movie."

"They're not a problem unless you try to molest them."

"Who would molest a moose?"

"Couple years ago some degenerate snuck into the moose enclosure at the Denver Zoo and tried to have intercourse with a female. They found him in the morning with his skull split open. They tried to downplay it."

"Naturally they would," Josh said.

They climbed above the tree line into a field of boulders, some as big as SUVs, following the serpentine trail. The air was bracing, a light breeze out of the west. They could see the top of Mount Sagamore gleaming like diamonds in the morning sun. Josh looked around. Not a cloud in the sky.

"Hard to believe they're gonna get thunder and lightning today."

"You can count on it. Something about the negative charge being attracted to the highest spot. Up at the summit, you'll see scars from lightning strikes."

Breathing heavily, Calloway sat on a rock and took a long swallow from his water bottle. "You climb this before?"

"No, but I've climbed enough fourteeners. They all get hit, all the time."

Heavy snow lay tucked under shelves and behind boulders, leftover from the previous winter, soiled gray. Something gleamed at the base of a boulder. Josh stooped and retrieved a discarded gum wrapper. He held it up.

"Pisses me off. Why come all the way up here and dump your trash? How much does a gum wrapper weigh?"

Kleiser made a stop sign with his hand. "Don't get me started."

Calloway was breathing hard. "You okay, boss?" Josh said.

"I'm fine. Just give me a minute. I haven't done this much exercise in years. This is good for me. I shouldn't have gone soft like that."

They reached the summit around eleven as heavy clouds crept in from the west.

Kleiser pointed. "There they are. Let's keep moving. You don't want to be up here when they arrive."

Just past the summit they looked southwest into a narrow valley with numerous outbuildings, including a barn, and corrals. The main house crouched out of sight below towering granite. In the clear mountain air, they could just make out tiny horses and people in the corrals, small as punctuation.

Josh pointed to the carbon fiber case on Kleiser's back. "Is that gonna fly? I mean if it rains?"

"Depends on how hard it rains. It's waterproof. I can zoom in real close with the camera, and it automatically records via satellite hook-up to my home computer. We'll also be able to view it in real time on our phones. I've got a dedicated site." He pulled out his phone and poked. "I'm sending you the app."

He put his phone away. "Keep moving. We're too high. Let's get down to below the tree line. We should be able to get within a quarter mile. They don't have anyone up on top of the mountain because who would come in that way?"

They descended. Pikas scolded them from rocks. There was more snow on this side, its melt forming a rivulet that grew the farther they descended so that by the time they reached the tree line, it was a rushing stream, no more than a foot across, but with dozens of tributaries from all over the mountain. Above, the clouds rolled in, rumbled, and the lightning began. They pulled up their hoods and put on their gloves, bushwhacking their way through the forest using Kleiser's GPS. They came to a massive anvil-shaped rock jutting over the ranch.

"We'll make camp here," Kleiser said, swinging off his packs. "The ranch is just below. It's a little too windy to put up the drone, but I'll get to it first thing in the morning."

"Can we make a fire?" Calloway asked.

"Ixnay. They could smell the smoke. You each have a NASA engineered mummy bag. You'll be fine."

Josh took off his pack, went through the woods, urinated, pulled out the phone and called Ninja on the satellite phone.

"What?"

"How's Fig?"

"Fig is estivating in supine splendor while I feed her Swedish meatballs."

"Okay. Later."

Josh began scraping up pine needles for a bed. "I'm going to freeze my ass off."

CHAPTER 34

ELECTRIC PORSCHE

Scipio needed a better flock to advance. The kids were too easy. They were feckless and spent their money on drugs. Only Amelia showed ambition, and only because she was so in love with him. The graven image. The false idol. You can't shit a shitter. He knew what he was. But sometimes, as he led his little band in prayer or meditation, he convinced himself he was that person, that saint sent to Earth to uplift the downtrodden and spread joy.

Yeah right.

With a driver's license that said David Scipio, he got a job parking cars at the St. Moritz Country Club in Bel Air. You want the money, you got to go where the money is.

Movie stars, moguls, sports legends met at the St. Moritz. Its restaurant was world class. Access was strictly controlled. No photogs allowed, but sometimes a friend of a friend, or the daughter of a big box merchant would take a candid on her phone and post it to social media.

Sean Sheen and Rebecca Forsyth Spotted Holding Hands at Toney St. Moritz!

Looks Like Luke Leek Has A New Toupee!

It's a Dog's Life! Muriel Takes Lhasa Apso Fernando To Toney St. Moritz!

Scipio had to take a parking test. He wore a laminated ID around his neck with his picture. He was instructed not to speak to the guests except for "Yes, ma'am," and "No, ma'am!"

"What if I'm unsure?"

The manager laughed. "Ask someone."

A natural mimic, Scipio effortlessly slipped into the role of the polished and respectable manservant. Jeeves by way of Alfred. First day on the job, Sean Sheen pulled up in his electric Porsche and tipped him a twenty.

"Park it where it's safe."

"Certainly, Mr. Sheen. Thank you, sir."

He earned a Masters in Philosophy from the University of Phoenix. He studied martial arts online, and at the Zhin Urdu Academy in Pomona. He was a natural. The one year he'd gone out for high school wrestling, he'd gone to the state finals. That weekend, he studied up on Sheen. He'd been a high school drop-out in Massachusetts working in a restaurant when one day he threw down his apron and said, "Fuck it. I'm going to Hollywood to be a movie star."

Sheen slept in his car, made the rounds, took any part he could get, joined the guild. A good-looking kid, the camera loved him. His break-out movie was *Night on the Town*, a risqué comedy in which four high school buddies pool their money and drive to Tijuana, determined to lose their virginity.

They paired Sheen with the thirtyish, devastating Laura Lackawanna, herself a childhood star looking for a way back. It was a combination of *The Graduate* and *Losin' It*, and both stars shone. Laura resurrected her career and Sean leaped to the A list overnight.

Soon, Sheen started his own production company. Boot to The Head Studios. He launched the *Death Trap* series, based on an old spy series from the sixties.

Over the weekend, Scipio plowed through the cinema of Sean Sheen. DVDs were a buck at pawn shops. *Demons from Hell. The Legend of the Purple Hand. Death Traps,* One through Five. Sheen did his own stunts. He was convincing. The internet was filled with his exploits, his fights with other stars, his girlfriends, his two wives, the time he broke up a mugging, the time he stopped a mob from looting a medical marijuana store.

Scipio brought up the video. The race riots four years ago, precipitated by cops killing a black man during the arrest. Three of the cops were black. The whole country blew up. On the third night, as the governor apologized to the looters and begged their forgiveness, the mob marched on a Melrose MMJ shop. Sheen was just coming out with an ounce of primo, six blunts, and enough THC gummy bears to tranquilize a hippo. As the masked looters approached holding torches, bottles, crowbars, Sheen sank into a fighting stance and yowled like an alley cat.

"Get the fuck outta here. I know these people and they're good people. You want to loot this store, you'll have to go through me."

"It's Sean Sheen!" cried a masked woman wearing a pink beret.

"Look, everybody! Sean Sheen!"

Out came the cameras. Many were the photo ops.

Sean Sheen: A Hero In Real Life!

The next time Sean Sheen drove up in his Porsche, Scipio was low into horse stance, midway through a powerful Okinawan kata. He popped up as soon as Sheen drove into view, although Scipio had seen him coming a quarter mile away.

"Welcome back, Mr. Sheen!"

Sheen, famous for his tough guy roles and private pursuit of martial arts, said, "What was that you were just doing?"

"That was an Okinawan karate form."

"Really. You know I practice. I've always been fascinated with the martial arts."

"I know, Mr. Sheen. I've seen your films!"

"Call me Sean." The movie star looked at Scipio's ID. "Dave. Hey, I gotta date, but let's you and me talk kung fu one of these days."

"Thank you, Sean!"

Sheen had never been nominated, but he was the number

one box office draw in the world three years in a row. Scipio didn't know about that right then. They never stopped
making actors.

One night, Sheen came out pin-eyed and crazy, teeth
like a wolf.

"Dave! What the fuck! Dave! Where's my car?"

"I don't think you should be driving, Mr. Sheen."

"What? Call me Sean. Relax! It's an automatic."

"Can't let you do it, Sean. How about I drive you?"

"You just want to drive my Porsche."

Scipio grinned. "You got me."

"Aw go ahead. I'll go back in and tell 'em what's going
on. Meet you out here in five minutes."

Sheen had a place in Malibu on a bluff overlooking the
ocean. Four car garage, gleaming white facade, floor to ceiling windows, pool, jacuzzi, tennis. The steel gate slid aside
at their approach.

"I got a man on the property at all times. You can't be
too careful."

The man in the gatehouse looked like business. Shaved
skull, steely demeanor, probably ex-military.

"Stop inside the gates. Lower your window."

Scipio did so. The man came over.

"Hal!" Sheen yelled in Scipio's ear. "This is Dave Scipio!
He's some kind of martial arts whiz! Dave, this is Hal Galp-
er. He's my guru. Hal holds black belts in seven disciplines.
You fought full contact in Japan, didn't you Hal?"

"That's right, Sean. Dave. Happy to meet you."

They shook through the open window. They drove up to the glass entrance.

"Just leave it here, Dave. I'll show you where you can crash."

"I can order an Uber, Sean."

"No, no. I want to talk to you. Come on. I'll show you a room. We'll talk in the morning."

CHAPTER 35

SLEEK FLANKS

An eye for an eye.

A man is never truly happy until he believes in something greater than himself.

Scipio rose at seven, padded through the silent mansion admiring the original Barry Windsor-Smith in the living room, the Barcelona ottoman and lounge, the honey tan Homer sofa, the lavish kitchen with a marble-topped island, induction stove, walk-in freezer, espresso machine, percolator, the Keurig, glass-fronted cabinets holding a dozen Mason jars of beans, cast iron pans hanging from the ceiling, flat screen TV, the rounded breakfast nook jutting into the garden like Buckminster Fuller's Dymaxion.

He opened the patio door and went out by the pool, and gazed out at tiny white triangles dancing in the morning sun on an infinite carpet of sapphires, flitting on the horizon. When he came back in, Hal Galper was making coffee in the kitchen.

"Sean asks if you can stick around this morning. He says he'll square it with the St. Moritz."

Galper whipped up some bacon and eggs.

"I've been with Sean for a while. He's a soft touch. I look out for him. He'd give you the shirt off his back."

"How did you meet?"

"I had a dojo. Shaolin Kung Fu. I studied Shaolin in China years ago, when you could still visit. Before that, I was in the Army."

"Seriously?"

"Yes indeed. It used to be a steady source of income for the Glorious People's Republic. Starry-eyed Westerners, hat in hand. Bowing and scraping, eager to clean the latrines. The monks especially loved the young ladies. Kung fu movies are China's gift to the world. Would any of us be studying were it not for Bruce Lee?"

Scipio poked a finger. "There's some truth in that. How long were you there?"

"Two years. When I got back, I began competing in contests. I trained with Danny Inosanto and Richard Bustillo. I got hired as a fight coordinator for a movie Sean was in, *The Black Olive.* Maybe you've heard of it."

"Nuh uh. But I've seen all the *Death Traps.*"

"I worked on those. Sean started coming to me for private lessons. Then, in the riots, they burned down my studio. I didn't know what to do, so Sean suggested I come work for him. I'm sort of a majordomo slash bodyguard slash gofer. I live in the guest house. I ain't complainin'. What are your plans?"

"You mean in general, or regarding Sean?"

"Both."

"Well, I'm not looking to break into the movies, although I admire his work. I plan to start my own religion."

"Say what?"

"Oh yeah. I have a master's in philosophy. I've studied all the great religions and I hope to found a truly honest and benevolent church that borrows from Christianity, Judaism, Buddhism, and the Tao."

"What about Islam?"

Scipio laughed. "Gotta draw the line somewhere."

Galper laughed. "Me, I was raised Episcopalian. Didn't take. I'm a godless sinner. Married three times. I figure if I can't make it work after three, to hell with it. I got a kid I rarely see, but I'll see a lot more of him. My bitch-ass ex has about driven him crazy and he's dying to come live with me. He's a huge Sean fan. I get to bring him on set sometime. What about you?"

"I'm seeing someone from my study group right now. I live in Rancho Cucamonga."

Galper put a hand to his ears. "Ouch. How do you get around?"

"Public transportation."

"Well fuck. Sean's got eleven automobiles. Let's see what happens."

"I hardly know him. I don't want to impose."

Galper regarded him sideways. "Riiiiight. Have you seen the gymnasium? Let me show you around."

They started by the pool. "This is a Roark Dexter Smith house."

"I don't know who that is."

"Smith was a visionary. Crazy as hell. He lived out here in a trailer for a month figuring out the exact alignment of the foundation. It's in tune with the tides, the magnetic poles, and the planets. Used to belong to the composer, Mark Wiley. Sean's been here nine years."

Galper pointed to a white deco cube with rounded glass corners. "That's where I live. Two bedrooms and two baths."

Galper showed him the garage, the gleaming burgundy McClaren, the silver Aston Martin convertible. Scipio longed to stroke their sleek flanks.

Galper opened the door. "Go ahead. Have a seat."

Scipio slid in and grabbed the wheel. He heard the engine whine, the double-clutching as he switched gears, the exhaust pop as he braked for the corner. All his life, he had wanted one.

"Come on. You gotta see the gym."

It was on the second floor, hardwood floors, a barre against a room-length mirror. On the other side, sheer glass looked over the ocean. Kettlebells, weight machines, sparring equipment, a twenty-foot ring raised a foot above the floor. They went to the barre and stretched.

"You want to spar a little?"

"Sure," Scipio said.

"Go into the dressing room. Put on some sweats. There should be a fresh jockstrap and a cup too."

There was a box of fresh jockstraps, a box of sealed mouthpieces in several sizes, and a box of cups. Scipio came out barefoot, wearing baggy trousers and a white muscle shirt showcasing his prison tats: a skull and a bald eagle. They put on sixteen-ounce gloves, head protectors, and mouthpieces. They bounced around. Galper gestured at the arms.

"You been inside?"

"Yeah. Two years. I was a wild and uncontrollable child. You couldn't tell me a thing. I had to learn the hard way."

"Okay, nice and easy. Show me what you got."

Scipio moved in easy, threw a roundhouse to the midsection. Galper danced back, they circled. Galper closed with a flurry bap bap bap! light as a mother's kiss. Scipio blocked two but the third got through, rapping him on the forehead. Scipio bobbed and weaved and threw an overhand right that connected behind Galper's ear. He grinned.

"Nice!"

He hoisted himself into the air with a flying knee that Scipio brushed aside, going low for a sweep, but Galper adjusted and landed on his feet. Scipio closed with a jackhammer jab that drove Galper back until he stopped and whirled, catching Scipio in the side of the head with a reverse crescent kick.

Scipio put up his hands. "Whoa! Didn't I see you do that in *Death Trap II*?"

"You have good eyes. I've been in all the *Death Traps*. I had a couple lines in IV. 'Look at my rat. Don't touch it. You may look at it but don't touch,'" he said in a thick Russian accent.

Hands clapped. Sheen stood just inside the door wearing swim trunks, tanned, toned body rippling, the legendary hair. "I knew you boys would get along."

"You want to join us?" Galper said.

"Nah. I just got up. I gotta get with Benny. Take about an hour. Dave, I'd like you to hang around. I want to hear about this new religion of yours."

CHAPTER

36

FLY LIKE AN EAGLE

The rain and the wind cut to the bone. Josh, Calloway and Kleiser clung to the side of the mountain huddled together in rain-proof parkas, too enervated to dig out their sleeping bags. The storm abated at midnight leaving behind a piercing wind. The morning found them on their sides like garden slugs, mouths open, poorly rested, dealing with waking dreams.

Josh was the first up. He made his way to the rivulet of melted snow and filled his canteen, used the propane burner to heat water for the instant oatmeal, pulled an apple and a bruised banana from his pack and ate them. The sun crept above the eastern horizon at nine. Kleiser pulled on a pair of shades and unpacked the carbon fiber case. There were two four-rotor drones inside, each the size of a pigeon. Josh picked one up. It weighed almost nothing.

"Charge'll last about two hours. I brought extra batteries,

but I have to use 'em sparingly. The facial recognition software will pick up either Scipio or Ashley and alert me. I use GPS to set up a pattern over the ranch."

"What if they see it?" Calloway said.

"There's always a chance. Hopefully they'll mistake it for a bird. It can zoom in from a thousand feet. If they do make it, they can try and shoot it, but that's gonna be a hard shot, and then we'll know."

"Great," Josh said. "Might it not be smarter to ease on down to where we can see the grounds and look for her ourselves?"

"Well, there's three of us and almost a hundred of them."

"I went to ninja school."

Calloway and Kleiser looked at him.

"Seriously. I went to ninja school."

"Fine. You want to creep down there and have a look be my guest."

Josh wore gray cargo trousers, waffle stompers, a green hoodie and gloves. He pulled the Beretta and binoculars from his backpack and stuck them in the hoodie's pockets.

"I can reach you with this satellite phone?"

"Unless there's a cosmic event."

Josh angled off to look for a way down. He'd gone a quarter mile when he spied a game trail snaking down at a forty-five-degree angle. He descended with his feet sideways, leaning uphill, holding onto jutting limbs, roots, rocks, anything he could grab. The sun warmed him so that he doffed the hood. It was in the forties as he descended on a zigzag path toward the God's Breath Ranch. He pulled off the hoodie revealing a gray knit long-sleeve pullover, shrugged on his backpack and inched downward. An anvil-like protrusion extended from a cluster of Douglas fir and bristlecone. The oldest living thing on Earth. The bristlecone pine. Some were five thousand years old. If he had one, he'd throw it a party.

The jutting rock gave him a commanding view of the ranch from the grand house on the right backed up against the cliff to the little valley and the dirt road winding down through the mountains. At this hour, a number of people were at work, feeding the livestock, tending the garden. He trained his binoculars on the long greenhouse. Hail must have smashed it countless times over the years yet all the glass was intact. They probably kept replacement glass in the metal pole barn. The garage was angled away so he couldn't see the doors, but it was big enough to house at least ten cars. The main house, on a hill, was a stately Victorian with a tin roof. The bunkhouse and barns had tin roofs as well. Nice little set-up. It reminded him of the marijuana farm in the mountains he'd visited years ago, tracking down a song for a client.

"Marissa."

Josh used his camera to take pictures of the compound. He put the camera away and picked up the binoculars again as a woman appeared from beneath the tin roof covering the main house veranda. Bingo. There she was, the first black face he'd seen. She wore a black cap, blue jeans and a light blue sweatshirt. He watched her cross the yard to a corral containing a half dozen horses and talk to a lean hombre in a cowboy hat who was hand-feeding a sorrel on the other side of the fence.

He watched as the cowboy and Ashley entered the corral. The cowboy said something to Ashley and handed her something, which she fed to the horse. She spoke to the horse, stroking its snout soothingly while the cowboy threw a saddle blanket over its back followed by a light Western saddle.

He showed Ashley how to mount, and then led the horse by its bridle around the corral while Ashley clung to the pommel. After one circuit, he handed the reins to Ashley. They were too far away to hear what was said.

Ashley tentatively rode the horse around the corral. It stopped, and at the cowboy's urging, she gently prodded it forward by leaning over the neck, and slapping its flanks. She sat up, holding the reins loosely, grinning.

Josh had always been afraid of horses. Look what had happened to Christopher Reeve. Give Josh a motorcycle any day. Ashley made several more circuits before dismounting, talking to the cowboy, and climbing out of the corral. He couldn't see the main house's front from where he lay. He would have to move clockwise around the cliff. Gathering his things, he shrugged into his backpack and headed up above the sheer rock face at an angle until he came to a ridgeline topped with bristlecone, juniper and aspen.

He'd gone a hundred yards when he came to a rock that jutted out like a rhino's horn. Taking off his backpack, he set it between two boulders, got down on hands and knees, and inched out on the horn. From here he saw the house. A man came out in blue jeans, pointed boots, a yoked jacket and a cowboy hat. The sun gleamed off a belt buckle the size of a saucer. Josh pulled his binoculars.

Scipio. Josh straddled the rock at the tip as he tracked Scipio across the yard toward the pole barn that served as the mess and the chapel. A wooden cross rose from the peaked tin roof facing the central courtyard.

A marmot leaped on his back. Josh spazzed and slid off the horn, falling ten feet to a steep, boulder-studded slope. He threw out his arms and legs to grab something, anything, but he was out of time and out of ground as he hurled off a precipice and fell toward a dense stand of Douglas fir. The first branches slapped him in the face and gut. He grabbed at anything, seized a branch that fell with him until it snapped. He grabbed a bigger branch that bowed him into the trunk, from where he fell another eight feet to the ground.

He lay there breathless and still, unable to move, feeling a warm trickle on his forehead, fearing the scrape of bone on bone. At last he dared to breathe. Cautiously he flexed his fingers, then his toes. Bit by bit, he realized that he was intact. His head throbbed. He sat up.

A man entered the clearing beneath the big tree holding a double-barreled shotgun. He was a lean, dark man with scarred eyebrows and the look of a soldier. He aimed the shotgun at Josh.

"Get up."

CHAPTER 37

THE DETECTIVE

Sean Sheen introduced Scipio to the actress Honey Parker and music mogul Rok Steddy, young, rich, searching, open to anything. Scipio began holding sessions in their houses where they would invite friends and acquaintances. The events were often catered. Beluga caviar. Wagyu beef. Ancient grains. Kale salad. The aroma of marijuana drifted through the rooms. Scipio forbade alcohol. Marijuana was a sacrament that opened the soul toward greater understanding.

Scipio bought Facebook ads. His followers stapled posters to telephone poles throughout Los Angeles, on bulletin boards in clubs and cafes, handed them out to kids at the bus station.

ARE YOU A SEEKER?
DOES TRADITIONAL WORSHIP LEAVE
YOU HUNGRY FOR GREATER KNOWL-

EDGE?
DO YOU FEEL A HOLLOWNESS WITHIN?
PLEASE JOIN US FOR A WORSHIP SEMINAR CONDUCTED BY REVOLUTIONARY THINKER SCIPIO AT SUCH AND SUCH A PLACE, AT SUCH AND SUCH A TIME REFRESHMENTS WILL BE SERVED

Rapper turned actor Yougenic, who played Jesus as a differently-abled lesbian of color in *Rhapsody in Pink*, was an overnight convert. Scipio never asked for money. The donations poured in and soon he could afford a loft in West Hollywood. He popped up at parties and premieres, dazzling with aphorisms, collecting followers like a flower child of the sixties gathering daisies.

Sheen put him on several movies as a spiritual advisor. Yougenic asked him to open for him at the Hollywood Palladium. His website and YouTube channel, *God's Breath*, featured advertisements for Chanel, Ralph Lauren, Aston Martin, Coach, as well as many charitable groups. He hired a signer for the deaf.

For five hundred dollars, he would consult with sinners, seekers, and people who happily forked it over just to meet him. Within a year he announced God's Breath Church and applied for tax-exempt status. Scipio moved into the old Reginald Conway house on Mulholland, and held court weekends with bacchanals that lasted until Sunday morning when Scipio led his congregation in worship and sought forgiveness for his gang of sinners.

Dot-com billionaire Carlos Crane told Scipio how to invest his money. He bought Disney right before Disney bought Marvel. *Slate*, *Salon*, and *The Huffington Post* interviewed him.

New Spiritual Guru.

A Fresh Take on God.

Does This Man Have the Answers for a Godless Age?

He wrote a weekly column for his website. Often, it took the form of aphorism or apocrypha. He frequently quoted the Apocrypha.

"If thou hast abundance, give alms accordingly, if thou have but a little, be not afraid to give accordingly to that little."

"A stubborn heart shall fare evil at the last."

"Observe the opportunity."

"Let thy life be sincere."

"I'm an Old Testament kind of guy," Scipio said, "But I also dig Jesus."

Rolling Stone wanted to put him on the cover, but sensing overexposure, Scipio demurred. He had labored in the vineyards of Babylon for ten long years. He had acquired well-heeled groupies who would carry out his every command. But he was no hothead. No race obsessed criminal. Sensing overexposure, financially secure, with more acolytes than he could handle, Scipio decided to remove himself from Sodom by the Sea and relocate to the heartland. In the mountains. Where it was clean. He looked at real estate from Montana to New Mexico and settled on Colorado.

He put the Mulholland place up for sale. One brisk February day, a stiff wind whipping up whitecaps, a private investigator arrived at Scipio's front gates. Scipio had asked around and everybody said that if you wanted the man who got things done, you got Dale Sorensen. Sorensen was a twenty-year veteran of the LAPD, ten of those a detective, and got out before the riots.

Sorensen arrived at the Scipio estate in a yellow Challenger, and waited, massive V8 burbling, as the gate contracted. Sorensen drove up the red brick turnaround and parked beneath the portico leading into Scipio's tudor-style house. Sorensen was a heavy-set man in a navy blue blazer with gold buttons over tan khakis. Scipio opened the door.

"Come in, Dale."

They sat in the living room looking out the multipaned windows at the city in the distance, the hazy blue Pacific.

"Would you like something to drink?"

"Gin and tonic," Sorensen growled.

Scipio clapped his hands and a young lady in a genie costume appeared.

"Jen, two gin and tonics."

"What's with the genie outfit?"

"We like to have fun."

Sorensen looked around. "I was here once on a call. Conway was slapping his fifth wife around. Looked different then."

"I had it redecorated."

Sorensen regarded the stuffed elk head over the stone fireplace. "You shoot that?"

"No, I bought it."

"So, you're moving to Colorado. Good hunting out there."

"I'm not a hunter, but I enjoy nature."

Jen returned with their drinks and a bowl of macadamia nuts.

"Thank you, Jen."

She trailed her fingers along his jawline and left. Sorensen's hedgerow brows rose.

"You must have known a lot of stars," Scipio said.

Sorensen picked up his drink and drained half before setting it down on a cork coaster. He waved in dismissal. "They're no different than you or me. Wait a minute. I take that back. They're a lot dumber. Most of 'em never finished high school. A lot of these stars, they come out here as wide-eyed ingenues determined to make it. Most don't. Some straighten up and go back to Wichita. Some turn to drugs and prostitution. The child stars are the worst. You know how many Power Ranger cast members have been convicted of murder?"

The detective held up three fingers.

"Conway was a lush, but the worst he did was slap his wife around. She had a mouth on her. I might have slapped her myself. I've found A-listers passed out in hallways. I once had a Laker on acid throw himself through a plate glass window to reach the pool."

"Was it Dean Scarborough?"

Sorensen drew an invisible zipper across his lips. "Come on."

"That's the only Laker I know."

"You've never heard of Kobe Bryant?"

"No."

"You didn't play sports in high school?"

"Dale, I was ten when my father was shot by a Chicago policeman."

"Sorry to hear it."

"I respect the police. We have some officers in our little group. This is not about the police, but this officer in particular. I want you to find him. I want to know everything there is about him. Here's everything I have."

He handed Sorensen a manila envelope. Sorensen opened it and slid out the contents, including several pictures of a young black officer. Rufus Calloway, Berwyn Police Department.

"May I ask your purpose?"

"I have reached a point in my life where I can finally forgive him. I want him to know."

"Have you conducted an internet search?"

"Yes. He retired from the force in 1994. No one knows where he is."

"I get two-fifty a day plus expenses."

Scipio opened the rosewood table between them and took out a checkbook. "I'm giving you a ten-thou-sand-dollar advance."

CHAPTER

38

STITCHES

Josh sat, head throbbing. "I think I have a concussion."

"What are you doing here?"

"I got caught on the mountain last night. Nearly froze my ass off. I knew there was a trail down off the mountain on this side so I thought it safer to come down this way. I fell when a squirrel or something jumped on my back."

The man looked at him. "You climbed Mount Sagamore alone?"

"Yeah. I do it all the time."

"Who are you?"

"Josh Pratt."

"Can you walk?"

Josh got unsteadily to his feet, leaning on an aspen. "What's with the gun?"

"It's a gun. This is private property. Why don't you come with me down to the ranch? We got a nurse practitioner who can give you the once over."

"Thanks."

The man gestured with the gun. "Go ahead. Follow the trail."

"What's your name?"

"Hal."

"I didn't know there was a ranch up here."

"You knew about the trail."

Josh made his way unsteadily down the trail. He had a massive headache but was otherwise intact. "I study maps."

"Where's your equipment? Don't you have a backpack?"

"Yeah. I took it off when I inched out on a promontory to take a look. That's when the squirrel jumped on my back."

"Marmot most likely."

As they descended through the pine and aspen, Josh warmed, and by the time they glimpsed the outbuildings through the trees, he was feeling pretty lucky for having survived the fall. The trail switchbacked down to the valley where the trees gave way to a high mountain meadow near the corral where Ashley was now riding the horse herself as the trainer looked on. Josh kept his head down and hoped she wouldn't notice. Galper directed him toward the long log cabin with the cross above the door. God's Breath members trickled in and out. The hall was filled with the aroma of coffee and bacon. Josh salivated.

"You want some breakfast?" Galper asked. "Let's get some breakfast."

They filled their trays and took a seat at an empty picnic table far from the door. After Josh had polished off his scrambled eggs and bacon, Galper carefully folded his hands in front of him.

"Do you have any identification?"

"Well yeah, but I'm just passing through."

"Humor me."

Josh dug out his wallet and showed Galper his driver's license. Galper examined it for what seemed like an eternity.

"Madison, Wisconsin."

"Yup."

"You're not the only person from Madison at this ranch."

"Really? Well, you know Madison's always been a kind of intellectual, searching town. I'm not surprised."

"Do you know an Ashley Calloway?"

For an instant Josh didn't want to say. It must have showed on his face. "Do you mean Heinz Calloway's daughter?" he said with what he hoped was astonishment.

Galper looked at him unblinking.

"Do you know her?"

"I've met her. Her dad and I are old friends. This is unbelievable!"

"Mr. Pratt, I'm going to have to ask you to stick around and answer a few questions."

"Excuse me? Are you a police officer?"

"No, but this is a private ranch and you're intruding."

"Well, I'm no expert, but I don't think you have the right to restrain me. Call a cop if you want."

"We are at the end of a nineteen-mile dirt road. The

nearest town, Callahan, has one police officer."

"Well, call him. What's the problem? I don't care what you're doing here. Look, if you're growing marijuana, it's legal. I don't care. I just want to be on my way."

"I understand that, Mr. Pratt, but we have security issues. Have you heard of the God's Breath Church?"

"Ashley's father is a friend of mine. I'm a private investigator. He hired me to find his daughter."

"Well, now we're getting somewhere. Why didn't you tell me that in the first place?"

Josh shrugged. "I was hoping to just have a talk with her. Her father is desperate to know if she's all right. Is she?"

"She's fine. I had dinner with her last night, but we have a policy that acolytes are not permitted any contact with their former life for at least six months. People come here seeking answers. Some of them are desperate. Some of them have been abused. This is a place of healing."

"I just want to make sure she's okay. Her father is worried sick."

"Often, family is the source of problems. Ashley told us that her father is cruel and controlling, like so many police."

"I don't believe she said that. What about the head guy in charge? Can I see him?"

"Possibly. I'll have to ask. I need you not to leave. Why don't you give me your wallet?"

"Why?"

"Well, I'm pretty sure you won't leave without your wallet."

"What do you care whether I leave or not?"

"We have some unresolved issues here, Mr. Pratt. You lied to me. That makes me suspicious. Now your subsequent story makes more sense, but how do I know you're alone? Hiking solo over the Continental Divide is a risky business."

"It's how I operate."

Galper held out his hand. "You can either give me your wallet and wait for me here, or I can take you to see Scipio."

Josh stood. "Let's go."

"That's a nasty gash. We'll get someone to clean it up."

"Got any ibuprofen?"

"I think we can hook you up. Come with me."

Galper led Josh down a short hall to an office with an open door. He knocked on the frame and entered. Inside, an older, heavy-set woman wearing sequined eyeglasses on a chain around her neck looked up from her computer. One wall was covered with bookshelves made from cinder blocks and pine planks. Behind her, the window looked out on a stock pond and the mountains.

"Vivian, Mr. Pratt has a nasty gash."

Viv rose from behind the desk. She wore blue jeans and a Broncos sweatshirt. She pointed to a straight back chair facing the desk. "Sit."

Josh sat. She delicately probed the gash on his forehead. She smelled of Chanel No. 5. "Looks like you could use a few stitches. I'm going to apply a disinfectant, you okay with that?"

"Sure."

"I'm going to leave you with Viv for a little while. I am instructing our security to detain you if you try to leave. Please don't abuse our hospitality."

Galper pulled his phone and stepped into the hall. Josh heard him talking quietly.

Viv went to a white metal cabinet with a red cross, removed a sterile needle and stitching thread. "This is going to sting, you okay with that?"

"Sure."

Josh waited patiently while she stitched up the wound, dabbing it with alcohol-soaked cotton. When she finished, she handed him a hand mirror.

Josh examined the professional stitches. "Looks good."

"You're good to go."

"Where do I go?"

"Hmmm," Viv said. "You have a point. Gladiator doesn't want you to leave. How about I show you to our library?"

"Does it have a computer?"

Viv giggled. "No, of course not. It's a real library, with wood shelves and books. Are you a reader, Mr. Pratt?"

"Yes."

"What do you like to read?"

"Westerns. I particularly like Louis L'Amour and Peter Brandvold who I think is L'Amour's heir."

"I like Westerns too. I'll have to check out this Mr. Brandvold. Come with me."

She led Josh down the hall to a high-ceiling room with a beamed ceiling, three walls lined with books. A window in the middle wall looked out on the pasture.

"There's a restroom right there. Why don't you just settle back with a good book until Gladiator comes for you? I recommend the Bible."

"I always enjoy reading the Bible."

He was deep into *Proverbs* when Galper returned.

Galper stepped back in. "Let's go, Pratt. Scipio wants to meet you."

ON THE TRAIL

Calloway and Kleiser lay on their bellies peering down into the valley. They saw the corral, the barn, and the two-story log building. But no Pratt.

"Now what?" Kleiser said.

"We're going to have to go down there. Hopefully, they'll listen to me."

"Wait a minute. I don't trust this Scipio as far as I can throw him. What's to stop them from just killing us and leaving us for the bears?"

Calloway stood up, binoculars dangling, staring at the sky, his face worn with concern. "I don't know. It's hard to believe that such enclaves exist in the United States, but after what I've witnessed in Madison over the past several months, I'd put nothing past them. On the other hand, we're armed. They might hesitate attacking two armed men."

"I don't think so. They're fanatics. Believe me, I know

the signs. And they have guns. Josh told us. I think the wise course is for us to retreat back the way we came, drive to a town with some kind of police force and tell them what's happening."

"That would take two days, at least. By the time we reach civilization, they may have acted."

"I've got a satellite phone."

"Show me how it works. I might be able to reach someone."

Calloway and Kleiser trudged uphill until they came to their little mess on the mountain, sleeping bags, backpacks, an empty donut wrapper. Kleiser dug through his pack and pulled out a rubber-wrapped Garmin with a two-finger antenna stub.

"Who we calling?"

"See if you can reach State Police Headquarters in Lakewood."

"How far away is that?"

"Pretty damned far. It's just a place to start."

Kleiser played with the phone and handed it to Calloway. "It's ringing."

"Colorado State Patrol. Sergeant Hathaway speaking."

"Sergeant, this is Heinz Calloway. I'm a police lieutenant from Madison, Wisconsin. I'm on Mount Sagamore looking down at the God's Breath compound. A week ago, my teenage daughter Ashley left to meet a man named Scipio who claims to be the leader of God's Breath. Have you heard of them?"

"Yes, I have. Please give me a minute to verify your status. Do you mind if I put you on hold?"

"As long as the batteries last."

"I'll try to be quick."

Calloway sat on a rock. Kleiser reached into his vest pocket and pulled out a blunt. "Do you mind?"

"Just keep it downwind."

Kleiser lit the doobie and inhaled, exhaling a luxurious cloud of smoke. "You know, ever since Colorado legalized pot, the price has gone down and the quality has gone up."

"Good to know."

"It's not just getting high. Hemp is superior to paper and cotton. The only reason marijuana was criminalized was because the big paper companies didn't want the competition. Hemp grows faster than lumber. A lot faster. You can harvest it without leaving an ugly clear-cutting scar."

"You don't have to sell me."

"So you're in favor of legalization?"

Calloway shrugged. "It's gonna happen whether I like it or not. Marijuana may be small potatoes, but I've seen people kill each other over botched marijuana deals. I've seen people kill themselves while they were high because they thought they could fly."

"Did you ever smoke dope?"

"No. My father was a police officer. I wish I could say the same for my daughter."

"Yeah, I can smell it."

The phone beeped. Calloway put it to his ear. "Lieutenant, would you mind verifying your birth date and badge number?"

Calloway told him.

"Okay. We received your missing person's bulletin, but here is the situation. Unless you can report a felony in progress or otherwise provide proof that they are breaking the law, we can't really respond. If you can do that, we can dispatch some troopers. If you need a medevac, we can do that, but only if someone's life is in danger. Where are you now?"

"We're above the compound. It will probably take us an hour to get down there, and we'll be more or less at the mercy of the group. My companion and I are armed, but so are the God's Breathers. They have a history of closing ranks against outsiders, and I find it disturbing that they would target my seventeen-year-old daughter. They're also holding a friend of ours, a private investigator named Josh Pratt."

"Do you know that for a fact?"

"He went down there a couple hours ago and we haven't heard from him since. They must have taken his cell phone."

"How's your reception up there?"

"Nonexistent. I wouldn't be able to talk to you without this satellite phone."

"So it's possible your friend may not be in trouble, and has just been unable to reach you."

"It's possible, but he's pretty conscientious. If he were free to move about, he would have returned."

"He may have broken his neck," Kleiser said.

"My associate informs me that Pratt may have broken his

neck. We don't know what happened to him."

"Well, why don't you go look."

Calloway put his hand over the mouthpiece. "He says we should go look for Josh."

"Why didn't I think of that?"

Calloway put the phone to his ear. "We'll go look."

"Can you transmit images?"

Calloway turned to Kleiser. "Can this thing transfer images?"

Kleiser gave him the thumbs up.

"Yes."

"You should be able to keep in touch via the sat phone. Call me if there are any developments."

"Yes sir. Thank you, Sgt. Hathaway."

They stuffed everything into their backpacks and headed down the mountain. They took a circuitous route to below where Pratt was last seen. At the base of the cliff, Kleiser crouched and examined some broken branches. "He might have fallen here. Looks like the branches broke his fall."

"Where is he?"

"Well, he didn't come back up so he must have gone down."

"Why wouldn't he at least alert us that he was alive?"

"That's a good question."

A game trail meandered toward the valley. They had gone a half mile when an adult black bear emerged from the forest, turned around sniffing, and stood up looking at them.

"Holy shit," Calloway said under his breath.

"Chill. It's just a black bear. They're more afraid of us than we are of them."

Kleiser waved his arms. "Beat it!"

The bear put its head down and disappeared into the forest.

"Do they have mountain lions out here?"

"Yeah, but they're even more chicken than the bears. Come on. Let's go."

An hour later, the trail emerged from the forest at the edge of the cliff affording them a view of the compound. A man riding a small John Deere pulled a wagon filled with hay toward the corrals. People came and went from a two-storied log cabin building, and tiny figures sat on the veranda of the big house beneath the cliff, to their right. Twelve men and women appeared to be practicing some kind of martial art on the flat earth between the oddly lavish Victorian mansion and the barn.

Calloway pulled out his binoculars and sat, carefully surveying, from left to right. "I see twenty-two people including those on the veranda. The man teaching those classes. That would be Gladiator."

Kleiser had read Josh's report. "We're no match for him or that gang. Not if they're armed. And even if they're not, what are we gonna do? Shoot them all?"

Calloway stiffened. "There she is."

Kleiser brought out his binoculars and focused on where Calloway was looking. A tall black girl hotfooted from the corral toward the mansion, up the steps and in the door.

CHAPTER 40

SMOOTH MEAT SANDWICH

Galper had traded his shotgun for a sidearm as he accompanied Josh across the parade ground toward the Victorian mansion beneath the cliff. A dozen men and women squatted in horse stance throwing punches to the cadence of a tough Latino with a Fu Manchu, his voice clear in the high mountain air.

"One!" he barked. The dozen threw a single punch. "Two!" they threw two. Kleiser nudged Calloway on the shoulder and pointed. A muscular man with a military demeanor accompanied Josh toward the main house. By the time Galper and Pratt passed the class, they were up to ten. Their stances looked good. Their concentration was excellent.

Galper followed Josh several paces back. "Up the stairs and right on in."

Josh glanced at the kung fu wooden man.

"Who uses the wooden man?"

"Scipio, me, some of God's Teeth."

The entrance foyer was spotless, with an antique coat rack, a Navajo rug on the hardwood floor, a Western landscape on one side showing the mountains reflected in a limpid lake, a painting of Jesus opposite. It was one of those paintings that might have come from a picture book, with a gauzy Jesus in a blue robe surrounded by children and animals. Josh thought Jesus looked a little like Jim Caviezel, who had played Jesus in *The Passion of the Christ*.

Past the foyer lay a large common area with an elegant hardwood staircase winding toward the second floor, a living room on the left, a hall on the right off of which lay a series of doors.

"Last door on the right," Galper said.

Josh went in the open door where a small, dapper man sat behind a polished maple Queen Ann desk consulting a computer. He stood and came around the desk, wearing jodhpurs, snakeskin boots, and a yoked shirt with mother of pearl buttons. He looked a little like Leslie Howard. He stood in front of Josh relaxed yet alert, feet slightly parted, hands clasped in front, shoulders back. He looked like he'd always been there.

He stuck out his hand. "Welcome to God's Breath Ranch. I'm Scipio. And you are?"

They shook. "Josh Pratt, sir. I was sent here by Ashley Calloway's father. He's very concerned about her."

"Why did you lie to Mr. Galper and tell him you were

just a hiker?"

"Sir, I was understandably trepidatious due to the church's reputation for vindictiveness."

"Trepidatious. Very good. Where'd you learn that? Prison?"

"Yes sir."

"I can spot a jailbird a mile away. Bet you're all tatted up."

"Yes sir."

"What if I were to tell you that Ashley Calloway is here of her own free will and has no interest in contacting her family at this time."

"I don't believe it."

"No. Of course not. Let me ask you this. If Ashley were to tell you herself, would that satisfy you?"

"It might satisfy me, but it wouldn't satisfy her father."

"I see. And who's her father?"

"Lieutenant Heinz Calloway of the Madison Police Department."

Scipio nodded. "As you are well aware, she has barely been with us for forty-eight hours, hardly the time one would need to brainwash a person. We do not brainwash our followers, Mr. Pratt. They come to us out of spiritual need, and it is only by satisfying that need that we hold them. There are no fences, barbed wire, or armed guards. That is what they have fled. Here there is freedom."

"If Ashley's here, I'd like to speak with her."

"That may very well happen, but not today. I think we need to know a little more about you, Mr. Pratt. You'll be our guest tonight."

"Are you holding me prisoner?"

"This is private property, Mr. Pratt. You are a trespasser. We are merely extending our hospitality until we are sure you're not a threat. The reason people seek us out is to escape the circumstances of their everyday lives. Some of them are trapped in abusive relationships. Some are addicted to drugs. Each and every one is searching for a spiritual awakening, something to pull them back from the abyss and give them a reason to live."

"Sounds nice."

"Have you eaten?"

"Not since breakfast."

"Hal, take Mr. Pratt to the mess hall and fix him up. After dinner, put him in the jail. I'll talk to Ashley. It's doubtful she'd want to talk to you tonight so I'll see you in the morning."

The sun sank in the west, easing itself into a craggy tub as Galper, always two steps behind, directed Josh to a one story log outbuilding. It looked older than any of the other structures.

Massive logs joined together by mortar on a concrete base.

"Step aside," Galper said, stepping up on the concrete. He used a key to unlock the heavy front door. Inside, a worn hardwood floor held a small wooden desk, something you might see in a school principal's office, an ancient pot-belly stove, and through an open door, a heavy metal cage.

"This looks like an old sheriff's office," Josh said.

"Years ago, this was a gold mining settlement. Quite a party town a hundred and twenty years ago. This is all that's left."

"Did they find any gold?"

Galper shrugged. "There's a chamber pot and I'll get you some bottled waters."

Josh looked at the jail cell. Rusted steel clasps bolted together in a basket pattern. No way was he going to bust out of that. He looked at Galper, watching him carefully from four feet away, hand on his pistol.

"Can I have a book?"

"Tell me what you want. I'll fetch it from the library."

"Do you have a biography of the Manson family?"

Galper pulled the iron door open with a screech and motioned. Josh stepped inside, sat on the aluminum cot as Galper slammed the door shut and locked the deadbolt. He went out into the front room and returned with two clear liter bottles of water.

"What happened to dinner?"

"I'll send something."

Josh was left alone in the cell in the fading afternoon light. A bare bulb hung above the cage. Josh looked around. Mouse droppings. Men had whittled messages in the floor over the years.

Nacho was here.

Beverly, I will always love you. Will.

Fukin asswips dont nowe what they got here.

The place didn't smell too bad considering. Pratt wasn't

the only recent visitor. He spotted several cigarette butts on the floor, and the latest whittle looked fresh.

Tell my parents I love them. David Wickless.

Josh was used to prison. He sat on the cot with his back against the cage wall. The cage was bolted through the wall with exterior flanges. Minutes later, a wan young man with a pierced nose entered carrying a cafeteria tray which he slid through a slot in the door.

"Thanks," Josh said. The tray contained a sandwich made with stale whole grain bread, smooth sandwich ham, a slice of Swiss cheese and an apple. The young man went into the outer office and returned with a blue down-filled sleeping bag which he stuffed through a one-foot square.

Josh examined his sandwich. A smear of yellow mustard. He wolfed it down and ate the apple. By now it was dark. He lay on the cot and pulled the open sleeping bag over him.

He drifted off. An insistent soft metallic clang on the window bars above his head. Josh sat upright and backed away from the wall. There was someone outside, on the back of the log cabin, banging a tin cup against the bars.

"Chainsaw," whispered a hoarse voice. "You there?"

"What the fuck! Who are you?"

"It's me, Toad!"

CHAPTER 41

THE PLAN

Calloway and Kleiser watched as a man wearing a sidearm marched Josh down the steps, across the compound to an old log cabin on the perimeter. Several minutes later, the man emerged alone.

As dusk fell, they noted armed men taking up their positions at the front gate and on the house's veranda.

"I count three," Calloway said.

"Me too."

"They can't be too worried about desertions. Where would they go?"

"They could conceivably hike out the dirt road, but they may have men farther down that we don't know about."

"Enticing a minor is a felony in Wisconsin. I've half a mind to go down there and arrest Scipio."

"But you don't have any authority here."

"I would be happy if he just took off."

"From what I know about this guy, he's got a really big ego. Possibly a god complex. He could decide to kill us both."

"And how would he do that without others finding out? I know his personality type. He's all about getting others to do his dirty work. I need to know if Ashley is all right."

"Hey, what do I know."

They sat in silence.

"We could go down there," Kleiser said.

"What if they have motion detectors?"

"They gotta feel pretty secure out here in the boonies."

"That mercenary group came out here."

"But they waited in town."

"So you think Scipio grabbed your daughter because your father shot his father."

"In the matter of motive, I'm no expert. I've seen people kill over a Klondike bar. Josh always talks about the Church of Payback. I think that might be Scipio's real religion."

More silence.

Calloway got to his feet, stretched with one hand on the small of his back. "Okay. I say we go down there. There's a ten-foot gap behind the house and the cliff."

"Oh come on, man. They're bound to have someone on lookout."

"I can't stand waiting around. My wife is going crazy. Here's what I think. We wait 'til morning, go down there, tell him who we are and why we're there. If he's rational, he'll give Ashley up. Enticing a minor is a Class Four felony. He can't take a chance on killing us. Too many people know where we are."

"Yeah, but we're in Colorado."

"What's he going to do? I'm her father. I'm a police officer."

Kleiser dug around in his backpack and pulled out two Keto Bars. Calloway ripped off the wrapper, stuck it in his backpack, and bit off a chunk. He chewed.

"Ugh. What is this shit?"

"It's good for you."

"All this paleo shit tastes like shit. What else you got?"

Kleiser pulled out two foot-long Slim Jims.

Calloway ate it like a wood chipper. He went to the stream, filled his canteen, and glugged.

Kleiser scooped up pine needles for a bed. "So we wait 'til manana?"

"Yeah, we'd better. They might shoot us in the dark."

They lay on their backs staring up through the fir branches at the brilliant night sky. More stars than Calloway had ever seen before. A hundred times more than he saw in Madison. This was due to their altitude, the lack of ambient light, and the lack of pollution. He was no camper. His idea of a vacation was a sandy beach in the Caribbean. One year he took Doreen to a Sandals in Jamaica. He was appalled by the open drug dealing he saw on the beach and never returned.

A star flared and traced a burning finger across the sky.

"Wow," Kleiser said softly, ten feet away.

"What was that?"

"That was a shooting star. Some fragment breaks off an asteroid or a satellite and enters the earth's atmosphere where it burns up from the friction."

"I have never seen that before."

Silence.

"Josh tells me you're a hacker."

"I'm an internet security analyst."

"Said you hacked the National Security Agency."

"Anything you say can and will be used against you in a court of law."

Calloway chuckled. "You're all right. I appreciate your helping me. Why do they call you Black Widower."

"I had a girlfriend named Stacy. We were in love. We were going to get married. She designed software, had a good job with Percolate. We had a condo in Denver. Her folks lived in Florida, so one year she decided she'd fly down to visit them over Christmas. I was slammed. It's not as if we didn't spend a lot of time together. We were together most of the time and we were getting on each other's nerves. So I said, go ahead. She booked a flight on United.

"I drive her to Denver. I know what happened from surveillance tapes, I didn't go in with her. They got this clusterfuck maze for the TSA. The fucking TSA man. The most beloved agency in America. I used to fly, but it got to the point that every time, every fucking time, TSA would pull me aside in Denver and give me the whole treatment. Go through my luggage, hand up the ass, the pat down, questions."

"Were you on a list?"

"No. I made sure of that. If you're on a list, I can get you off. That's why they pay me the big bucks. Anyhow, she gets to the gate. She was a petite redhead in blue jeans carrying a backpack. And they pull her aside and give her the full Monty. Meanwhile, one aisle over, four Arabs in headgear and flowing robes waltz right through.

"Stacy barely made the plane. It takes off. Fifteen minutes later it explodes over Eastern Colorado killing all one hundred and twenty-seven people aboard. They later determined it was a bomb. Duh."

"Jesus! I'm so sorry! When was this?"

"Two thousand and nine. Eight years after nine eleven. I used face recognition software and TSA records to learn the identities of the agents who gave Stacy the strip search, and the ones who waved the Arabs through. I went after them like a colony of fire ants. Turns out one guy had downloaded two thousand kiddie porn images. Another owed his ex-wife tens of thousands of dollars in child support. How they got hired I'll never know. I got 'em fired. It wasn't much. It was the best I could do. I'm not a killer."

"I don't fly much. Last year Doreen and I spent a week in the Bahamas. World of Neptune, with the dolphins and the hundred-foot slide. They don't hassle me because I'm a cop. I guess when you want to wear a badge, you take what you can get."

"Fuckin' TSA, man. They make prison guards look like elite troopers."

"Could you tap into their surveillance network down there, if they have one?"

"Not from up here. What's the plan?"

"Let's go down there in the morning. I'll hold my badge and see where that gets us."

"I got my drones."

"Okay. Let's try and get some sleep."

Calloway stayed awake a long time staring at the stars.

CHAPTER
42

COYOTES

"Toad!" Josh said. "How the hell are ya?"

"I've been sober for four hundred and fifty-three days."

"Congratulations!"

"I still smoke a little reefer. The reefer here is horrendous."

"Understandable."

"Man, I couldn't believe it when I saw Gladiator parade you across the yard. I've been waiting to speak to you. What are you doing here, man?"

"The girl Scipio brought. Her father's a friend of mine. I'm here to get her back."

"That girl looks like a model? The black girl?"

"Yeah. Her name's Ashley. Can you get me out of here?"

"I don't know man. I'm doing okay here, you know? They've become my family."

"Come on, Toad. It's a cult! Like Manson or Jim Jones."

"No really, man, they do good work. I've seen it. There

are people here who would be dead if not for Scipio."

"I don't want to mess with his thing, but Ashley doesn't belong here. She's seventeen. Enticing her across state lines for immoral purposes is a felony."

"Do you think he's fuckin' her?"

"I think that's the game. Why, I have a theory. I think my friend's father killed Scipio's father."

"Say what?"

"A long time ago, in Chicago. I think Scipio is actually Brian Pils."

"Hey, I heard about all those people you fucked up. You been representin'."

"I'm not the same man you knew, Toad. I've accepted Jesus into my heart."

"And you still killed all those people?"

"Goose says you still owe him two hundred dollars."

"Yeah, man, I forgot about that. "

"Can you get me out of here?"

"This thing is pretty solid. I was thinking maybe get the Ram, hook a chain up to the ball hitch and the other end to these bars. Worked for Butch Cassidy."

"This cage still has four walls, and the way they're fastened, it would take a welding torch or some kind of massive machine to open it up. The other option is getting the keys."

"No can do, man. Gladiator's got the keys. I might as well just put a gun to my head."

"What about the beatings?"

"I've seen 'em. They asked me to participate but I told

them I didn't feel good. They test everyone for smack, coke and meth once a month. We're all clean, man. What's it like in the real world?"

Josh looked around. The ranch was silent save for the eerie yodeling of a coyote. "It's nuts. They shut down the whole country. Everybody wears a mask. They rioted in Madison over that black guy in Minneapolis. Burned down State Street. There's nothing there anymore. I don't know if they'll ever come back."

"What's State Street?"

"Never mind, man. College town. It's hard to explain. You know about the riots, right?"

"No. What riots?"

"Don't you watch the news?"

"No, man. All the TVs are closed circuit. We can watch DVDs. That's about it. And they all gotta be approved by Scipio. *Seven Years in Tibet*. No Westerns."

"Do you have a cell phone?"

"No, man. You got to turn in your phone when you join. Then they test you every couple of months to determine your enlightenment factor. You've got to get to Stage Ten before they give you your phone back. Reception's for shit up here anyway. They got a landline, but only Scipio's allowed to use it."

"So, you're completely cut off from your former lives."

"Yeah, well that's the point, isn't it? That's why I'm sober."

"Do they know you were a Bedouin?"

"No, man. They have a tat removal service here. First day I arrived, I cleaned up. 'Course I couldn't get rid of them all, but I got rid of any gang or prison affiliation. They can do the same for you."

"There wouldn't be much left."

"What can I do?"

"Get to Harrison and tell them I'm being held against my will."

Toad looked pained. "I have a life here, Saw. I'm afraid if I leave, I'll fall back into bad habits."

"Do you think Scipio is capable of murder? Are there any unexplained disappearances? People who were here one day and gone the next?"

By Toad's silence, Josh knew he'd struck a nerve. "Were any of them young women?"

"Shit."

"Who? How many?"

"Right when I got here, Scipio was carrying on with this chick, she couldn't have been more than twenty. You know the kind he likes. Tall and willowy, straight blonde hair. One day she flies through the front door in tears, got a big smack mark on her face, Scipio right after her. Caught her before she got to the stairs, dragged her back in. Hell. About thirty people saw it. Never heard from her again. The next day, he addresses the camp. Some shit about Fiona having her theta levels scrambled. So, in the middle of the night, Scipio agreed to drive her to Salida. Says he gave her a couple hundred bucks and put her on a bus to Pueblo. Didn't sound right, and nobody comes or goes the Teeth don't know about it. But we were afraid to ask, right? You don't question Scipio."

"Anybody else?"

Toad looked pained. "Look, man, I got a good life here. I don't want to give it up. I even have an old lady."

"Does Scipio approve? Do you have to get permission before you fuck?"

"Let me think about it."

"We took an oath, brother."

"That was a long time ago, Saw. We're both different people now."

"You got that right. Don't call me Saw. That was the old life. The things I've done, I wonder if God will ever forgive me."

"But isn't that why you became a Christian? So God would forgive you?"

"Yes, and I believe that He has. But here, in my own mind, you think about the things you've done. Christ's absolution can never erase those memories."

"Let me think about it. I'm one of the Teeth now. I got obligations. Anything I can bring you while you're holed up in here?"

"A welding torch and a hack saw."

"Right. Okay. I gotta go. I gotta check in. I'll be back."

Josh sat alone in the jail cell listening to the coyotes howl. After a while, he got down on his knees and prayed. "Lord, I'm not above asking for help. But before I do, please look after my friends Heinz and Kleiser, and return Ashley unscathed to her family. If you do that, you will make me a happy man. And if there's anything left over, get me out of here. Thank you. Amen."

CHAPTER

43

SURROGATE

Galper came for Josh at nine. He unlocked the door with one hand on his sidearm. "Let's go."

As they walked across the broad parade ground, people barely glanced their way. Acolytes swept steps, pushed wheelbarrows filled with rocks and construction equipment, worked on fencing. Beyond the corral in the meadow, a group of five sat in a circle, legs crossed, eyes shut, palms pressed together.

Galper marched Josh up the stairs, down the hall, into the office, where Scipio sat behind his desk wearing a gray worsted jacket, white shirt and red tie. Ashley sat on a leather sofa, legs crossed, a cup of coffee on the table in front of her.

"Hello, Ashley," Josh said.

"Hi, Josh. I'm sorry you had to come out here."

"Your father is worried sick."

"I'm fine, Josh. I came of my own free will."

Scipio clapped his hands together. "Sit. Would you like coffee?"

"Sure."

Scipio nodded to the table, which also contained toasted English muffins and individual jelly packets similar to those found in a waffle house. "Help yourself."

Josh mixed in two half and halfs and three sugars and sat on the sofa. Galper sat on another sofa across the room.

Josh looked across the desk. "Is she free to go?"

Scipio tilted a hand toward Ashley. "What say you?"

"Josh, I'm here of my own free will. It's something I had to do. Please tell my folks I love them and I will get in touch with them when it's time."

"Is she allowed to phone her parents?"

"She's free to do whatever she likes."

"'Cuz I heard you had no phone service up here, and you have to get permission to use the landline."

"Those are lies."

"Ashley, why don't you phone your mother right now?"

"I'm not ready to do that."

"It would put her mind at ease."

"You can tell her I'm fine, Josh."

"If I ever get out of this place."

Scipio cleared his throat. "You come to my house. You eat my food. You steal from me."

"That sandwich? They gave it to me."

"You're here to steal this girl, aren't you?"

"Is she your property? Is she free to leave? Am I free

to leave?"

"Mr. Pratt, you have a criminal history. You were a member of a violent motorcycle gang. You came here uninvited and lied about it. You are an agent of mischief."

"I went to prison. I turned my life around. I believe in Jesus. Isn't that one of your tenets? Don't you call yourself a Christian?"

"We believe that Jesus was a great prophet, but God's Breath draws inspiration from many sources."

"What I don't get is what's your interest in a seventeen-year-old high school student?"

"She reached out to me. We talked for months and it soon became obvious we had a special bond. She wanted to come. She wanted to join God's Breath. God's Breath exists to help people reach their full potential. We are teachers and advisors. By the time Ashley leaves, if she chooses to do so, she will have grown exponentially, as a person and as a spiritual being."

"Does anybody ever leave? Can you give me the names of acolytes who have left amicably? Give me ten names. No. Give me five names. Let me talk to them. If they vouch for you, I'll trouble you no more."

Scipio stared unblinking. "The Lord hates a liar. You've already lied to us, when you said you were just out hiking. That was a lie. I believe you're here at her father's behest."

"But isn't your name a lie? Isn't your real name Brian Pils?"

Scipio remained still. Josh saw a tiny light flare and fade in the cult leader's eyes. "You were convicted of atrocious assault. Yet here you are, born again. Won't you extend that courtesy to others?"

"Yeah," Galper said. "What's that mean? Atrocious assault?"

"I cut off a guy's arm with a chainsaw. I'm not proud of it. I pled guilty and did my time."

"Well, you must be some kind of badass," Scipio said.

"I never said that."

"I find it interesting that you were a member of the Bedouins, a one percent biker gang, listed by the FBI as involved in drugs and weapons trafficking."

"There are no Bedouins. Does your flock know that you served two and a half years in Joliet for statutory rape? That you were convicted of aggravated assault and armed robbery?"

Josh felt Galper shift uncomfortably. Ashley leaned forward, arms on knees.

"Is that true?"

"I have no idea what he's talking about. Who did you say I was? Brian Potts?"

"Pils. Brian Pils."

"Do you have any proof of these allegations?"

"Not with me, but if you give me access to the internet, I can pull it up."

"Mr. Pratt, you are an uninvited guest. You are disturbing the ranch's tranquility and in particular that of this young girl who has come to us seeking peace and enlightenment. You come to my house. You eat my food..."

"That sandwich again?"

Scipio's face darkened. He wasn't used to being inter-rupted. "Joshua sent two spies to Jericho. Following God's law, they killed every man, woman, and child, as well as the oxen, sheep, and donkeys. Was this necessary? Was it just? What if the Israelites had offered to settle the matter via one on one combat? Might they not have spared the city? Now here you are, Joshua, threatening our city. Would you kill every inhabitant if you had the chance? Certainly you are capable of such an action."

Ashley squirmed, itching to say something. Josh knew the feeling. Being part of a group, afraid to speak for fear of a backlash. He'd held his tongue too often back in the day. He'd done a lot of bad things.

"I'm here because Ashley's father, whom I've known for years, asked me to come and see if she was all right."

"Ashley, are you all right?"

She looked down. "I'm fine."

"Is she free to leave of her own free will?"

"Any time."

Josh looked at Ashley. "How about it, sis. Your folks are worried sick."

"I'll call them later."

"You know how cults work. They may or may not let you call, and if you do, it will be monitored. Isn't that one of your rules, Brian? That acolytes are permitted no contact with their former lives for, how long? A year? Two years? Forever? You know, I spoke to a few people who left the cult. They described an atmosphere of mind control, humiliation, and special privileges. I'm surprised nobody's done a big article on you yet. There are plenty of journalists who would be interested. But you've so terrorized your apostates that they live in hiding. Because you're still after them, aren't you? Your real church is the church of payback. Isn't it?"

Scipio smiled humorlessly. "I will give you an opportunity the residents of Jericho never had. Surely you can hold your own against Mr. Galper, who is ten years your senior."

"Huh? You want us to fight? Why don't *you* fight me, Brian? I hear *you're* a badass."

"You're just a surrogate, right? You didn't come here on your own. You came here because this girl's father told you to. You can fight my gladiator and if you win, I'll let you go. Ashley can do whatever she likes."

"And what if I lose?"

"If you lose, you'll be dead."

CHAPTER
44

GOOD AND EVIL

Calloway woke with a crimp in his neck. The down-filled sleeping bag was warm enough, but the ground was hard, even with the layer of pine needles he'd scraped together. Kleiser was still sawing away when Calloway woke, walked into the woods and pissed against a tree. As he zipped his fly, he looked around, astonished to find himself in such natural beauty. His last vacation had been three years ago. He and Doreen had flown to Cabo San Lucas, stayed in a hotel for a week, sunning on the beach, hitting the blues clubs at night. Doreen had even paraglided, pulled behind a powerboat a hundred feet in the air.

He'd never been to the mountains. He'd heard that Colorado was the healthiest state in the union, and what with all the up and down, he didn't doubt it. Retirement gleamed like the pot of gold at the end of the rainbow. He wasn't one of those guys who would rattle around without a sense of purpose. He loved police work but enough was enough. He and Doreen had socked away enough for a comfortable retirement. They would travel, visit all the states they'd never been, hit the national parks, maybe even go to Disney World. Doreen worked as a librarian at the downtown library, but since the lockdown, she didn't have much to do. She'd put in her twenty too. He wanted to show her the forest, but not as he'd seen it. Doreen wasn't much for camping. Her idea of roughing it was a Best Western.

They'd done okay. Terry had just finished a two-year stint in the Marines and was working for Hotwire, a media company. Calloway worried about his boy living in California, which lurched from crisis to crisis. Drought. Fires. Homelessness. Riots. A disappearing middle class. San Andres Fault. Godzilla. They'd been threatening to secede for years.

Terry didn't worry him. He'd raised that boy right. It was one of his proudest achievements, teaching his son to be a man. Girls were different. Maybe he should have spent more time with Ashley, and she wouldn't be in this situation. But that was her mother's job, wasn't it? Fathers raised sons, mothers raised daughters, unless they had no choice in the matter. He wondered where he'd failed, that his darling girl would go running off with some internet guru she'd never met. He well knew the urges of the young, the dramatic gesture, the abrupt life change, the sudden bad decision. As a police officer, he'd seen countless young people destroy their lives in an instant. Let's rob a gas station. Race you to town. I can drink more than you.

At UWM, where he had majored in criminal justice, Calloway knew an ur-hippy named Jay Pant. They were sitting around a dorm room one night when a shady cat named Zbigneif blew in with a zip-lock filled with acid. He held the bag out like a home owner greeting trick-or-treaters.

"Who wants a hit?"

Jay Pant, who had a wild splurge of curly black hair, stuck his mitt in the bag, grabbed a handful, and washed it down with a Diet Coke. He was never the same after that. He dropped out of college and joined a hippy commune. They lost touch and Calloway rarely thought of him until twenty-five years later, when the remains of a body found at an abandoned farm in Nebraska, was identified as Jay. They matched the skull to his dental X-rays, dating from his final visit to the dentist before he left for the commune. He had gone without a dentist for ten years.

Calloway leaned back and inhaled. Ain't that somethin', he thought. Fresh pine air, all those stars, a man could become used to the mountains. Maybe they'd move out to the country. Some of those small upper Midwest towns were heaven, but not Madison. Madison had become unsafe. Gangs roamed the streets. State Street looked like Hiroshima. The store owners had thrown in the towel. The last spate of riots had lasted a solid week. The mayor ordered the police to hang back, give the "protesters" "room to destroy."

Calloway thought it a damn strange way to run a city, but he hadn't voted for him. Chicagoan Saul Brogden came as a student, studied political science, ran for alderman while in his twenties, advanced through the ranks until finally, he became Mayor For Life. The bearded, mustachioed Brogden wore worsted sports jackets with leather elbow patches, smoked a pipe, and spoke in a smooth, controlled manner that belied his radical policies. Calloway had seen it coming ten years ago, when the City Council turned down the PD's request for more funding, for more officers. Crime was going up, but the number of personnel had been frozen at four hundred and twelve for ten years.

The City Council looked like Jay Pant's hippy commune. The lone conservative member, Walter Roland, was the only who ever wore a suit and tie to meetings. The rest wore tie-dyes, dashikis, berets, grass skirts, accordion pants, burkas, a full range of cultural appropriation. There had also been a minor scandal several years ago when an alderperson who had billed herself as Black was forced to admit she was a nice Jewish girl from Grosse Pointe.

No, he wouldn't miss it. Silence pulsed in his ears. He was so used to the constant sound, even in his bedroom on Madison's posh west side, the silence unnerved him. He looked around. A bluebird landed on a Douglas fir. Wouldn't it be great to live right there, in the mountains? No water, no electricity, no supermarkets—It was just a dream. A lot of people did live in places like this. They'd seen the houses and the mailboxes on the way up. God knows what they did in winter.

Scipio's house would do nicely. Maybe Calloway should have been a cult leader instead. An odd scruffing sound caught his attention. A black bear rubbed its flank against an aspen, causing the limbs to shudder and rain gold leaves. Calloway fingered his nine mm Beretta.

POLICE VETERAN SHOOTS BEAR

The bear looked at him, sniffed, and ambled away. He could always bring Doreen to Rocky Mountain National Park, if they made reservations five years in advance. All the parks were operating at half capacity due to the virus. Everyone was mobbed. RMNP was the most mobbed. After forty-six months of lockdowns, Americans were desperate to get outside.

Kleiser was up when Calloway returned, heating coffee over a can of Sterno. Kleiser had policed the site, packed his bag, everything neat and trim, backpack lying next to the carbon fire drone case.

"Have a cup of coffee. I propose we break camp, choose a spot and launch a drone. See what we can see."

Calloway crouched and poured coffee into one of Kleiser's plastic cups. "Sounds like a plan."

The sound of a public address system filtered up through the trees. "Children of God's Breath. This is Scipio. You are invited to witness an extraordinary event. We have an intruder, a man sent by a cop to spirit away one of ours. Most of you have yet to meet Ashley Calloway, the newest member of our tribe. Please welcome Ashley to God's Breath."

"Welcome, Ashley!" rolled up through the trees.

"Please come the parade ground where we will witness a battle between good and evil. Between this wicked intruder, and our own Gladiator, Hal Galper."

CHAPTER 45

AMATEUR HOUR

One hundred people lined the parade ground, standing outside a fifty-foot ring of stones. Inside was a smaller, ring twenty-five feet in diameter. They would fight in pants. No shirts, no shoes. Scipio stood on the veranda wearing gray Dockers, sunglasses and a striped referee shirt, his hair swept back and gleaming. He looked like a James Bond villain. He handed Josh a mouthpiece. Josh waved it away.

"No thanks." He looked at the stones. "Are those part of the fight?"

"They define the ring," Gladiator said.

"What happens if one of us falls and bashes our head in on one of those rocks?"

"I guess the fight would be over."

"What happens if you pick up a rock?"

"I'm not using rocks and you're not either."

"How do you feel, being used as an attack dog?"

Galper walked to the end of the veranda, stripped off his shirt, shoes and socks, and stretched, using the rail for balance. It was a crisp cool morning, the temperature in the forties. Josh shivered as he removed his shirt and the breeze caught his sweat. He'd been sweating since he arrived.

Two of God's Teeth stood at the base of the stairs, armed. They looked like gym rats, with hulking shoulders and arms, wearing gray work pants. One was six-two with short black hair, the other the same height but built like an ox, wearing suspenders. They kept glancing at Josh.

Josh trained with Nelson Ferreira at Zhong Yi Kung Fu on East Washington when he could, and he ran almost every day. He was in shape. But being in shape and fighting an experienced combat veteran were two different things. Josh could hold his own in a street brawl, but he probably wouldn't do very well against any mid-level professional fighter. Galper had years of experience. He was not a professional fighter but he'd been in street fights. Josh could read it in his face.

Scipio strutted down the stairs wearing a headset that broadcast through the public address system. Speakers mounted on poles and the roofs of outbuildings, like a military base.

"The only rules are, no biting, no fishhooks, eye gouges, or kicks to the groin. The contest will continue until one combatant is no longer capable. You all know Galper. Many of you have trained with him. Galper is a proud veteran of our armed forces. He has earned our respect and love.

His opponent, Josh Pratt, is a former gang member, now a private investigator. He sneaked into our compound yesterday claiming to be an innocent hiker out for a stroll. When you begin your relationship with a lie, it's all downhill from there. He is here to spirit away our newest member, Ashley Calloway. Ashley's father is a cop."

Boos and hisses.

"If our uninvited visitor wins, he is free to go, albeit without Ashley. If Galper wins, we will hang on to Mr. Pratt until we decide what to do with him. Now, since I am a practitioner of mixed martial arts, we will have three five-minute rounds with a one minute break between rounds. If no victor emerges, we will do it again tomorrow, and every day after that until we have a clear winner. Val has agreed to treat Galper between rounds. Is there anyone here willing to help our interloper?"

Silence. Scipio looked around. Josh stared at Toad. Toad swallowed and stepped out of the crowd.

"All right, Toad," Scipio boomed. "If you can fix a car, you can fix a man. Get Toad a bucket of water and clean towels."

Scipio was living the dream. He pointed to opposite sides of the circle. "Fighters! Are you ready?"

Josh shrugged. Galper hopped from foot to foot, opening his mouth to reveal a yellow mouthpiece.

Scipio chopped air. "Fight."

Galper shuffled forward in a boxer's stance, left foot forward, shoulders hunched. Josh threw a front kick that fell short. They circled. Moving his head like the metronome of a Grandfather clock, Galper shuffled in and threw a combination. Jab, cross, hook. Josh ducked, caught the hook on the arm, but Galper's left hook sunk into his ribs like a pile driver. The same ribs that Ryan Gherke cracked. Lowering his guard to protect his ribs, Josh swallowed the pain and circled, matching Galper's head movement with his own. Josh ducked beneath Galper's jab and threw a wild looping right hand that struck his opponent on the temple. Galper staggered, danced back and grinned.

When Josh was eighteen, a prospect, Goose had given him boxing lessons. "You come forward and throw five fast jabs in a row, one of them is bound to land."

Leaning forward, Josh lifted his left foot. Gravity propelled him. He swung his left elbow in a tight little arc, catching Galper's jab, popping up, pistoning his jab. One two three four five. And what do you know, the last jab landed. Galper pivoted and threw a sidekick that Josh partially blocked, but the blow forced him back and Galper was on him like a swarm of wasps, landing vicious jabs and hooks. Josh bulled his way in, grabbed Galper behind the neck, and drew him into a knee to the gut. Galper leaped and spun, striking Josh in the side of the head with his right elbow. Josh fell to the ground, hooked Galper's left ankle and jerked.

Galper grabbed Josh's leg on the way down and climbed up his torso, in an attempt to take his back. Josh spun, throwing his left elbow into Galper's sternum. They rolled.

Galper went for a headlock but Josh threw a vicious elbow straight up into Galper's jaw.

Scipio blew a piercing whistle, ran in and smacked both men on the back. They parted and returned to their corners. Galper limped a little on his left foot.

Josh sat on an overturned five-gallon bucket while Toad wiped blood off his face with a wet towel. "Watch out for that jab. I think he'd rather box, but the dude can kick. And he knows jujitsu. Don't wrestle. Keep it on your feet. Move your head and jab."

Scipio blew the whistle. As Josh stood, Galper ran at him, throwing himself into a reverse spinning roundhouse that whistled over Josh's head, skimming his buzz cut. Josh spun counterclockwise, his roundhouse kick catching Galper on the thigh. A solid strike with the ball of the foot. They danced around. Josh faked a jab and slammed his right instep into Galper's calf. Galper had lifter's legs. It was like striking a leather sofa.

Galper faked a cross and threw his roundhouse, striking the same spot he had before. Pain radiated through Josh's body, but the rib held. It was stronger where it had healed. Galper went for the takedown, landing Josh on his back in the dirt. Josh grabbed Galper around the neck, brought his right leg up and went for a triangle, but Galper anticipated, postured up, raining down elbows and punches. Josh waited until Galper had separated his hips, pulled from behind the shoulder, throwing a knee into his butt and scooting down beneath his legs, turning and rolling out.

Panting, they stood. Blood trickled from Galper's nose and mouth. He smiled tightly.

Two men ran out of the crowd and seized Scipio by his arms. Calloway ripped off the leader's headset and put it on his own head. Holding up his badge, Calloway boomed, "Police! Stay exactly where you are."

CHAPTER
46

TENSE MEETING

"Daddy!" Ashley squealed, flying down the veranda steps into her father's arms. There was a moment of silence as the entire camp watched.

"Teeth!" Scipio shouted.

Half a dozen men stepped out of the crowd holding handguns. Back to back, Calloway and Kleiser held their weapons at their sides.

"This is a police matter," Calloway said. "I'm a police officer from Madison, Wisconsin. I have informed the Colorado State Police that Scipio is holding a minor child and they are sending officers. It doesn't matter if she wants to be here or not. She is a minor. If there are any other people here being held against their will, produce them immediately. If you try to stop me or my deputy, you will be interfering with a police matter. Disperse now."

"Bullshit!" Scipio spat. "This man is a cop in Wisconsin!

He has no jurisdiction here!"

Calloway found himself enjoying the advantage of the public address system. "As I said, the Colorado State Police are on their way. I urge you to disperse. Do not try to leave the compound. There's only one way out of here and by now, there will be cops waiting for you on the road."

"Scott! Check the police scanner!"

A tall man with a receding chin broke from the crowd and headed for the dormitory. Scipio marched up the steps, went into his house, and returned a minute later with a bullhorn. Seconds later, Kristin followed him out, hanging back, her face a mask.

"These three men are interlopers," he boomed from above. "There are three of them and one hundred and nine of us. Supreme Theta status to whoever brings them to me."

The crowd milled and murmured. They didn't know whether to shit or go blind. They had been indoctrinated to obey this man's every command, but that was without reality. Now reality was there in the person of Lieutenant Calloway and his two companions. Calloway pulled his Beretta from its holster.

"Make no move against us. This whole place is wired for video, isn't it? Look at all these cameras. Anybody who makes a hostile move toward us will be recorded, apprehended, and prosecuted. All we want is my daughter. Permit us to leave, and you have no problem."

He turned off the mic and turned to Ashley. "You ready to go?"

Biting her lip, she nodded her head.

Six men, including the two teeth at the base of the stairs, formed a circle around Calloway, Josh, Kleiser and Ashley, holding pistols in both hands, in shooter's stances. The ox in suspenders said, "This is sovereign land. We came here to escape the world of police and petty jealousies. Drop your weapons. I don't believe the State Police are on their way."

"Aaron!" Scipio barked through his bullhorn. "Take their weapons and bring them to my office."

Josh backed up against Calloway. "What's the plan?"

Calloway looked around. "We can't shoot our way out of here. There are too many of them."

"Fuck," Josh said. Calloway and Kleiser allowed themselves to be disarmed. Josh's pistol lay in his backpack somewhere on the mountain.

Calloway turned his mic back on and

looked around. "How come the only black faces I see here are hers and mine?"

His mic went dead. Ox gestured. "Let's go."

They followed Scipio into the big house, into his office overlooking the grounds.

"Aaron, Paul, Ryan and Greg, stay with us. Shut the door."

Kristin entered. "What the fuck, Scip? What the fuck is going on?"

"These men have invaded our sanctuary with the intent of kidnapping our newest member."

"You know, Scip, I've stood by while you banged every underage groupie in the joint, but now you're roaming around the country recruiting."

"Paul, get her out of here. Put her in the jail."

A Tooth with long blond Thor hair wearing blue coveralls gestured at the slim woman. "Kristin, let's go."

"You motherfucker," Kristin spat.

"Come on, Kristin. I'll carry you if I have to."

She turned on Scipio hissing. "You won't get away with this."

"Sister Kristin needs counseling. Her theta levels are dropping. Make sure she has breakfast."

She shook off Greg's hand and left. Paul shut the door behind them. The three Teeth stood in a semicircle covering Ashley and Calloway, on the sofa, and Kleiser and Josh, who sat in chairs facing the desk.

"You have no right here," Scipio said.

"You kidnap my underage daughter and say I have no rights?"

"I didn't kidnap her. She asked me to come. She asked me to bring her here. Perhaps you are not the parent you thought."

"Scipio," Ashley said in a firm voice. "I've changed my mind. This was a mistake. Let us go and we'll cause you no trouble. My father knows what he's doing. If he said the Colorado State Police know he's here, he's not lying. Stop now before you do something you'll regret."

"You little cock tease," Scipio sneered. Something rippled beneath Calloway's face.

"Why no blacks? You got a problem with black people? I see some Asians, maybe some American Indians, but no African Americans. 'Cept my daughter. Maybe you like a little dark meat, is that it? Bored with the usual assortment of underage white bread? I look around, I see mostly white people. In fact, you're the whitest person here. You call yourself Scipio? You should call yourself White D. Eisenflour."

Josh snorted. Even the Teeth snickered.

"Bleach Pierpont IV. Vanilla ISIS. You know who else hated black people? Charles Manson. You and Chuck got a lot in common."

"I do not hate black people," Scipio hissed. "I've always despised cops who think they're better than everyone else. Your father killed my father."

"I heard that."

"So here we are. Ashley was nothing but a means to an end. And here we are. My followers will obey me no matter what I tell them. If you were to disappear, nobody would ask."

"And we won't be the first, will we?" Calloway said. "What happens when they bring some cadaver dogs up here to sniff around?" He half-turned to address the gunmen. "Anyone ever go missing overnight? And all of a sudden they're a non-person and it's forbidden to even mention their names?"

The Teeth gave no sign.

"Are you men willing to commit murder for your almighty leader? Does he share the wealth? Do you have to get permission if you want to have sex?"

A troubled, knowing look passed among them. Someone ran up the front steps. Seconds later there was a knock on the door. Paul opened it to admit Scott, the tech guy. "State cops headed this way."

"Thank you, Paul. You may go."

The door shut.

"It would be too easy to kill you," Scipio snarled. "I want you to suffer as I suffered when your father took my father away from me."

"He was a rapist and a thug. Like you, White D. Eisen-flour."

Scipio pulled a fat revolver from the desk drawer. "Ashley get up. Get up or I'll plant one in your old man's knee." Scipio stood, came around the desk, and pointed the gun in both hands at Calloway's knee.

"Don't do it, sweetheart."

Ashley tore herself away and stood. "It's all right, Dad. I'll be all right."

Calloway surged from his seat. Aaron jerked forward, grabbed him by the back of his collar, and threw him forcefully back on the chair.

"We're leaving. You men hold them here until the state police arrive. Then you do what you have to. Remember all I have given you. Remember what you were before you came to me. Do this for me, and your names will be inscribed forever in the God's Breath Book of Life."

Aaron, Ryan, and Craig leveled their weapons at Calloway, Kleiser and Josh at point-blank range. Scipio grabbed Ashley by the wrist, yanked her out of her seat and left, slamming the door behind him.

"I thought there was only one road in and out," Josh said.

Aaron laid his pistol barrel across Josh's temple. "Shut the fuck up."

"You don't ever build a fortress without at least two ways out," Ryan said. "That's Sun Tzu. You can look it up."

"Listen," Craig said. He was a heavy-set redhead with a beard. "I don't know about you guys, but I got warrants. I really can't hang around here if the State Police are gonna show."

"You'll do what the boss said," Aaron said. "You signed a contract."

The sound of a V8 rolled through the open window.

The door to the office exploded inward. Toad stepped inside carrying a double-barreled sawed-off and blew away Aaron's head.

CHAPTER 47

SUNDAY

Ryan spun, squeezing off five shots. Toad collapsed, firing his second round, striking Ryan in the thigh. Ryan grunted, and blood sprayed as he sank to the floor. Keeping his pistol in front of him, Craig backed out the door, shaking his head. They heard him run down the hall and bang through the front door.

Josh leaped over the sofa and knelt at Toad's side. Toad was dead, his eyes staring glassily at the ceiling. A brother to the end. Shouts from outside. Kleiser remained where he was, a Buddha among barking dogs. Calloway sprang to his feet. "Come on."

Josh looked at Kleiser. "You coming?"

Kleiser's voice was calm. "You go. I'm going back the way we came in."

Josh picked up Aaron's .357 magnum S&W and went to the window. A crowd gathered at the base of the stairs, uncertain of what to do. Craig stood at the top.

"It's over. Scipio screwed the pooch. The state cops are on the way. Aaron's dead. Ryan's bleeding out."

"What the fuck?"

"Noooooooooo!"

"What about Scipio?"

Craig strode down the steps. "You can wait here for the state police if you like. I'm outta here." He beelined toward the garage, where one of the doors had retracted into the ceiling showing an empty bay.

Josh and Calloway ran down the steps toward the garage. As they approached, a second door rose with a mechanical whirr. Galper jumped into the driver's seat of the Aston Martin and pushed the button. The V8 engine roared to life. Josh leaped in front waving his arms.

"Hold on! Hold on! He's got Ashley."

Galper waited. "What do you want me to do about it?"

"Is there another way off this mountain?"

"There's an old forest service road four miles south that cuts through the San Juans and comes out near Buena Vista. There's an aluminum gate across the entrance, but it's not locked."

"Is that where you're going?"

"Fuck no. This diva would never make it over the pass. You want to catch up with Scipio and that girl, take the forest service road."

"What car did he take?"

"The Road Runner. You can't miss it. It's bright blue.

Now if you'll excuse me, I'm not waiting around. Take that Cayenne. The key's in the ignition."

Josh stepped out of the way. Galper put the Aston in gear and chirped tires on the flat concrete floor, fishtailing through the parade ground headed for the main gate leaving a cloud of dust in the air.

Josh and Calloway got in the Porsche and fastened the seat belts. The key fob lay in the center console. It was one of those new vehicles where you didn't turn a key, you just had it nearby and pushed a button. The engine roared to life, the fuel gauge swinging to near full. As they worked their way to the main gate, they paused for God's Breathers running around like headless chickens, carrying backpacks, children, some of them heading for the garage to commandeer the remaining vehicles. They panicked. In the space of a day, everything fell apart. They'd lost their leader. They'd lost their god. Josh wondered what went on there that so many of them appeared so desperate to avoid the police.

The SUV absorbed the gully whumpers with aplomb. They rolled past the dormitory, the greenhouse, the corral, the recently harvested corn and wheat fields, with the massive insect-like watering harnesses standing idle. It was late morning and the temperature was in the mid-sixties, warm for that time of year.

Calloway pointed to a police scanner mounted beneath the glove compartment. "Lookee here." He turned it on and turned the dial. Static and squawking.

"We don't know if the state cops are on their way or not," Josh said.

"No sir."

"Damn it. We should have taken Kleiser's satellite phone."

"Too late for that. Look. There it is."

Josh slowed for the aluminum gate and turned off onto a rutted dirt trail that meandered through the state forest. Calloway got out and opened the gate. He got back in. Josh mashed the accelerator and the big SUV bit down with all four wheels, drifting through the corners.

Calloway grabbed the passenger grip. "Damn, son! Where'd you learn to drive like that?"

"I took a defensive driving course a couple years ago. I thought I was going to get security work. I 'bout shit when you called Scipio White D. Eisenflour. And that shit about Manson."

"I can talk ghetto when I gotta."

Josh drifted around a curve nearly colliding with a Douglas fir and stood on the brakes, startling a bull elk which trumpeted and disappeared into the forest. Calloway poked at his phone, then put it away. He glanced at the dashboard. Sixty miles an hour on a straight that had them jerking at the limits of the restraints, a hairpin curve back into the trees.

They emerged from the trees atop a bluff with a view of the switchback road climbing the mountain. They saw a flash of blue before it disappeared into the trees.

"There he is," Calloway said.

Josh pushed the big SUV to the limit, smashing over boulders, feeling the springs bottom out in the ruts. If Scipio got to the highway, he might disappear. The Porsche was fast, but it wasn't as fast as a tuned Road Runner.

Josh white-knuckled the wheel. "This is all about payback. Your old man killed his old man so he's gonna get back at you no matter what. What a fucking waste. He builds this organization, gathers all these people, and for what? He may actually have done some good here if he got people off dope and had them working together. And he throws it all away at the Church of Payback."

Tiny firecrackers through the open windows. The Road Runner backfiring. They could hear Scipio double clutching. As Josh wrangled the Porsche around a curve, the rear end broke loose and whanged into a tree.

"Shit."

"Keep going."

For an instant they were airborne. The Porsche landed on all fours as they strained against their seat belts. As they dove into a thirty-degree grade, Calloway grimaced as he held on for dear life. They broncoed down the mountain, a strip of asphalt appearing briefly between the trees. Highway Twenty-Four.

Fifteen minutes later they emerged from dense forest at the rim of the two-lane blacktop. The Road Runner's tires had left a trail to the south. Josh shimmied onto the asphalt and accelerated. Calloway tried his phone, clucked in disgust and turned on the radio.

John Denver singing "Take Me Home, Country Roads." Calloway turned the dial. FM reception was spotty. AM blared Spanish and *Come to Jesus* sermons.

"What day is it?" Calloway said.

"Fuck if I know. Sunday?"

HOT WHEELS

The Porsche came up on a Winnebago with Illinois plates towing a Jeep, two bicycles clamped in a cantilevered bike carrier, and an aluminum motorboat upside down on the roof. The road curved to the right through a narrow mountain pass.

"Great," Josh said, hanging off the left side of the Jeep trying to see. A Mack Truck hoved into view. Josh pressed on the brakes and tucked in behind the caravan.

"We gotta get around it," Calloway said.

"Wait."

They trailed the caravan at sixty miles an hour. Josh felt the steam rising from Calloway's forehead. For ten agonizing minutes they inched along until the road opened up into a downhill straightaway with a passing lane going in the opposite direction. Josh floored it, surged around the massive trailer reaching a hundred and ten miles an hour before cutting in front. The Winnebago laid on the horn. Josh kept going. They had no idea how far ahead Scipio was. The road turned too much. They didn't even know if he was still on the road. They'd passed a couple scenic turnouts but there was no place to hide, and no roads extended into the mountains on their right. As they swept clockwise around the fir-lined mountain, they glimpsed a blue car passing from right to left a mile away across a gorge. As Josh turned counterclockwise, they glimpsed a ribbon of blue at the bottom of the canyon.

Calloway eeped as Josh turned too fast and the wheels momentarily broke loose. The heavy vehicle drifted toward an Armco barrier beyond which lay a two-hundred-foot plunge. The left rear bumper kissed the barrier with a clang, the vehicle scrambled on gravel, caught traction, and whanged down the road.

"What?"

"Nothing."

Neither spoke. The only sound was the whoosh of wind through the open moon roof, and the *brrrrrt* of tires on blacktop. Despite the cool air, Josh sweated through his shirt. Calloway pulled a plastic bottle from the door pocket, unscrewed the cap, drank, and passed it to Josh, who slowed down to drain the bottle.

They turned a corner. Two bighorn sheep stood in the middle of the highway looking at them stupidly. Josh applied the brakes as slowly as he could without losing control of the vehicle, but the sheep just stood there. At the last minute, they leaped out of the way, running up the scree and scrambling up the sheer face of the cliff. The Porsche came to a cockeyed stop in the middle of the highway.

"Come on!" Calloway urged.

Josh swerved the vehicle into the right lane as a semi roared by going north, its blast lingering in their ears long after it had disappeared. There was little traffic. Josh drove with grim determination, feeling the weight of the vehicle, feathering the gas an inch shy of disaster. They pulled onto a long stretch parallel to the river. Far ahead, the blue Road Runner disappeared around a curve. The speedometer crept to one hundred and thirty.

They turned the corner and saw the blue Road Runner, closer now, running along the river with a high mountain meadow on the right. Josh focused on the blue. He'd learned a long time ago that the way to go fast was to look where you wanted to go and keep it smooth. Smoothness was the key. The faster you went, the more any change in vector or velocity affected you.

"SHIT!" Calloway barked.

The blue Road Runner tumbled off the road like a Hot Wheels car thrown by a six-year-old. It rolled over several times before coming to a halt in the middle of the meadow, right side up. Josh concentrated on his driving. After long seconds, the driver's door opened and Scipio fell to the ground. They were a quarter mile away.

"Come on come on..." Calloway chanted through clenched teeth. Josh pulled off the road, wallowing over the ruts and stopping ten feet from the smashed Road Runner. Calloway was out the door before they stopped moving. Josh followed. They raced to the passenger door. The window was open. Ashley sat dazed in the seat, a gash on her forehead leaking blood.

Calloway tried to open the door. The tumble had crimped it shut. Together, he and Josh yanked and the door blew open with a shriek. Calloway leaned in.

"Baby, it's your daddy. Can you see me?"

Ashley focused and nodded.

"Don't move. Something might be broken. Just sit there a minute. Breathe. Is anything broken? Don't move. Just feel yourself, starting at your toes. Flex your toes. Are you flexing your toes?"

She nodded.

Josh stood and looked toward the slopes where Scipio, still wearing his striped ref shirt, entered the trees. He thought about going after him, but for what? Whether or not the state cops had reached the compound, they were sure as hell on their way now. Kleiser would have made sure of that. Josh hurt all over. He wasn't running after anyone.

For ten minutes Calloway talked to his daughter while reviewing every limb. Finally, he unlatched her shoulder harness. A highway patrol car pulled off the road onto the crushed grass and stopped. A big trooper in shades and a Smoky hat got out and walked toward them.

"Heinz Calloway?"

Calloway turned. "That's me, officer." He reached for his

badge and identification.

The trooper's name was Jacobsen. "Who's in the vehicle?"

"My daughter Ashley."

"How is she? I'm going to call an ambulance."

"I don't think she broke anything. She's a bit banged up."

Jacobsen fingered his shoulder phone. "Jane, this is Jacobsen. I'm at mile forty-four on Highway Twenty-Four. We're gonna need an ambulance to transport a juvenile female." He nodded.

"Okay. They're sending an ambulance. I'm glad your daughter is safe. Sir, may I see some identification?"

Josh already had his driver's license out. "Scipio ran into the trees."

"We've known about the compound for years, but we were unable to act. No one was willing to file a complaint."

"What changed?" Calloway said.

"Apparently there was a shooting this morning with several people dead."

"We were there," Josh said. "Neither one of us was involved in the shooting."

"Okay. Why don't you tell me what happened? And later, we're going to have to go down to Salida and take a formal statement."

Jacobsen passed between them and leaned in. "Are you all right, young lady?"

"I think so."

"Sit tight until the EMTs get here. They may want to strap you to a board."

Ashley felt herself, moved her legs, swung them out. "I think I can stand."

"Why don't you just wait for the EMTs?"

"Really, officer. I'm fine. Let me out."

Jacobsen stepped back. Ashley stood. Calloway hugged her.

"Ouch!" she said.

Calloway put an arm around her shoulder and led her away.

"Did he touch you?"

"No, not really. He wanted to. Oh Daddy, how could I be so stupid!"

An ambulance hove into view, lights blinking.

CHAPTER 49

JIGGETY JOG

Jacobsen fronted Josh. "What happened, Mr. Pratt?"

They sat in Jacobsen's cruiser with a recorder on the console.

Josh ran it down, from Ashley contacting Scipio online to their departure from the compound.

"I just don't get it," the trooper said. "She's a smart girl. She loves her family. What would make someone like that run off with a complete stranger?"

"Men like Scipio are experts at telling people what they want to hear."

One of the EMTs motioned to Josh. "Let's take a look."

Josh sat on the ambulance tailgate while the EMT probed. "These stitches look new."

"Brand new."

"And then what? You walked into another door?"

They watched while the EMTs strapped Ashley onto a

collapsible gurney and slid her into the back of the ambulance. Calloway came over.

"I'm riding with my daughter. Josh, I don't know when we'll see each other again." He put his hands on Josh's shoulders. "Thank you, brother."

Josh embraced him. Calloway broke away and got in the ambulance.

"Looks like you did a good thing here," the big trooper said. "Why don't you ride with me. You can give us a statement in town and we'll put you up at a Best Western. How does that sound?"

"What's happening at the ranch?"

"Should be state patrol. Someone texted us pictures of two bodies. Gunshot victims. It takes a while to get up there."

State Patrol HQ in Salida was a nondescript four-story red brick building with hexagonal corners. Josh sat in a bland meeting room with a fake wood floor, pictures of the Rockies on the walls, and a signed picture of Peyton Manning.

"Who sent us the pictures?"

"I'm not at liberty to say."

State investigator Darrell Cummings, who looked like a refrigerator with horn-rimmed specs and a walrus mustache, folded his hands across the oak table. "Why not?"

"He doesn't want to get involved."

"We'll let that go for now. You'll have to stick around for a day or two to identify people and fill in the gaps."

"I got nothing else to do."

Jacobsen gave Josh a ride to the motel. The staties set up a temporary HQ at the ranch. Other staties and forest service personnel searched for Scipio. Now that they had his real name, they found several outstanding warrants including sexual assault and menacing. The weather turned bad. Snow fell in Salida. After two days, Jacobsen drove Josh to the Salida Airport where he caught a Frontier to Denver and switched to Southwest for Madison. He arrived Wednesday afternoon, phoned Ninja from the airport, and called an Uber.

The Uber driver arrived in a Leaf, a balding man, with long scraggly hair like Uncle Creepy. He wore plastic Mardi Gras beads around his neck and a tie-dye Grateful Dead T. He chirped to a stop curbside, jumped out, and grabbed Josh's backpack.

"Get in man! You ride up front with me. I don't go for this class bullshit."

Josh slid in. The driver entered the address into his phone.

"Exit the airport and head south on Packers Avenue."

"That broad sounds like my ex, man. She would never shut up. I still hear her voice when I'm asleep."

"Why'd you split up?"

"She said I wasn't living up to my potential. I got a PhD in psychology but here I am driving an Uber. I tried the corporate thing, man. It just didn't work out. Worked for Wisconsin Physicians Service. It was a bad fit. They clutched a viper to their bosom."

Josh laughed. He stuck out his hand. "Josh Pratt."

"Eugene Felder. Came here in '79 to go to school and never left. I was on the City Council for two years until I lost to that fascist creep, Musgrave."

"No politics, Eugene. You a Grateful Dead fan?"

Felder grinned and flipped a switch. "Uncle John's Band" chimed in.

"Fucking masterpiece," Josh said.

"You got that right. People bitch about the Dead. 'They're just a jam band, man.' No, they're not just a jam band. All you gotta do is listen to this record."

"Been listening to it all my life."

They cut through town. Josh glanced toward the university as they crossed State Street. Most of the storefronts were boarded up, covered with graffiti. BLACK LIVES MATTER. DEFUND THE PIGS. HIPPITY HOPPITY—END PRIVATE PROPERTY.

"You believe this shit, man? When I went to school, we demonstrated, sure, but we didn't burn shit down."

Felder took South Wash to the Beltline and headed west. "Look at this shit, man. Looks like a fucking cloverleaf. When I came here, Madison was still a small town. Now it's spreading like some kind of invasive water plant. Look at all these roads. You can't even see the Arboretum anymore."

"Tell me about it!"

By the time they reached Ptarmigan, the Dead were on "Black Peter." Ninja's Cherokee sat in the driveway. Josh tipped Felder ten bucks.

"Thanks, man!"

Fig started barking as Josh walked up the drive. He opened the door and sat to embrace the furry explosion slobbering all over his face. Ninja came out of the kitchen holding a beer, wearing pleated pants, a black pullover and a black beret.

"Fuck happened? You look like you were in a fight."

"Yeah. We found the compound, got Ashley back and I got my ass beat. Now there are cops all over the place."

"You didn't mention me, did you?"

"No, of course not. I didn't even mention Kleiser, although they know he was there. They know someone was there. They just don't know who."

"Good luck tracking that guy."

"Got any plans?"

"Don't worry, man. I ain't hangin' around much longer. Just got to line up a few shots. I'm workin' on it."

"Where you going?"

"Best you don't know. But hey, I did manage to rip a new track while I was here. I even got Fig a part. You want to see?"

"Yeah, gimme a minute. I gotta call Ray."

She answered on the first ring. "Get your ass over here."

"Baby, I'm drained. I haven't slept in two days. Let's do it tomorrow."

"Okay, but Sid is waiting to piss on your shirt. Are you okay?"

"Just beat up. I'll tell you all about it."

"Well okay. I love you."

"I love you too."

Josh showered. There was a dent on his bed where Fig slept every night. He had just pulled up the blankets when Fig landed on the bed with a soft thump.

TROUBLE

Tuesday morning Josh went for a jog. He only did two miles so Fig wouldn't hurt herself. He showered, fed Fig, and cooked bacon on his old gas stove top. Bacon splatter covered the stove top. Josh loved bacon, but it always made a mess. That was part of the price you paid for cooking your own bacon. Ninja emerged blinking like a mole.

"Do I smell bacon?"

"No."

"Gimme some."

They sat at the kitchen table eating bacon and English muffins.

"This is good coffee. Where do you get it?"

"Big Lots. You need to pony up a bill for services rendered."

"Aw, hell no. What are you gonna do? Put it on your IRS return? Listen, I needed a place to go and you gave it to me.

Let's just call it even."

"When you moving on?"

Ninja took his time chewing and swallowing. He washed it down with coffee. "Ain't that just like a white man. Use a nigga and cast him aside."

Josh rested his chin on his clasped hands. Ninja flashed his dazzling teeth.

"I gotta keep it on the down low on account I have irritated Johnny Torreo. He's one of those Sicilian mother-fuckers. They never forget and they never give up."

"You could buy a motor home."

"You funny. I'm looking for a rental property. I've got aliases that'll fool anyone. I don't suppose you want to buy a rental property."

"I'd like to help you out but I can't be dragged into your personal vendetta. I'll ask around. I might know somebody."

"I like this town. I really do. I could live here."

"Let me see what I can do."

Josh phoned Calloway. "How you doing?"

"I feel great! I turned in my two-weeks' notice. Ashley's been accepted at Cornell. Doreen and I are gonna sell this place and move out in the country. Raise some chickens."

"Are you serious?"

"You bet."

"What about Scipio?"

"The feds have issued a nationwide alert for Brian Pils. Income tax evasion. You believe that shit? All the shit that man has done, they're gonna stick him on this."

"That's how they got Capone."

"Amen, brother. We're meeting with the feds today. I couldn't have done it without you."

"Yeah yeah."

"Doreen wants you to come over for dinner."

"Can't tonight. Got a hot date."

"That Ray, she's fine."

Josh rang Ray's condo at six pm, holding a bottle of Freixenet. It was a cheap Spanish champagne, but it came with a cork. Ray met him at the door wearing nothing but a filmy black negligee.

"Oh no!" she said, touching his stitches. "What happened?"

"I fell out of a tree."

Josh barely managed to close the door behind him before they got in a lip-lock that led them staggering into the bedroom. Josh kicked the door shut behind him to prevent Sid Vicious from pissing on his shirt.

As they lay in each other arms in the afterglow, Ray said, "There's a demonstration tomorrow at the capital to defund the police. I want you to go."

"That ain't my thing, baby doll."

"Please. I'm asking you."

"Can't do it. You know Heinz Calloway is one of my best friends. That's where I was this past week. Rescuing his daughter from a cult."

"Do you love me?"

"You know I do."

"Then do this for me."

"No, that's not me. I don't demonstrate. I'm a very private person."

Ray pulled away, sat up and put on her panties, pants, and a Figure 5 T-shirt. "You disappoint me."

"You knew I was an unreconstructed troglodyte when you met me."

"Do you vote?"

"Not yet. But I've been meaning to."

"Will you at least vote for the progressive Dane candidate?"

"Sure."

"All right. I'll let you stay."

Josh saw her whole life in an instant. How she got this way. The Madison school system, staffed top to bottom with progressives out to change the world. The professor parents. He a sociologist, she a historian. Josh feared to look at their course titles. Ray was an only child. More would put too great a burden on the ecosystem.

They'd sent her to a private boarding school when she was fourteen, St. Agnes in Delafield, where earnest young teachers preached the evils of capitalism.

A man's vote was private. That's why voting booths had curtains. He hoped she wouldn't ask for proof. Ray was what every red-blooded American male wanted in a woman. Curvy, beautiful, smart, fun. But nothing was perfect and he wondered just how far she'd go trying to get him to embrace her politics.

Josh believed in the biker code. Your word was your bond.

Do what you say you will. Be there when you do it. There was a little wiggle room. No biker would insist he keep such an absurd promise. Josh had yet to vote, but just hadn't got around to it. He didn't watch the news, and pretended it didn't exist. He didn't even know if he was eligible.

Growing up with his hoodlum father, Josh wasn't even aware of politics. He was too consumed with dread and hunger as Duane blew one opportunity after another, dragging him from cheap tenement to trailer park to flophouse, always one step ahead of the law. Josh had grown up with a lawless mindset. The Bedouins had no love for the police. It was only after he'd gone to prison and met Pastor Dorgan that he changed his attitude.

He believed in the biker code. How could he support any politician, whose word was as evanescent as a soap bubble? He knew enough about politicians to know they all lied. They had to. It was a requirement of the job. As always, it was a matter of degree. Who lied the most? Vote for the other guy. He was aware of very few politicians who had ever met a payroll or worked with their hands. They went into politics because it was a way to get rich without working. Sure, campaigning and governing were work, in the sense that you had to plow through reams of bureaucratese and put up with tons of bullshit. You had to get out there and press the flesh, kiss some babies.

On the other hand, you got your name in the news, you didn't have to drive anywhere, you were protected by an armed detail, and you grew mysteriously rich. People went into politics for power and money. All that crap they spouted about serving their constituents and caring so much violated one of Josh's Life Rules.

Show don't tell.

You want to do good work. Do it. But spare others the press release and video. Josh didn't watch football, but he was aware of a number of NFL pros who quietly, sometimes secretly, supported charities, sometimes sneaking into hospitals to visit with young fans.

Most knelt during the national anthem.

Ray returned and handed Josh a plastic glass filled with champagne. "I'm nuking a pizza. Come on! The Packs are playing the Vikings tonight."

"I thought we'd go to the Crystal, catch Dalton Seaberry."

"He won't come on until nine at the earliest. Listen, if you live in Wisconsin, you have to support the Pack. It's the law."

Sid Vicious ran in. Josh picked up his shirt. "All right. But Imma need a spray bottle to keep Sid off my ankles."

CHAPTER
51

MCFARLAND

The Crystal was at fifty percent capacity. Every other booth and bar stool was roped off or had a warning label. Josh and Ray took the last two stools as Dalton Seaberry took the stage, at nine-thirty. The old man with a seamed face, a worn tan sport jacket and a brown fedora sat on a wooden chair cradling his legendary guitar, Priscilla. There were rumors he'd cut a deal with the devil.

His drummer was an ancient gnome with a full beard in denim coveralls, the bass player some kid with long blond hair cradling a Fender. From the opening chord, electricity swept through the building. Seaberry shed ten years, bending over his ax, using a bottleneck slide, singing in an aching tenor that fell into the sub-basement. Ray squeezed Josh's arm hard enough to leave claw prints.

Everybody loved the blues.

During the break, Ray wrapped her hand around Josh's

arm. "The folks want us to come to dinner. How does Friday sound?"

Josh's stomach lurched. Worst Case Scenario: married with two young children, a bigger house, a mortgage, a straight job. Was this not what Jesus sanctified? Who said life was supposed to be easy? Well, what could it hurt? He could act like a pig. Her parents would tell her to find someone more suitable.

"All right."

She almost lovey-dovey-ed him off the stool. "Oh, they'll love you, Josh! Let's spend the night at my place and go together!"

"Why don't you spend the night at my place? Sid Vicious does better by himself than Fig." He'd never told her where Fig's name came from.

"Oh, you miss your doggie. Okay. Are you coming back to my place?"

At ten the next morning, Josh kicked out in Steve Fleiss' parking lot in a two-story stucco office building on East Wilson off the Square. Red letters on a white background read: THIS PARKING LOT IS RESERVED FOR CLIENTS OF THE FLEISS AND BRAUNSCHWIEGER LAW FIRM. ALL OTHERS WILL BE TOWED.

He went up the atrium steps to the second floor. Marsha, the vivacious redhead who'd worked for Fleiss ever since Josh had known him, looked up from her desk and smiled. "There he is."

"Hey Red."

"Go on in. He's waiting for you."

Josh entered Fleiss' office that had a skylight and a window looking out on King Street. One wall contained a floor-to-ceiling bookshelf with space for the little trophies every politically active lawyer earned. March of Dimes. United Way. A blank space that used to belong to the Boy Scouts. Pictures of Fleiss with Mayor For Life Saul Brogden, Aaron Rodgers, Brett Favre, Davante Adams, UW President Eleanor Clift.

A framed sampler said: THE LAWYER'S PRAYER: DEAR LORD, PLEASE LET THERE BE SUFFERING AND STRIFE AMONG YOUR PEOPLE LEST YOUR SERVANT STARVE.

"No, I'm not getting a dog. Why don't you bring your dog over and have him piss around the perimeter?"

Beat.

"All right. Here's what we're gonna do. I'm going to order some coyote piss off the internet and we'll use that. Okay. Later."

Smiling, Fleiss turned toward Josh. "I have all these brown spots in my yard. My yard guy says it's rabbit piss."

Fleiss' yard guy was a landscaper and convicted felon whom Fleiss had represented. As with many of his clients, he accepted services in lieu of cash. Landscaping to auto repairs to house cleaning. "Hey, congratulations on saving Calloway's daughter."

"What have you heard?"

"Only that you got her back safe, and there was a shootout that left two people dead. In other words, a typical Pratt adventure. What's up?"

"Got this guy staying with me who's a valuable asset. He's a hacker. He hacked the Pentagon. There's nothing he can't get into. He's been living at my place and now he wants to rent."

"So why come to me?"

Josh waggled his fingers. "This guy ain't exactly Joe Dirt. He's off the grid. He can't use his real name. ID isn't a problem. He can come up with whatever. His money's good. And he could be a valuable asset for you too. Say you want to trace someone, a witness. Whatever. This guy can do it."

"I'm not a landlord."

"Yeah, but you know a lot of landlords."

Fleiss represented several landlords trying to evict non-paying or troublesome renters.

"What kind of place is he looking for?"

"Some place discreet. Out in the country."

"I'll ask around. I would like you to deliver a subpoena."

He poked the intercom. "Marsha, do you have that subpoena for Mr. Combs?"

A minute later Marsha swished in, handed Josh the subpoena, and swished out.

Josh read it. The petitioner was Casper M. Doughty of Sun Prairie. The respondent was Alvin Combs, who was required to appear in court. Combs lived in a trailer park in McFarland.

"My client was driving on the Beltline when he did

observe the respondent, Mr. Alvin C. Combs, toss a beer bottle out of his vehicle which sailed gracefully through the air and struck my client's windshield dead center. Fortunately, my client had a witness and was able to note the license plate number."

"Tell me about Combs."

Fleiss slid a sheet of paper across the desk. Aggravated Assault, mail fraud, cruelty to animals. Combs had served two years for the assault charge.

"Sounds like a fun guy."

"That's why I pay you the big bucks."

Josh tucked the subpoena in his jacket pocket. "I'm on it."

He took John Nolan Drive to the Beltline to Highway Fifty-One. McFarland was a farming community clinging to the east side of Lake Waubesa, population eight thousand. It had a few Indian mounds. Cruising through town, Josh saw a two-wheeler approaching and threw out the biker's signal. The rider responded. It was only after they'd passed Josh saw that the other vehicle was a scooter, and cursed himself. It happened to every biker.

The Willamette Trailer Park lay on Grevioux Road on the southeast side. Josh passed through an arched entrance, down Willamette Lane and stopped at a clean double-wide with a FOR RENT sign in the window. He wrote down the telephone number, got on his bike and rode to Combs Trailer. An old Panhead sat out front and a tarp-covered car in the back. Josh kicked out next to the Panhead. The muted rumble of his two-into-one summoned Combs, who stepped out on the prefab porch, two steps up from the concrete slab.

"Nice Panhead," Josh said.

"Thanks. What you riding?"

"It's a '98 Road King."

"What all you do to it?"

Josh took a deep breath. "Engine: 88 with oil cooler. Changed the cams to S&S gear drives with a .510 lift. Took out the fuel injection and replaced it with an S&S Super-E, Yost Power Tube, S&S manifold and Pingle High Flow petcock. S&S Teardrop air cleaner cover with a K&N filter. Screamin' Eagle Hi-Performance ignition unit with a 6200 rpm rev limiter. Accel SuperCoil, Firewire plug wires and spiral wound metal core wires. Accel Platinum tipped plugs. Five-speed tranny with Barnett kevlar clutch, self-adjusting hydraulic chain tensioner. Screamin' Eagle dualies. Progressive springs in front with higher viscosity, Progressives in back. Changed the rear swingarm bushings to "STA BOW" nylon high density. SBS semi-metallic disc brake pads and the brake lines are stainless steel braids. Went to tubeless wheels."

Combs came down for a closer look. "Nice!"

Josh handed him the summons. "This is for you."

Combs looked down, then looked at Josh with sadness. "How'd you find me?"

"They got your license plate."

Combs stuffed the summons in his hip pocket. "Yeah well."

CHAPTER 52

MEET THE PARENTS

The McRaneys lived in a two-story red brick colonial in University Heights, down the street from Frank Lloyd Wright's famous "Airplane House," which surmounted the hill. They had one of those *We Believe* signs in the front yard.

Josh pulled his Chrysler into the driveway. Bad enough their daughter was dating a biker. No need to rub it in their faces.

The McRaneys emerged all smiles. Ray hugged her father, then her mother. "Folks, this is Josh Pratt."

Josh wore a Duluth Trading Company Wrinkle Fighter with the sleeves rolled up to just below the elbow, exposing his inked arms. He was freshly showered, shaven, and anointed in Tom Ford Tuscan Leather, a gift from Ray.

"Pleased to meet you, sir."

"Call me Hal."

"Ray has told us so much about you!" Marianne McRaney

gushed. "Come on in. Let's go out on the back porch."

The patio was surrounded by old-growth elm and oak, their neighbors visible through the trees. It had a gas grill, wrought-iron benches, a round table with an umbrella in the middle.

"Would you folks like some drinks?" the professor asked. He was a tall, silver-haired patrician in stressed blue jeans and a Hawaiian shirt decorated with coconuts and surf.

"You know what I like, Daddy."

"I'll have any local beer," Josh said.

Marianne sat on an upholstered sofa and smiled at them with crimson lips. "So you're a private detective. I don't believe I've ever met a private detective."

Ray sat next to Josh on a wicker love seat, clutching his arm. "Josh is my knight in shining armor."

"How did you become a private detective?"

"I stumbled into it. I started delivering summons for a lawyer friend and I became interested. I never really had a profession, but there does seem to be a need for my services."

"Who's your lawyer friend? We know a lot of lawyers."

"Steve Fleiss."

Marianne wrinkled her nose in disgust as McRaney came out the patio door carrying a tray. He set the tray down on a glass table between the sofas and handed Josh a cold bottle of Capital City Autumnal Fire.

"Figure a guy like you drinks straight from the bottle."

Ray poured white wine for herself and her mother. McRaney had a martini. They held up their glasses.

"Cheers," McRaney said.

They clinked. They sipped.

"Josh was just telling us how he became a private investigator."

"How's that?"

"After I got out of prison, I began delivering summons for my lawyer. It sort of mushroomed from there."

Alarm flared in Marianne's eyes. McRaney set down his martini. "Why were you in prison, if you don't mind my asking?"

"Not at all, sir. My father abandoned me when I was fifteen. When I was a young man, I joined a motorcycle gang. They were the only family I ever knew. I'm ashamed of the things I've done, and I've tried to make amends. I spent four years in Waupun for atrocious assault. I cut off a man's arm with a chainsaw. I tell you this not to shock you, but because I'm a different person now. I have accepted Jesus Christ into my heart and soul and believe in honesty."

Sickly smiles settled on the McRaneys.

"Well, Ray thinks the world of you," Marianne lamely repeated.

"I try to be worthy of her respect, as I shall try to be worthy of yours."

"And how did you meet?" Marianne said.

"Louise Lowry introduced us. She and Dave are my neighbors across the street."

"Oh!" Marianne chirped. "We know the Lowrys! Hal's on the Alumni Committee."

"That's right," McRaney said. "Good people. You live across the street? We've been to their house."

"I live in the yellow ranch-style. They say it's better to have the cheapest house in an expensive neighborhood than the most expensive house in a cheap neighborhood."

McRaney smiled quizzically.

"I'll have you over."

"What did you think of *Kiss Me Kate*?" Marianne asked brightly.

"Loved it. Never was much into musicals. The only musical I saw was *Paint Your Wagon*."

"I'm not familiar with that one," Marianne said.

"Lee Marvin and Clint Eastwood. It's the only time you'll catch them singing."

Marianne raised her glass. "We had hoped that Ray would follow us into academia, but I must say, she has done very well for herself, keeping dance alive in this city."

"It's never too late to get yourself a BFA in dance, darling."

"Thank you, Daddy. I will take that under advisement."

"Did you get the grant?"

"No, Daddy. Everything is on hold until after the virus goes away."

"We thought about asking you to wear masks tonight, but Ray assures me you're healthy."

Ray ran her hand along Josh's shoulder. "He's very healthy."

"Ray says your both professors. What do you teach?"

"I teach Psych 225. General characteristics of scientific

method; use of experimental, observational, and correlation-al research designs; research methods used in psychological science; illustration of core issues in research methods taken from several areas of psychology; lecture, demonstration, and experiments."

"I teach History of European Sexuality," Marianne chirped. "Well, come on in. That pot roast isn't going to eat itself."

They sat at a polished oval walnut table with fresh flowers in a vase and four settings of silverware, linen napkins, wine glasses, and water glasses.

"Sit," Marianne said. "Everybody sit. I'll bring the food out."

The dining room off the kitchen had a cocoa carpet and a marble-topped credenza with a silver samovar beneath a gilt-framed painting of a schooner heeled over in rough seas, with iridescent waves. Josh sat opposite McRaney, who sat at the head of the table. Marianne and Ray swooped in with salads. Josh guessed the green stuff was kale and arugula.

"So, Josh," McRaney said. "What are you working on now?"

"I just delivered a summons to a man in McFarland."

"Oh, come on. Ray told us how you rescued the police-man's daughter."

Josh waved it away. "It was no big deal."

"As you may have guessed, we don't favor a militarized police."

Ray and Marianne returned with platters of pot roast,

potatoes, and carrots. "We don't favor any police force," Marianne said. "There are better ways to deal with violent crime."

Marianne went back and returned with two platters, one of which she placed in front of Ray. "If the police would just go away, crime would just go away."

McRaney tucked his white linen napkin beneath his chin and picked up his knife and fork. "We're very proud of our City Councilperson, Mkwume Ndaga. He's one of the co-sponsors of the bill to defund the police."

Josh smiled. It was going to be a long evening.

CHAPTER
53

KUNG FU MUSICAL

They went to Josh's house after dinner. Dr. Dis blasted from below. Josh went down the stairs and saw Ninja dancing among his terminals, one screen showing virtual currency charts, another open on Big Butted Mamas, a third on Dane County Rentals. He wore earbuds. Josh tapped him on the shoulder and he snapped into a low karate stance, laughed, took off the buds.

"Sorry. Didn't hear you come in."

"Dude, Ray's here. Can you chill the speakers?"

"Of course." Ninja turned the sound off.

Josh handed Ninja a slip of paper with the phone number for the trailer, and the address. "This place is for rent. It's in McFarland. No one will look for you in McFarland."

"Where's McFarland?"

"Southeast of here. It's a white bread farming community, but I did see one black family."

Ninja stuck it in his pocket. "Yeah, thanks."

Fig scratched outside the door and whined while they made love. Josh let her in and she jumped on the bed in a frenzy of licking. She settled down at the foot of the bed.

"The folks really liked you!'

"How can you tell?"

"If they don't like someone, they always have a word with me before I leave."

She lay with her head in the crook of Josh's arm.

"I'm astonished."

"Really? How come?"

"I'm unreconstructed."

Ray laughed. "Maybe that's what they like about you."

"I doubt it."

"Can we watch the news?"

"Why?"

"I want to see how the demonstration went."

Josh smacked himself in the forehead. "How could I forget!"

He turned on the flat screen attached to the wall. WMAD's ten o'clock broadcast began with staccato thriller music closing in on the serious mien of Rachel Ostrander, a mixed-race beauty with great hair.

"Good evening. We have just learned that a police officer has been shot near Elver Park. The assailant surprised him in his cruiser and hit him in the chest and the arm. The officer has been transported to Madison General and is expected to survive. Meanwhile, we have this footage of the alleged assailant."

Grain black and white footage showed the herky-jerk approach of a man in a hoodie. Marched right up, took aim with one hand and fired four times, ran like hell. Josh noted the man held the pistol sideways, gangsta style

"The alleged assailant is believed to be a male in his mid-thirties. Anyone with information about this person, please contact the Madison Police. We go now to Mayor Brogden's press conference, with police chief Lucinda Akers, at the City-County Building."

Mayor Brogden was a Charlie Chaplin-esque figure in a baggy suit with a scruffy mustache and hangdog hair. Chief Akers was a portly black woman in a blue uniform.

Brogden looked at the camera. "Shooting police is unacceptable. It is not a demonstration. We will not rest until the perpetrator is apprehended and punished to the full extent of the law. Officer Kahn is an honored member of our Community Outreach Program, who works with underage offenders in boxing, gymnastics, and baseball. He has an exemplary record, a wife, and two children. If anyone knows anything about this incident, I urge you to come forward."

Dozens of hands shot up.

"Katy," the mayor said.

The camera zoomed in on Katy Varner, sleek in a long-sleeved dark blue dress, black hair brushed to a high sheen. "Mr. Mayor, Elver Park is known for gang activity. Why was Officer Kahn alone at that time? Is it MPD policy for officers to patrol alone in their vehicles?"

"We are currently experiencing an officer shortage due to an unusually high number of retirements and transfers."

The chief stepped up. "We are offering a five-thou-sand-dollar reward for anyone whose information leads to the apprehension of the alleged perp."

Hands shot up.

Josh muted the sound.

"Listen," Ray said.

"What?"

"*Kung Fu Musical*. Young Russel cruises into town on his one-wheeled skateboard determined to start his own martial arts school and runs into a group of kung fu guys who follow the Way of the Snake. If he wants to teach, he has to fight all the kung fu guys! At the skateboard park! On skateboards! The first song is 'Bouncing Off Walls.'"

"Enter the Dragon got my tail waggin'," she sang in a clear tenor. "Next came Jackie Chan, the man with the plan! Bouncing off walls, Jackie's got balls! He trained for years with Biggie Smalls!"

She threw off the sheet and leaped to her feet.

"Those kung fu guys have more muscle than wise, throw down the gauntlet. Fight for the park or deal with the tauntlet."

Ray choreographed as she sang, halting, laughing, starting over. Josh laughed too.

"What happens next?"

Ray put her arm on the dresser. "He gets his ass handed to him. Then Vanessa the lady cop rides up on her motorcycle and chases everyone away."

"A lady motorcycle cop. I like it."

"Of course! Russel immediately falls head over heels for Vanessa who tells him to get out of town. Like Rambo."

"Russel skates off singing, 'Confessin' to Vanessa.' He seeks the wizened sage who lives in a trailer."

"The Mr. Miyagi part."

"He finds Elmer Kludd passed out in a sty. Russell cleans the trailer and when Elmer wakes up, he attacks! Anticipating the old man's savagery, Russell yanks the throw rug out from under him and he lands on his ass. Looks around. Realizes Russell cleaned the trailer. You've heard of *Drunken Master*. This is *Stoned Master*. The higher he gets, the more impossible his kung fu. They sing, 'Do You Wanna Marijuana.'"

"Next month is Squab's Invitational, an international kung fu extravaganza sponsored by Squab Financial. The winner gets a million bucks, a contract as Squab spokesperson and a lifetime supply of squabs. The town meets in the park to sing 'Squab Job.'"

"What happens next?"

"I don't know. I thought maybe you could help."

Josh laughed. He wouldn't know where to begin. "All I can do is tell you about the movies I liked."

"Ooh. I'd love to see them."

"Some are pretty bloody."

"The bloodier the better."

The TV silently showed a crowd milling around in front of the City-County Building holding up signs. DEFUND THE POLICE. END RACISM.

"Turn it up!" Ray said.

The camera closed in on a cresting wave of blonde hair. "Several hundred people gathered today outside the main police station to protest what they see as systemic racism and the militarization of the police. The demonstration was peaceful. Councilperson Mkwume Ndaga was one of the featured speakers."

Close in on a black man with high cheekbones wearing a knit green, red, and black cap. "It has been proven in study after study that the police are ineffective in reducing crime. It has been proven time and again that the police themselves are often the instigators or root cause of crime."

"Don't see you," Josh said.

"I was at the back of the crowd."

"Can I switch channels?"

"Go ahead.

Josh flipped until he found *The Masked Singer*. Dude dressed like a giant rabbit singing "Sweet Home Alabama," the audience cheering and booing, judges mugging it up, looking at each other in consternation. Josh thought he was pretty good.

Nick Cannon wore a beet-colored jacket over a black shirt. "I can't believe you sang that!"

Ken Jeong pumped his fist. "Yeeeee-HA!"

Jenny McCarthy shook her head grinning goofily. "I have to admit, he's got a voice. It kind of sounded like Harry Connick."

Ray snored softly. Josh turned off the television, gently extricated himself, went to the bathroom. Fig followed him in, whining to be petted. Josh sat on the bathroom floor and put his arm around the dog's neck. "I think I'm pretty easy-going, don't you?"

Fig licked him.

He'd never considered getting married and having a family, but now he realized that that's what men did. Jesus didn't come to him all at once. He came bit by bit as Josh realized the truth in His words. Father Dorgan called it the accumulated wisdom of the ages and lamented that men were born without tribal memory, the whole crawling out of the muck trial by fire thing. He'd never really lived with a woman but he was thinking about it. He tried not to engage in magical thinking. If only Charlotte Newton had lived… But she hadn't.

Would Ray insist on marriage? Wasn't that rather bourgeoisie? Would Sid Vicious get along with Fig? He tried to work it out. He guessed that most men made these calculations sooner or later. Duane sealed the deal. All Josh had to do was look at how Duane had lived and do the opposite.

Josh tried not to think about the women he'd abused over the years. Before he went to prison. He bowed his head. "Lord, forgive me."

He hadn't thought about his father in over a week.

Was he moving too fast? He'd only known Ray a couple of months. But a man should be able to figure out if a woman is for him in a couple of months.

But first, he had to get Ninja a place of his own.

CHAPTER 54

THUMB IN THE BREEZE

John Haber was a contract trucker out of Madison City, Iowa, who drove for several of the road firms when they were short. His latest contract found him picking up a load of circuit boards in Santa Fe and driving them to Jackson, Wyoming. Haber's rig was a 2018 Mack Anthem with a 425-horse engine which he'd bought to replace his '91 Peterbilt, with 285,000 miles. Haber had been driving continuously since the virus hit, with only occasional weekends off with his wife Jennifer and fourteen-year-old son Nathan.

Haber had delivered canned corn to supermarket distribution centers in Philadelphia, New York, and Boston. He'd carried aluminum skiffs to Louisiana, lumber to Idaho, and hand tools to Harbor Freight. On this particular October afternoon, he was carrying circuit boards, acetylene torches, fire extinguishers, and hand tools from a Denver warehouse to Goodell's Hardware in Riverton, Wyoming.

Haber never was much of a drinker. He smoked a little pot. He loved his family, his truck, and the Green Bay Packers. On long hauls, he listened to George Strait, George Jones, Dwight Yoakum, Waylon Jennings, Patsy Cline, the Carter Family, and Loretta Lynn. He didn't have much use for the new stuff, except for Toby Keith. And as for the Commie Chicks, or whatever they called themselves, these days, they could go pound sand.

Haber listened to Sirius XM radio. They had a show called Country Time which knew what he wanted to hear. He was on Highway Two-Eighty-Seven rolling through the Shoshone National Forest listening to Merle singing "Mama Tried" when he spotted the hitchhiker standing in a clearing at the base of an incline.

Contract truckers had to sign an agreement that they would not pick up hitchhikers, but Haber had spent much of his youth hitching around the west and had always had a soft spot for the noble knights of the road. He was an independent. The contract didn't apply to him. He feared no man. He kept a .357 in a hidden holster under the dash. He slowed down to take a look. The man wasn't a beggar. He didn't press his palms together or hold a sign saying GOD BLESS. He wore clean blue jeans, and a black leather jacket over a blue work shirt, a North Face backpack at his feet. When Haber pulled over with a squeal, the man didn't suddenly pick up his pack and run like a fool. He hoisted it onto his back and strode purposefully down the shoulder until he could boost himself up through the door.

"Where you goin'?" Haber asked.

"Boise. Thanks for stopping."

"I'll get you part of the way. Just toss your pack in the back there."

The man was middle-aged, but he was no hobo. His face was clean-shaven, his hair neatly combed. He looked like he took care of himself.

"Name's John."

"Lance Broderick," the hitcher said, offering his hand.

They began the ascent into the Rockies.

"Whatchoo doin' out here, Lance?"

"I am headed to my new parish. I'm a pastor. Next stop, Fortney Baptist. I am due on Monday. The day before I was going to leave, my engine blew up. It was an old car and I had no insurance. I gave the church my word I would be there, and I intend to keep it. I'm not a man who turns back at the first sign of adversity."

"Why din'tcha ask the parish to rent you a car? Surely they would have done that."

"John, I seek no riches in this life. I seek only to follow God's will. From talking to the current deacon and the church's board of supervisors, I get the impression that it is not a rich church. 'A faithful man will abound with blessings, but whoever hastens to be rich will not go unpunished.'"

"Ain't that the truth. I been truckin' all my adult life. I ain't a rich man, but I'm not poor either. I own my own home, got a loving wife and son."

"Amen, Brother John. The love of money is the root

of all evil."

"Now we got the gummint who wants to get rid of paper money altogether. They want everyone to go cashless, charge everything, so they can keep track of us."

"I hear you, Brother John. It's what they call the New World Order. One government, headed by the United Nations, most likely."

"Don't even get me started on those motherfuckers, excuse my French."

Broderick chuckled. "I've heard worse. I wasn't always a man of God."

"We all know what New World Order really means. The Joooos."

"Well, I have to confess, I have a credit card, but I pay it off every month. I'm not about to give those usurers anything extra."

"Yeah, I got one too. For business expenses. Easier to keep track."

"What are you hauling, Brother John?"

"Acetylene torches, circuit boards, fire extinguishers, and hand tools."

They crested the hill and began a long downward segment. A sign said RUNAWAY TRUCK RAMP, HALF MILE.

"You ever have to use one of those?"

"No, sir. I keep my rigs in tip-top condition. Know a guy who used one once. Saved his bacon."

They passed the ramp jutting upward at a thirty-degree angle. A sign said BOGANVILLE, FIVE MILES. It was three pm.

"I don't normally stop for meals but I'm ahead of schedule and this place has some good barbecue ribs. You want to join me?"

"That's very generous, Brother John, but you must allow me to pay. I can't let your kindness and generosity go unrewarded."

"You sure you can afford it?"

Broderick chuckled. "I'm not indigent."

"Well, all right. Thank you."

"No. Thank you."

The highway straightened onto a high range, rolling past cattle grazing in brown fields, snow-capped peaks visible on their left. They passed a threshing machine crawling down the road in the opposite direction. A billboard said, PETERSEN TRUCK STOP/MOE'S BBQ/SHOWERS/ FACILITIES/TRUCKERS WELCOME.

The Petersen Truck Stop sign towered fifty feet over the highway. The truck stop was a white commercial block with vinyl siding, five fueling islands, three for cars, two for trucks, and a sprawling parking lot, one side jammed with cars sporting license plates from all over, the other designated for trucks, with three long haulers parked parallel to each other fifty yards behind the building.

Haber expertly eased the Mack between the long white slots and shut off the engine, not noticing as Broderick slipped his hand into the pocket of his cargo pants and removed an ice pick.

"What kind of truck is that?" the preacher asked.

As Haber turned to look, Broderick secured the driver's head with his left arm and thrust the ice pick into his right ear. There was a moment of resistance before the cartilage popped and the ice pick penetrated the driver's ear, killing him instantly. Broderick pulled Haber down and looked around. No one had noticed. The preacher quickly searched the driver's pocket, finding a fat wallet filled with cash. A quick count showed over five hundred dollars, mostly in twenties. Broderick removed a bottle of Clorox Wipe-Its from his backpack and carefully wiped down every surface in the truck he might have touched.

A methodical search of the cockpit turned up the Smith & Wesson, which the preacher put in his backpack. He waited until no one was around, let himself quietly out of the cab, walked around the back of the truck stop far from the cameras, climbed a fence surrounding a pasture, walked through the pasture until he was out of sight of the truck stop just past a bend, and stood by the side of the road with his thumb in the breeze.

CHAPTER
55

CADAVER DOGS

Saturday, Josh drove Ray to her dance studio, returned and raked leaves. He was scooping them into a plastic garden bag when his phone rang. He didn't recognize the number.

"Josh Pratt."

"Mr. Pratt, this is Horace Wipf."

"How are you, Mr. Wipf?"

"I'm happy that you were able to rescue that young lady, but we're afraid that Scipio might come here."

"Why would he do that?"

"Scipio will put it together that you spoke with us."

A cringe of remorse shook Josh.

"Sir, I think he's got bigger things to worry about right now, like getting out of the country. And why would he come after you? I'm the one who got the girl out."

"I know it sounds irrational, but he's not a rational man. I'm just telling you what Lee says. He's talked to some of the others and they all feel the same way."

"Well, I don't know what to tell you. If I've brought any harm to you, I deeply regret it. If you're that concerned, take precautions."

"We are."

"I'll put my tech guy on it, maybe we can track him down."

"Let me know."

"I certainly will."

Josh broke the connection and saw that Calloway had called.

"Whassup?"

"Cadaver dogs sniffed out four graves at the compound. They've been sent to the Chaffee County coroner. Won't know who they are for a while, but two look like the bodies of adolescent girls."

A bolus of dread settled in Josh's stomach. "How you doing?"

"Chief wants me to hang on for two months."

"That's not your problem."

"I know. I don't know what to do. I'm talking it over with Doreen."

"Ashley?"

"I really got to hand it to her. She went back to school with her head held high. When people ask her about it, she says she's writing a book."

"Ha! That's not a bad idea."

Josh stuffed the leaves into two Hefty trash bags and dragged them to the curb. Although he was not part of the HOA, Albert Waste Management picked up all his trash. Some of their employees were bikers. Trash pick-up was Monday.

Inside, the basement was dark. Still sleeping. Josh fried some bacon and Ninja appeared like a groundhog, blinking in the light. After his guest had had coffee, Josh asked him, "Can you find Scipio with the face recognition stuff?"

"I can try. But he's hip to that shit. You saw the precautions he took the few times we were able to get him on camera."

"I'll get hold of the surveillance cameras from the compound. Should be plenty of material with which to work. How goes the house hunt?"

"Eager to get rid of me?"

"I love you like a brother, but I'm used to living alone."

"I hear ya. I hear ya. I'm the same way. Got a line on a promising rental in Brooklyn. Gonna check it out tomorrow."

"You'll stand out like a cockroach on white bread."

"Don't mind, don't care. I stick to myself most of the time anyway. Longer I stay, the more danger I put you in."

"Seriously?"

"Man, I'm tellin' you, Torreo doesn't mess around. Those contracts stay open until they're filled. Right now he's got better things to worry about, like a grand jury investigation."

"What's his deal?"

"Loan sharking, human trafficking, drugs. Mostly meth. People think the Mexicans run that shit, but it's the mafia too."

"Oh come on."

"Seriously, bro. They never did go away. Everybody's worried about the Russians and the Ukrainians, but these eye-talians, man, they never give up. You hear about vendettas going back centuries. It's a Sicilian thing. "

"You watch too many movies."

"I'll make him an offer he can't refuse."

"Yeah, well see if you can find that shitbird. Or any evidence he's left the country."

"On it."

Josh went into his office and checked his mail. The usual offers from Nigerian princes and the widows of Zambian generals. He went to Facebook. He had three friend requests from voluptuous young women with unlikely names. They all used the same eye makeup. He went to the Bedouins' page. There were very few Bedouins left, and most were old and retired. They used the page to keep in touch. Goose was the administrator.

Josh wrote, "It is with a heavy heart that I announce the death of Brandon 'Toad' Tortollini, who gave his life last week to save us from the cult leader Scipio. You may have heard news stories about Colorado State Police investigating a shooting at the God's Breath compound. I was there. I was one of the people Toad saved. Toad had been a cult member for years but in the end, their brainwashing could not overcome his devotion to our brotherhood. Please post your memories here. Sincerely, Josh Pratt."

Josh dug through his scrapbooks and found an old

color picture of him, Toad, Goose and several other Bedouins grinning outside some rural roadhouse. He ran it through his scanner and posted it on the page. He paused with the heavy book open on his lap and turned the pages. There he was with some cutie whose name he couldn't remember. There were too many pictures like that. He felt a deep sense of shame.

Fig came in, laid her snout on his leg and whined. He ruffled her fur. "I'm good. Want to go for a run?"

Fig woofed and wagged her tail. They suited up. They ran. Josh picked up a neatly tied bag of dog poop. Bag in hand, he picked up the pace. Fig had no trouble. They did two miles and turned around. On the way back, they passed two young men on one-wheeled skateboards, rolling toward town. They waved. Josh waved back. The skateboards cost eighteen hundred bucks. They looked like fun, but they weren't motorcycles.

He showered, changed into fresh clothes and went into the basement. Ninja sat at the long table before his two monitors, bopping to music on headphones. The room was filled with marijuana smoke. Half a doobie lay in an ashtray. Ninja wore a burgundy hoodie with the top down, cream Veja sneakers and artfully ripped jeans.

Josh tapped Ninja on the shoulder and the hacker popped up and around, wild-eyed.

"Don't do that, man!"

"I thought you were a ninja."

"I can't ninja all the time."

"Find anything?"

"Naw. That cat is gone. Hey, Imma drive to Brooklyn and check out that house. Want to come?"

Josh's phone rang. Ray. She was weeping.

"What happened?"

"Kayla's dead." A sob bubbled in his ear.

"What?"

"A friend of hers found her this morning. She didn't go to work last week and they started to worry...oh my god."

"How did it happen?"

"She was strangled with a lamp cord. He took her car."

CHAPTER 56

WRONG GUY

Josh turned to Ninja. "Stop what you're doing. I need to find a guy named Perry Lee who lives on Ferris Avenue in Monona. He's got a criminal record."

Ninja held up a finger. His hands flew. A black and white court document appeared onscreen with full face and profile, vital data, and a list of convictions: aggravated assault, auto theft, rape, possession with intent to distribute, and resisting arrest.

Josh went into his office and picked up his notepad, went downstairs. "He's driving a black and gold 1968 Pontiac Firebird Trans-Am, Wisconsin license plate PL6690."

"Don't you think he's changed that by now?"

"Those cars are rare. There can't be too many rolling around in pristine condition. This one's got a gnome doll glued to the dash."

"Maybe he sold it."

"See what you can find. What am I paying you for?"

"You ain't payin' me."

"Invoice me."

Ninja barked. "Not likely!"

"Well, figure out what you want. Deduct room and board."

"Yeah, yeah. Leave me alone now."

Kayla was dead. Just like Fig, Cass, and Polly Furst. And Bricklin. She was another one, even if she did volunteer to help take down the terrorist training camp. If he hadn't intervened...No. It wasn't his fault. He hadn't killed her. He hardly knew her. It made no sense that Perry Lee would kill Kayla to get at Josh. Nor was it his job to bring her killer to justice. He buried his face in his hands.

"Lord, help me."

Fig laid her muzzle on his thigh. He took her out on the deck and brushed, accumulating enough fur for a scarf or a hat. The weather had taken a turn toward winter with overcast skies and a stiff breeze knocking leaves to the ground.

"Got it!" echoed out the door. Ninja appeared holding a laptop. He set it on the picnic table facing Josh. "Is this it?"

The high-quality image showed a black and gold 1968 Firebird parked outside a Buffalo Wild Wings, the view from a camera mounted on the building. Josh could just make out the gnome on the dash.

"Where?"

"Seven Two Eight Beaver Dam Parkway."

"How old?"

"Twenty minutes."

"Can you come with?"

"Should I bring a gun?"

"No. I want you to record the encounter."

"What else I got to do?"

It was four-thirty by the time they pulled into Pothier Place, the upscale strip mall on Beaver Dam Parkway. The Buffalo Wild Wings occupied a corner slot next to a Red Wing Shoes with a GOING OUT OF BUSINESS banner in the window, a boarded-up storefront, and Walsh Liquors. Josh pulled into a slot a row behind the Firebird and dialed 911.

"What is your emergency?"

"Ma'am, my name is Josh Pratt. I'm a private investigator from Madison. Yesterday, a young woman named Kayla Bissel was found strangled in her apartment in Madison. Her car was stolen. I am looking at that car right now. We are in the parking lot of the Buffalo Wild Wings at Seven Two Eight Beaver Dam Parkway."

"One minute. Please remain on the line."

Hums and clicks.

"Mr. Pratt, could you verify the vehicle's license plate?"

Josh read her the plate.

"Officers are on the way. Please take no action yourself."

Ninja elbowed him and pointed. A baldy in a black leather jacket exited the bar and headed for the Trans-Am. It wasn't Lee.

"Fuck," Josh said to the dispatcher. "Dude's getting in the car."

"Take no action. Officers are on their way."

"I'm going to follow him."

"Sir, this is police business. Do not interfere."

Josh followed several car lengths back, leaving the phone on speaker. "He's headed east on Thirty-Three."

"Sir, do not follow the vehicle. This is a police matter."

They cruised out the commercial strip. McDonald's, Arby's, Carl's Jr., Pizza Hut, KFC, Popeyes, all doing great business because sit-down restaurants had been limited to fifty percent capacity. Flashing lights appeared in the rearview. Seconds later, they were overtaken by three BDPD cruisers. Two tucked in behind the Trans-Am whooping while the third pulled in front. The Trans-Am pulled over into the parking lot of a boarded-up hot tub retailer. No one was buying hot tubs.

Josh pulled in behind them and parked fifty feet away. Four cops swarmed the Pontiac, guns drawn. They weren't wearing masks. The bald man exited the driver's seat, was whirled and cuffed and taken to one of the cruisers. A cop gave Josh a hard look. Josh got out of his vehicle and stood there, waiting for the cop to come over.

The florid, slightly overweight cop's badge said Cooper. "You the guy that called it in?"

Josh had his ID ready. "Yes sir. I knew the murder victim."

Cooper glanced in the Chrysler. Ninja smiled and waved.

"Who's your passenger?"

"My associate is an internet tracking expert. It was he who located the vehicle in Beaver Dam."

"Sir," Cooper said to Ninja, "would you step out of the vehicle and show me your ID?"

Ninja did so. Cooper took their IDs. "Wait here." Cooper returned to his vehicle.

"Who are you today?" Josh said.

"Art Cameron, 2657 Richardson Street, Fitchburg."

"Did you just make that up?"

"No, you thilly. I did it the day after I arrived. I'm a computer consultant. I work for Epic Systems."

They watched while police searched the Firebird, pulling a pistol and a bag of dope from the glove compartment and dropping them in evidence bags. Cooper returned and handed back their IDs. "Dispatch said you knew the victim."

"She was a casual acquaintance."

"Mind telling me why you bothered to track the vehicle?"

"My girlfriend Ray introduced me to Kayla. I felt sorry for her. She had an abusive boyfriend. I'm here to support my girlfriend who believed the boyfriend killed her. But this guy ain't the boyfriend. I never saw him before."

Cooper stared a minute. "All right. We appreciate the assistance, but in the future, once you phone it in, stay out of it. You're putting yourselves and others at risk by chasing him like this." He handed them back their IDs.

"Thank you, officer. Our involvement is over."

"We may want to ask you some questions. How can we get hold of you?"

Josh handed over his card. "May I have yours?"

Officer Cooper gave him his card. They got in the Chrysler and drove to Madison.

CONCURRENTLY

Josh dropped Ninja off on Ptarmigan and drove to Rise Up, where Ray was working with five dancers, three women and two men, thin, inked, and pierced. She excused herself and they went up to her office overlooking the street from the second floor.

"Kayla's killer is a man named Arnold Rennsalaer, a career criminal who served four years in prison for armed robbery."

"I don't understand."

"Neither do I, but we are working with the Beaver Dam police to see where their paths crossed, how he even knew about her. If Perry was involved, we'll find out and I'll turn that information over to the police."

"Can't you just kill him?"

Josh grinned. "Whoa, girl! What happened to respect for all living things?"

"As a favor to me."

"What if Perry had nothing to do with it?"

"He's still a scumbag."

"Agreed, but that ain't my thing."

"You've killed people before."

"How do you know that?"

"I did my research. You led a raid on that terrorist training camp near Dodgeville. Six people died."

Josh spread his hands. He'd gone there for vengeance, for the death of Polly Furst. And because of his actions, Bricklin, one of Nelson's students and a leader in the Madison Women's Self Defense Initiative gave her life.

"God doesn't want me to kill. I try to avoid it."

"Don't give me that God shit."

"I don't require that you believe, but you have to respect my belief."

Ray frowned, then laughed. "You're a riddle wrapped in a mystery inside an enigma."

"I'm a simple man."

"Yes, yes you are. And that's what I love about you. What about that kung fu guy?"

Nelson Ferreira taught Zhong Yi kung fu at his school at 3361 East Washington Avenue. He'd been teaching in Madison for twenty-five years, and had moved three times. Nelson was six feet tall and weighed three hundred pounds. He'd learned kung fu in his native Brazil, and led his team annually to Hong Kong to participate in the Lion Dance Competition. Until the virus.

The governor decreed that all must wear masks in any

commercial establishment and was thinking about requiring them at home. Behind drawn drapes, Nelson led his students in traditional training without masks. Five local martial arts schools had shut their doors due to government regulations. Six gyms had declared bankruptcy.

A health nut, Ferreira preached the gospel of exercise, fresh air, and a sound diet. Because Zhong Yi was beautiful, a third of his students were women. Classes included women's self-defense.

Josh and Ray arrived at eleven in the morning. The school had a closed sign in the window and the door was shut, but it opened even before Josh could touch the handle. Nelson stepped to the side, a massive gray-haired cuddly bear wearing a traditional Chinese kung fu suit. Dark blue with white trim and frog clasps.

"Ray, Nelson."

Nelson placed his palms together and bowed. "How can I be of service?"

"I've always been interested in Eastern martial arts" Ray began, "and I hope to study with you. But what I'm really looking for are kung-fu dance moves for a show I'm putting together, *Kung Fu Musical*."

"Do you have a script?" Nelson said.

"Not yet. I've just started writing. I should have something in a week. I have a list of songs and I'm looking to add more, and I want to have a big dance number where two competing schools are showing off their moves, like *West Side Story*."

"Well, we do a lion dance. Would you like to see it?" Nelson brought out three folding card chairs and set them up in his office. He cued up the flat screen and they were in Hong Kong, revelers lining the streets, bright colors, and here came the crimson, big-eyed lion, six feet dancing. It thrust hither and thither, delighting children and adults until the street suddenly cleared and its path was clear. It faced another lion dance.

The film ended.

"No! It can't end there. What happened?"

Nelson shrugged. "We had a party and we all got drunk."

"It's marvelous, but I want something more trad Broadway. Like Bob Fosse."

Nelson sat bemused.

"*Cabaret! Sweet Charity!*"

"Sorry."

"I will loan you my DVDs. You'll love them. In the meantime, I'd like to sign up. How much is it?"

"Why don't you come take a class and see if you like it?"

"I'm sold, buddy. You don't have to twist my arm."

"We have a class tonight at six, but I'm asking students to park across the street in that Budget Host and use the back door. The governor will shut us down if he learns we're training."

"Oh, the governor wouldn't do that!"

Nelson was as placid as a panda.

"Okay, I can do that."

"Wear loose fitting clothes."

Josh and Ray drove toward the dance studio. "How do you stay open?"

"The Wisconsin Arts Board gave us a grant. I think they put in a word for us. I just hope nobody comes by during a performance and sees people without masks."

"I'm surprised it hasn't happened already."

They pulled up in front of the theater. Ray pulled Josh in for a kiss. "Will I see you later?"

"Can you come over to my place?"

"Can't tonight. I've got a Zoom meeting with some backers."

"You can do that at my place."

"Let me think about it. I'll call you."

He got home at four. Fig woofed him in the door. Ninja was out on the deck wearing earbuds and working on his laptop. Josh stepped in front of him and he looked up startled. He removed the earbuds.

"Arnold Rennsalaer and Perry Lee served concurrently at the Jackson Correctional Institution, 2012 to 2014."

"Ahuh. Maybe I should talk to Perry."

"Maybe you should wait and hear what Rennsalaer says to the Beaver Dam cops."

"Ahuh. I'd like you to put up some cameras in front and back."

"What's wrong with Fig?"

"Fig ain't always here."

"I might have the equipment with me."

"Give me an invoice?"

Ninja grinned. "You know that ain't gonna happen."

Josh called Cooper and left a message. Cooper called back fifteen minutes later.

"Officer Cooper."

"Rennsalaer and Perry served time together."

"How do you know that?"

"My tech guy. You can verify it. Jackson, 2012 to 2014."

"Thank you."

"Listen, there's something you should know." Josh told Cooper about his encounter with Perry.

"You're not going to do something stupid, are you?" the cop asked.

"No. Just thought you might want to talk to Perry."

CHAPTER

58

LOOKIN' FOR A HOME

On Sunday, Josh put on an electric vest and leather jacket and rode to First Baptist Church of Mt. Horeb, an old wood country church with a steeple and a bell. Josh sat in the back row. Pastor John, an aging longhair in shirt and tie, gripped the podium looking out at his congregation. The church was half full, every other seat blocked off for "social distancing."

Half the congregation wore masks. The governor had restricted religious services by executive fiat to ten people. Josh looked around. A hundred people were gathered in the small wood-framed white church, with a bell tower over the entrance.

"Render unto Caesar that which is Caesar's," Pastor John said. "And to God the things that are God's. The Constitution clearly delineates the separation of church and state. In the 1892 case *Church of the Holy Trinity Vs. United States*, Supreme Court Justice David Brewer wrote 'no purpose of action against religion can be imputed to any legislation, state or national, because this is a religious people.' John Adams, one of our Founding Fathers, said, 'Our Constitution was made only for a moral and religious people. It is wholly inadequate to the government of any other.'

"Now here we are, hundreds of years beyond the founding. Are we still a moral and religious people? Can a nation survive when the majority no longer worship God, or even recognize Him? How casually modern man casts aside the hard-won wisdom of the ages. I can't speak for other religions, but Christianity survives because it has something to offer. Christ's love. It does not demand obedience. Except for the Jesuits, of course."

Laughter.

"The United States is at a spiritual crossroads. It has been for decades, but lately it seems as if everything is coming to a head. There are states that will arrest you for attending services. They say it's due to the spread of the virus, and yet these same states turn a blind eye toward the nightly riots."

Josh ate it up. Father John had surprised him. He'd always assumed the old hippy was a liberal. The pastor had changed. How could one live through the events of the past couple of years without changing? The virus had killed their way of life. Josh knew dozens of musicians who were now on welfare, or working for the handful of big box stores that still hired. One only had to walk down State Street to see the devastation wrought not just by the virus, but by the riots.

When the service ended, Josh rode home. Ninja was up

on a ladder mounting something beneath the garage roof. Fig sat at the base wagging her tail and barking.

Ninja came down.

"Can you see it?"

Josh peered up under the eaves. "What am I looking for?"

Ninja grinned. "The hornet's nest."

Josh peered at the dead nest, the size of a softball, vacant since he'd nuked it last year with Raid. "Holy shit."

Ninja picked his laptop up off a green metal chair on the front stoop, opened it and brought it over. The screen showed Josh and Ninja looking down at the laptop.

"I downloaded the program onto your office computer. Just click it on and you can scroll through the feed. There are four cameras, one on each side of the house. It cycles through every five seconds and stores it on your hard drive. I set the hard drive to wipe itself clean once a week. I programmed it to recognize forms and mass, anything bigger than Fig. Something shows up, it sends you an alert."

"Give me an invoice."

"What you got in that gun safe?"

"Ah, no man. You ever ride?"

"Ride what?"

"A motorcycle."

"No. Why?"

"I could sign that Harley over to you."

"Ah no, man. That ain't my thing. Hey, I think I found a place. Landlord's driving up from Janesville to meet me this afternoon. You want to check it out?"

The empty farmhouse sat on two hundred acres in Green County outside Monroe. They passed huge green combines in fields. Numerous fields had been plowed under. They passed long-abandoned barns with sagging roofs, and pastures dotted with Guernsey and Holstein. They pulled onto a dirt road at 4771 West Buckskin Road. The one-story pale green farmhouse with dusty picture windows was similar to Josh's. A new F-150 was parked on the gravel turnaround.

As Josh shut off the engine, a man came out of the house. He was middle-aged with the start of a paunch, wearing gray carpenter's pants and a blue work shirt. Thinning hair surmounted a friendly face.

"Mr. Patterson? Howard Salen," he said offering his hand.

Ninja shook. "How'd you know it was me?"

"Just a guess."

Ninja grinned. "I like him."

"Josh Pratt."

They shook.

"The property belonged to my parents. They farmed potatoes. I've spent the summer fixing it up."

"What do you do with the land?" Josh asked.

"I rent the fields to Monsanto. Come on in."

They entered the house which smelled faintly of dust and lavender. The living room held a worn fabric sofa with lace doilies on the arms, an ancient RCA cathode-ray television beneath a framed Terry Redlin print.

"Three bedrooms, two baths. My sister and I grew up here. We've been coming up here on weekends for thirteen years, my wife and two daughters. Finally had to put Pop in an assisted living facility. Mom passed away nine years ago. Now the kids are all grown up and moved out. This used to be mine."

He opened the door onto a small empty room with a sliding closet door, a Farrah Fawcett poster taped to the wall over where the bed used to be. Another wall held a *Star Wars* poster.

They went next door. "This was June's." The sister's room was bare except for a David Bowie poster. Last was the master bedroom at the end.

"I gave the furniture to the Salvation Army, except this wooden bed frame. Figured anyone who moved in would want their own mattress. Took the box springs to the dump. I never did see the purpose of box springs."

"Yeah, I don't get 'em," Josh said. "Got a futon sits on plywood sits on cinder blocks."

The kitchen had a tile floor, Formica counters, an avocado green Westinghouse fridge and a gas stove. "Everything works. Dishwasher, washer, dryer, garbage disposal. It's eleven hundred a month."

They went out on the rear deck, looked across the narrow pasture to the tree-covered ridge. "It's peaceful out here, except for planting and harvesting. You got coyote, deer, badger, maybe a few bear. Well, the rent's eleven hundred a month, and I got utility bills going back ten years so you can figure your expenses. I'll require a one-month security deposit in addition to the rent."

"It's very nice, Mr. Salen. Can I let you know?"

"Don't take too long. I got another showing this after-noon. What is it you do?"

"I'm an IT guy. I write programs for small and mid-sized companies."

"Got a card?"

"Ah, no, I didn't think to bring one."

They paused for a minute looking around. A cow lowed in a neighboring pasture. A chevron of geese flew by honking.

Ninja thanked him for the show and they headed back to town.

"What was wrong with that place?" Josh said. "Why didn't you snap it up?"

"Mr. Salen was too nice. What happens if my shit blows up out here? I don't want to drag him into it. I prefer to rent from some faceless corporation."

Josh said nothing. As they headed north on Sixty-Nine, Ninja gazed out the window at the rolling hills, the farm-houses, the red barns and silos.

"Don't worry, captain. I'll be out of your hair soon enough."

CHAPTER 59

A BOLD PROPOSAL

They stopped at Woodman's where Josh bought a pork loin and salad fixings. He fed Fig, marinated the pork loin in orange juice concentrate, brown sugar, sesame oil and soy sauce. He called Ray.

"Hi!" she said, breathless.

"What's going on?"

"I've been doing kung fu all day! I'm exhausted! Sensei says I'm a natural."

"Did you figure out your dance number?"

"No, but I learned how to kill man with one blow. *Dim mak*, the death touch."

Josh laughed. Nelson was nothing if not practical. "How'd you like to come over for dinner?"

"What are we celebrating?"

"Dinner."

"Can I shower at your place?"

"What a question!"

"I don't have any clothes."

"I've got clothes."

"You talked me into it."

It was dark when Ray arrived, parking her Prius next to Ninja's van in the driveway. She crouched to hug Fig, stood to hug Josh.

"Ninja's out back grilling the tenderloin."

"How long is he going to be here?"

"He'll be gone soon, I promise."

"What can I do?"

"Play polka music. He hates that."

"No, I mean to help."

"You could make the salad."

They sat at the old stained maple dining room table with the ARC sideboard beneath a framed Jeff Slemons print of Big Daddy Roth style monsters in hot rods. After dinner, Ninja cleaned off the table and did the dishes while Josh and Ray watched the evening news in the living room.

After dinner Ninja went downstairs. Josh and Ray watched *What's Your Problem*, a popular game show in which contestants vied for the most pathetic complaint. The host was a smiling, square-jawed Midwestern type with a tidal wave of brown hair wearing a Brooks Brothers suit. "Good evening, folks, and welcome to *What's Your Problem*, the show where we get down to the nitty gritty of just what is setting you off. Please welcome our reigning champ and major whiner Ramona, the librarian from Scranton!"

A petite woman in a blue dress wearing cats eye glasses strode out waving.

"And let's give a big-problem welcome to our newest contestant, computer programmer Brad Hu from Omaha, Nebraska!"

Hu wore thick black glasses, black hair cut short, a dark blue suit with a slide rule poking out of the pocket. Smiling and waving, he took the podium across from Ramona.

Ninja came up wearing blue jeans, a plaid shirt, carrying a tackle box and a fishing pole.

"Imma go fish."

"Where?" Josh said.

"Monona Bay. I hear that's a good fishing hole for gills and crappies."

"I didn't know you fished," Josh said.

"You didn't know I can play chess either. Mind if I take Fig?"

"You can take her, but keep her on a leash. And don't feed her any fish."

"I don't even eat those fish myself."

Ninja stooped to put a leash on Fig, who wagged her tail excitedly. On television, Brad Hu decried individual fruit labels.

"You want to eat an apple, it takes five minutes to get the label off and sometimes you damage the fruit. Peaches are even worse. Whose bright idea was it to stick one of these labels on a fruit that bruises so easily?"

The audience gave him a seven.

Next up was Ramona from Scranton.

"Ramona," the host crowed, "what's your problem?"

"People who fall asleep at stoplights."

The host fell to his knees and clenched his fist over his heart. "Tell me about it!"

Fig and Ninja left. Seconds later, they heard him rev up the car and head toward town. Josh turned the TV off. Ray swung around to straddle him and they made out like teenagers before Ray got up and led him into the bedroom. While Ray was in the bathroom Josh put on a Smokey Robinson record.

Ray came out wearing a cheerleader's skirt, jumped on the bed, and held Josh down at the wrists, growling like a lion. She planted herself on him and they stared at each other without moving until Josh couldn't stand it anymore and flipped her over onto her back. His phone beeped. He ignored it.

He filled his hands and head with her.

Shuddering, they came. It had never been this good with any of the women he'd been with before, except maybe Fig Newton, and now Ray was clouding her memory.

"I've been thinking," she said.

Uh oh. Duane always told him, "Pussy is like voodoo. It can make a man do anything." He waited.

"Don't you want to hear what I have to say?"

"Go ahead."

"You don't sound very enthusiastic."

"I can't wait."

"Well if you're going to have a roommate, why not me?"

Josh was silent too long. She pulled away and glared.

"What?"

"I'm thinking about it."

"Seriously?"

"I've been thinking about it. All this time, I've always lived alone. It would be a big change for me, but I recognize that you're the girl for me and both our lives might be better if we lived together."

Ray threw herself down on him, smothering him with kisses.

"I want the moment to start when I can fill your heart, with more love and more joy than age or time could ever destroy..." Smoky crooned.

"He'd better not bring those fish back here," Josh said.

Ray swatted him. "What is wrong with you?"

"You look ravishing tonight."

"Better."

There it was. Time to grow up. Be a man, take a woman, spawn. Others had done it. He could do it. She was gorgeous, a hellcat in bed, secure, and self-supporting. On the other hand, she was always pushing that political shit. They hadn't talked religion. She knew where he stood. He thought she might be a nature worshiper. Gaia. Druids. Who knew?

He hadn't shared a bed with a woman in years. Not since Fig. The dog slept at his feet on the bed every night. He could always get a king size.

"Mr. Pratt," a voice hissed from the shadows.

CHAPTER
60

STALLING FOR TIME

Josh pushed Ray behind him and sat up.

"Who the fuck are you?" Ray said.

"His name is Brian Pils. He thinks he's Scipio. I meant to ask you. Why name yourself after some obscure Roman general?"

"He wasn't obscure. You're just not well-educated." Scipio stood in the entryway wearing a black leather jacket that fell to mid-thigh and a black Scheels Auto cap, his face hidden. He held a revolver in his right hand. Josh's guns were locked in the basement. Legally he wasn't allowed to own weapons. He wished he'd kept one in the bedside table drawer. If Ray moved in with him, she could register them in her name.

Scipio hooked a wooden chair with his toe and sat, the gun unwavering.

"What are you mad at me for?" Josh said.

Scipio's smile had a dip in the middle, like Steve Mc-Queen. "You upset my apple cart. I had a nice little thing going until you came along. First, I'll take care of you, and then I'll kill that nigger whose father killed my father."

Scipio never let his followers see this part of him. Josh was afraid. Afraid for Ray and for himself. He was glad Ninja had taken Fig fishing. Ninja would give her a good home. Tectonic plates shifted in his skull.

I am not a victim. Keep him talking.

"Calloway really got to you, huh? It is pretty strange that you have no black people among your followers. Why is that, do you think?"

Scipio showed his teeth, perfect with pointed incisors. "You and the prison shrinks, eh? I'll bet they had a ball with you. I learned a lot in prison. I had the whole library. *Border-line Personality Disorder. The American Psychiatric Association Diagnostic and Statistic Manual of Mental Disorders. The Power of Positive Thinking. Dianetics.* That's where I learned, I learned a lot. Beats the hell out of these college educated Chads and Karens. All these Chads and Karens. They made me rich. All these Hollywood movie stars, living in ten-million-dollar mansions, they never graduated high school. They were easy to snow. They all have deep-seated feelings of insecurity. They know they playact for a living, and they get paid millions. They know the people who pay to see them live McShreveport or Peoria and are happy if they can go to Disney World once in a lifetime."

"I heard Sean Sheen can really fight."

"Sean would have no trouble holding off an aggressive fan. Against even the lowest ranking professional fighter, he would fold like a cheap suit. You're quite the street fighter. Never seen anybody give Halper that much trouble. I wonder how you'd do against me."

"Did you train?"

"I learned in prison. They call it the jailhouse rock. I had a hard time, my first five months. Got reamed out pretty good. I hooked up with the Aryan Brotherhood and in between blow jobs, they taught me pretty good. I knew you were in prison the instant I saw your tattoos."

"How do you think you'd do against the lowest rank professional fighter?"

"Pretty good."

"Let's find out."

"Not in this life."

"You gonna shoot me?"

"I might cut you. I know twelve different ways to kill with a single incision."

"Then what are you going to do? Try to get out of the country? They've frozen all your assets. How much cash can you carry?"

Scipio stood. "Don't worry about it. Let's go downstairs. It's quieter."

He stood in the corner and motioned Josh and Ray to go ahead.

"You mind if I put some pants on?"

"Go ahead. I don't want to look at your junk. You too.

What's her name?"

"Ray," she said, reaching for her panties. They put on underwear and their jeans. Ray pulled a Norton T-shirt off the dresser.

"Let's go."

Ray went first. When she got to the living room she ran to the door, unlocked it, and fled into the night. Josh whirled around, seizing Scipio's right wrist. He smashed an elbow into Scipio's face, got both hands on the wrist, forcing the gun away. Scipio was amazingly powerful. They staggered around the living room, Josh's finger between the hammer and the cylinder. Scipio headbutted him, smashing his nose. Tears filled Josh's eyes and his vision blurred. They staggered back and forth, as if engaged in some primitive dance, knocking over chairs and the coffee table, sending a china plate, brake assembly and drive chain to the floor. The plate shattered.

Josh swung the gun arm, first one way then the other. Scipio used his free hand to reach for Josh's testicles. Josh brought his right knee up and struck Scipio in the ribs, eliciting a gasp. Ray would go directly across the street to the Lowrys. That's where she and Josh had met. Josh prayed they were home. If they were, and she called nine one one, it would be at least fifteen minutes before anyone arrived, out here at the far southwestern corner of the city.

Josh used his height to hook Scipio behind the ankle and bowl him over on his back. Before Josh could get on top, Scipio grabbed the drive chain and whipped it across Josh's face. Scipio got up and kicked Josh in the side of the head, driving him to the hardwood floor. Josh lashed out with his foot, catching Scipio on the calf, causing him to lurch forward. Josh thrust his hips into the air aiming a kick at Scipio's face, but Scipio dodged to the side, reaching for a brass lamp. Josh grabbed a triangular shard of a plate and swiped it across Scipio's calf, drawing blood. The pistol lay under the sofa, a foot in. Josh lunged for it. Scipio leaped in the air and came down with both feet on Josh's back. Josh instinctively rolled away from the sofa, seeing the heel of Scipio's boot descending.

He rolled toward Scipio, tripping him. Scipio fell toward the sofa. Josh sprang up and whirled, but Scipio twisted away squirrel-like and leaned back panting, holding the pistol in both hands.

"Go...in...the basement..." he gasped. "Or I'll shoot... you in the knee...and I'll track down your bitch girlfriend if it's the last thing I do."

Josh put a hand to his face. It came away with blood and grease. "I could make it worth your while. I got cash."

"How much cash?"

"I got half a million dollars in a safe in the basement."

"Show me."

Josh went through the kitchen, turned on the lights and went down into the basement, Scipio five steps behind. Scipio took in the basement with its red shag rug, lurid black light posters of babes on choppers, and the computer table dominating the room. It was warm in the basement and smelled faintly of ozone.

"What is this?"

"I got a tech guy staying here. He'll be home soon."

"Well, we'd better get busy then. Where's the money?"

Josh pointed to the big Liberty centurion beneath one of the basement windows opening onto a rear window well. Scipio motioned toward a door.

"What's that?"

"Utility room. Washer, dryer, heater."

"Get on your knees. Open the safe. Don't pull it open more than one inch or I'll shoot you in the spine. I can't miss from here."

It wasn't as if Josh could reach in and grab a chambered pistol. None of the guns were loaded. He was just stalling for time. He had no cash in the safe. The ceiling creaked softly.

CHAPTER 61

FULL HOUSE

Scipio rushed to the base of the stairs and shut off the light.

"Too late. They'll have seen it through the window."

They heard at least two men moving around the house. They came to the head of the stairs. The lights went back on.

"Whoever's down there," said a strange voice, "come on up or we gas the room."

For an instant there was silence.

"You think we're joking, here's a taste."

Something heavy bounced down the steps and spewed green gas that caused Josh to weep and cover his mouth. He ripped open the door to the utility room, went inside and shut it. He turned on the light. It was a small room containing a washer, dryer, furnace and water heater, with an industrial metal shelf holding power tools.

Scipio pounded on the door. A trickle of gas crept under the edge. Josh ripped open the single window. It wasn't big enough for him to exit.

Scipio shot out the lock. A shard of wood stuck in Josh's cheek. He yanked it out. The door swung inward. Scipio came through, bringing with him the stench of the trench, and shut it, jamming a box of books against it to hold it shut.

"All right," the voice at the top of the stairs said. "We're comin' down. We got masks and we got an industrial fogger. It'll fit under any door. So you can come out now or you can stay in there and choke to death."

"What do you want?" Scipio choked through the door, coughing.

"Where's Ninja?" The voice was just outside now, muffled by a mask.

"Who the fuck is Ninja?" Scipio hissed at Josh.

"I have no idea."

"There's no ninja here! You got the wrong house! Leave now and we won't call the police!"

A white plastic nozzle poked beneath the door.

"Give 'em a blast," a man said.

The nozzle hissed, releasing a cloud of toxic gas that felt like acid on Josh's skin. He yanked the box away from the door and opened it. Two men wearing hazmat suits stood in his basement, one holding an automatic, the other a hand-held commercial fogger. The man with the gun motioned toward the stairs.

"Take it slow. There's a guy in the kitchen waitin' for us."

Josh went first. A thin, cold-eyed man in gray dockers,

black T and gray sports jacket sat at the breakfast table hold-ing an automatic, his phone leaning against a wood napkin holder. He stood, motioning them to precede him into the living room. The basement door slammed shut. While the cold-eyed killer watched them, Josh heard the men taking off their suits. The blinds were closed so he couldn't see if there were lights on across the street. The two men entered the room. One was middle-aged, at least six-two, with massive shoulders and a burgeoning belly wearing a Calvin Klein suit, white shirt open at the collar, gold chain nestled in his spring-like chest hair. The other was younger, face like a ferret, long hair slicked back. he wore a gray suit too.

"Don't lie to me," Johnny Torreo said. "Nobody keeps a computer set up like that unless they're a pro. Where's Ninja?"

"Who the fuck is Ninja?" Scipio demanded.

The cold-eyed man whacked him in the temple with his gun.

"Who the fuck are you?" Torreo said.

"I'm Scipio."

Torreo sneered. "The Roman general? I don't think so."

"His real name is Brian Pils," Josh said. "He's a rapist and a murderer."

"Well, we're looking for Ninja. Where is he?"

"Gone fishing," Josh said.

"At night?"

"It's the best time."

The cold-eyed man drew back his gun. Josh held his

hands up. "It's the truth! He went fishing. I don't know when he'll be back. How'd you find us?"

"Ninja thinks he's the only dude who can trace a phone? I got a guy can track a satellite call to Pluto."

"Listen," Scipio said. "I have nothing to do with this. I came here to waste this motherfucker for sticking his nose into my business."

"Sounds like you and me got a lot in common."

"Damn straight. I'm a wanted man. I'm trying to get out of the country."

"Nobody's going anywhere until we figure this out. Is that spook coming back?"

Josh shrugged. "He comes and goes as he pleases. I may not see him for days."

"Why do I get the feeling you're lying to me?"

"I got nothing to do with you. Ninja said he needed a place to stay. He didn't say why. And I needed a hacker."

"You got any beer?" Torreo said.

"In the fridge. Six pack. Bring it out."

The ferret-faced man returned with a carton of Point. There was silence while each ripped off the caps and drank.

"Tony, go downstairs and take a look at that shit. He left the fuckin' computer on. I think he'll be back soon. See what you can find."

"Johnny, it's like a gas chamber down there. I can't breathe."

"Use the fuckin' mask, numbnuts."

Tony went into the kitchen. They heard him going down

the stairs. He came back up.

"Johnny, there's a big safe down there."

"It's a gun safe," Josh said.

"What's in it?" Torreo said.

"Duh."

"All right, let's open it up."

"Are you going downstairs with me?"

"We'll all go. Pete, you stay here."

"What about me?" Scipio said. "You don't need me. I'll just disappear."

"You're coming too."

Red and blue flashing lights filled the living room through drawn blinds and the door window, followed a second later by heavy pounding.

"OPEN UP. POLICE."

Torreo looked at his boys.

BANG BANG BANG.

Josh strode to the door and threw it open. Three MPDs in vests, guns drawn, rushed into the room. Scipio ran through the kitchen into the back yard. Josh stood in the middle of the room with his hands on his head. Calloway entered wearing a rumpled suit, his badge on his belt and motioned Josh out the front door.

"Did Ray call you?"

"Yes. She's across the street."

Josh looked across the street, up the hill at the Lowrys, who stood outside their front door with Ray, recording on her phone.

"What's going on?"

"Scipio tracked me down. Broke into the house. Ray got away and phoned you guys. About ten minutes later, these guys showed up looking for Ninja. The guy in the suit is Johnny Torreo, some mobster from St. Louis. Ninja doxxed him over a girl. Ninja had to get out of town so he came here. Torreo's still pissed, apparently. Scipio just scrammed through the back door. He's probably cutting through White Oaks right now."

A fusillade of barking from behind the house. Every dog in the neighborhood joined in. Josh worried about Fig. Thank God she wasn't home when Scipio sneaked in.

More police arrived. They separated Torreo and his boys, cops taking them to separate cruisers.

Ray ran down the Lowrys' driveway, across the street, into Josh's arms.

"Thank God," she said. "Thank God."

Three reports echoed from behind Josh's house.

"That came from Phil Bass' house," Josh said.

CHAPTER

62

THE LATE SHOW

Josh buttonholed Calloway. "I know him. I'd like to come along."

"Let's go."

Calloway led two squad cars down the street to the gated entrance to White Oaks.

Josh pointed. Calloway turned onto Verdine drive, a cul-de-sac with three mini-mansions arranged in a semi-circle. Phil Bass, a big man with a wave of silver hair, sat on the stoop outside his house, his newly purchased revolver on the ground in front of him. Priscilla sat next to him, her arm around his shoulder. One of his three garage doors was open

Lights flashing, the cruisers stopped on Bass' brick turn-around. Bass stood with his hands in the air.

"Who fired the shots?" Calloway asked.

"I did. About ten minutes ago, a man broke into our

garage. When I went out to confront him, he threatened me
with a shovel. I only bought this gun for self-protection last
week. I never dreamed it would come in handy."

Josh nodded. "It's all true. I can vouch for Mr. Bass."

Bass gave him a look, part gratitude, part accusatory. This
was the third shooting Josh had brought to White Oaks.

"Are either of you injured?" Calloway said.

"Just shaken up."

Two officers drew their pistols and approached the open
garage door from either side.

"Sorry, Phil. I hate that this keeps happening."

"It certainly is exciting," Priscilla said.

"The home invader is Brian Pils, aka Scipio," Josh said.

Moments later, one of the officers stepped out and drew
a finger across his throat.

"The coroner is on his way," Calloway said.

Bass wiped his forehead with a handkerchief. "We seldom lock our doors. This is a very peaceful neighborhood.
He must have come in through the back garage door, which
opens on our yard."

Josh felt like crawling into a hole. *I was here first.*

Calloway entered the garage. He came out. "It's Pils.
Roger, Brian Pils. What's his hometown?"

"Midlothian or Berwyn," Josh said.

The cop sat in his shop and looked up Pils' record. The
printer chugged out five pages which he handed to Calloway. Calloway glanced at them.

"Nice mug shot."

The picture showed a much younger Scipio with long scraggly hair staring blank-eyed at the camera.

Josh phoned Ninja on his last burner.

"What?"

"How's Fig?"

"She's fine. Listen. We drove by about a half hour ago and kept on going. I would just as soon avoid the police. What happened?"

Josh gave him the condensed version.

"Wow," Ninja said. "I am so sorry, man. I don't know how he found me. He's better than I thought. If I thought for one second I would lead that motherfucker to your place, I never would have come."

"Don't worry about it. It's all for the best. Torreo is in custody and Scipio's dead. When can I have my dog back?"

"Man, there are still cops all over your place. Can I return her to you in the morning?"

"Put her on for a minute."

A moment of silence. "She's here."

"Who's a good girl? Who's a good girl?"

Fig barked excitedly.

"Where will you spend the night?"

"I'll get a motel room. She'll be fine. You know I'll keep her safe. She'll be home tomorrow."

"Yeah, me and Ray may join you. Call me when you get a room. They shot my house full of tear gas or some shit."

"Seriously?"

"Oh yeah. Your boy came prepared."

Calloway stood with hands on hips waiting for Josh to finish. Josh tucked the burner in his pocket. "You need me anymore?"

"Need you to come downtown tomorrow and make a statement. I guess we're finished here, but the crime boys are still going through your house. You can stay at my place if you like."

"Thanks, Heinz, but I think Ray and I are going to take a room tonight."

"Where's Ninja and Fig?"

"Just spoke to them. They're cool."

"I would like Ninja to come down and give us a statement."

Josh clucked. "Rotsa ruck."

"Look. If you know where he is, you have to tell me. Otherwise, you're impeding the investigation."

"I don't know where he is."

Calloway stared at him for a sec, then shrugged. "I'm hanging it up. Can't wait to go fishing."

"Say, Heinz, what do you know about people fishing in the lagoon off John Nolen Drive?"

"It's an old tradition. Many blacks drive over from Milwaukee to fish there. I wouldn't eat any fish caught in the lagoon. Illinois is extraditing your father in the deaths of the Williams family at the Hardison Motel in Rockford. They're picking him up tomorrow."

"Good."

"They lifted his prints off the duct tape you saved."

"I used to wonder what it was like to grow up in a real family with two parents who loved me. Some people are born lucky."

"Tell me about it. You may have to testify."

"That's fine."

"You want a lift back to your place?"

"Let's go."

Josh got in Calloway's car and phoned Ray. "Where are you?"

"I'm across the street. The Lowrys offered us their guest room."

"I thought we'd go to a motel."

"Oh come on, Josh. What's wrong with the Lowrys?"

"They've already done so much for me."

"They want us here. Louise is practically cackling with glee. One of her hookups finally worked out."

"All right. I'll grab some stuff and come over. Are the cops still at my place?"

"Yes. They're down to two cars."

"See you shortly."

Calloway dropped Josh off in front of his house. The front door was wide open and all the lights were on. Josh went inside, where three crime techs wearing bootlets and gloves bagged evidence including the gas canister from the basement. Josh went into his bedroom, got some fresh underwear and his shaving kit, went into his office, closed down all his programs and shut the computer off.

Ray, Dave and Louise sat on lawn chairs on their front

stoop as Josh trucked up the driveway.

"Sorry," Josh said.

"Don't be," Dave said. "Beats watching *America's Got Talent*. You know where the guest bedroom is."

Ray sprang up and hugged Josh. The Lowrys went to bed. Ray and Josh went in the basement. The guest bedroom contained a queen-sized bed attached to a full bath. Ray was all over him.

"Let me get clean."

"No," she said. "I like you dirty."

CHAPTER

63

SIGNS

When Josh and Ray walked across the street Monday morning, Fig greeted them with a fusillade of barks. Josh and Ray knelt and showered Fig with love. Ninja was gone. It was as if he'd never been. The basement was immaculate, his bedding in the laundry hamper, the computer table folded and put in the utility room. The gun safe was untouched. All the dishes were done. A stick-it note on Josh's computer said, "I'll be in touch."

In the kitchen, Ray blinked and swiped her eyes. "What's that smell?"

"Tear gas."

"The cops used tear gas?"

"Not the cops. Johnny Torreo."

"Oh."

Josh phoned Calloway. "Any word on Arnold Rennsalaer?"

"I'll get back to you."

"When's your last day?"

"I'm hanging on until November. The department's short-handed."

Ray showered, put on fresh clothes. "I have to go. We're starting rehearsals today."

"You finished it?"

"Not quite! I'm still stuck on the final act, but I have enough, and I want to get started. Come on by if you get a chance."

"I'll call you."

She kissed him and left. Josh felt terrible about Phil Bass. This was the third shooting in White Oaks and they were all his fault. But he was there first. Josh drove to Woodman's and bought a case of Freixenet. He drove to Bass' house, parking on the curb in front. Police tape ringed the garage. The house was a two-story red brick Georgian with white trim and a three-car garage, the type of house in which a university president might live. There was a *WE BELIEVE* sign in the front yard.

Priscilla answered the door. She was a petite blonde with sharp features.

"Josh," she said. "What's this?"

"It's a case of cheap champagne. It's Spanish, but it has a cork. This is for all the trouble I've caused."

She stepped back. "Come on in."

Josh followed her in and set the case of champagne on the marble counter in their kitchen. Pots and pans hung from the ceiling next to a skylight. The back yard looked out on effusive Autumn color. It looked like a bowl of Trix.

"What happened? You look terrible. What did that guy have to do with you?"

Josh sat at the breakfast nook. Priscilla held up a mug.

"Yes, please."

She plugged in a Keurig and handed him the mug. He added cream and sugar. "You know about Ashley Calloway?"

"Yes. I'm so relieved you found her."

"The guy who broke into your garage last night was the guy who took her. He's just another dime-a-dozen cult leader like Jim Jones or Charlie Manson. He was very successful. Had this big compound up in Colorado. That's where we found her. Did you read about it?"

"Just what I saw on the news. What were you doing there? Wasn't that a matter for the police?"

"Heinz is an old friend of mine. He asked me to look into it."

"Well obviously, you're very resourceful. Our friends are always asking about you."

Josh spread his hands. "I would really prefer a nice normal life. But when someone comes to me with a situation... and especially a friend."

"Would you excuse me for just one minute?"

"Certainly."

Priscilla left the kitchen. A tawny cat wound around Josh's ankles purring. He reached down to scratch its ears.

It leaped up on the bench next to him and crawled into his lap. He gazed out the window at the fall colors, seeing a marble bird feeder and a fieldstone patio. The gas grill was covered with a green tarp.

Priscilla returned with a whiff of perfume. She picked up a mug and slid in opposite him, focusing her vivid green eyes. Was she wearing contacts? She'd freshened her make-up. "It was so bizarre, the way you met Phil's brother Bruce."

"You know, I'd seen his Grand Symphony Sedan on the Square. I'd always meant to go out and take a look at his shop."

"He and Phil could not be more different. We worry about him, living out there all by himself."

"Introduce him to the Lowrys. They'll fix him up."

Priscilla laughed. "That's a good idea. We only see Bruce at Thanksgiving and Christmas. We really should have him over more often."

"I'll check in. See how's he doing. Why don't you fix him up?"

"I don't know any eligible single women. None that would have him. Bruce isn't very tactful. He really doesn't care whom he pisses off."

"I admire that in a man."

"Not like Phil. Phil is the consummate gentleman. He has to be, doing what he does. Being a developer these days takes diplomacy, charm, and a deep understanding of human nature, all of which Bruce lacks."

"Yeah, but he's a genius."

"So they tell me. What's it like, being a private detective?"

"It's boring. I deliver summonses. Mostly, I walk my dog and stay in touch with old friends on the internet. My girlfriend runs a dance theater. They're doing *Kiss Me Kate*."

A furrow appeared between Priscilla's eyes. "You have a girlfriend?"

"The Lowrys introduced us. Ray McRaney. Rise Up Dance Theater. They're doing five more shows. Place is never so filled you have to wear a mask."

"I see. Careful there with Snerdly. He'll cover you with orange fur."

Josh looked down. Cat hair spread around the cat, like pine needles. "I'm used to it. I'll just vacuum off when I get home."

"You know, Josh, I'm always here if you want to talk to someone."

"Thanks. I appreciate that."

"Phil won't be home for several hours."

She laid her hand on his. "I admire what you do very much. Without you, ours would be just another boring neighborhood."

"I would hardly call it boring. I like boring. Mostly, I just want to be left alone."

"I just want you to know, if you want to talk to someone, I'm here."

"Thanks, Priscilla. Hey, I gotta run."

"Of course. I'll see you out."

As they reached the front door, her hip brushed against

his. She put a hand on his arm. "Why don't we have you and your girlfriend over for dinner?"

"That'd be great."

Josh stepped out onto the stoop.

"It was great seeing you, Josh. Drop in any time."

"Thanks, Priscilla."

As soon as the door shut he broke into a sprint. When he got home, he changed into sweats and running shoes and set off at a jog, Fig at his heels. He did two miles, keeping an eye on Fig to see if she limped. When he got home, he showered and put on fresh underwear and shirt, the same jeans, covered with cat fur. He sat on the sofa in the living room and ran the shop vac over his lap while Fig went into the bedroom. She didn't like the vac.

There was a moment there when he was tempted. He bowed his head.

"Thanks, Lord, for giving me strength."

He went into his office and checked his mail.

Unique Pearlz wrote: "Good pm. Is nice chatting with u u have a very nice profile pics."

Vera Felicity wrote: "Hello how are you doing today handsome."

Dominique Rose wrote: "Hello i saw your profile on facebook and i can't stop thinking about you please contact me urgently please."

Letter from Goose. "Saw! What the hell happened? Very sorry to hear about Toad. He was a brother to the end. Goose."

Josh wrote back, giving Goose a brief summary and assuring him that Toad would get a proper send-off. Back in the day, when the Bedouins lost a brother, there was a wild bacchanal with an ambulance standing by. Josh found a local sign company where you could design your own sign and they would deliver.

Josh spent several minutes designing his signs.

CHAPTER

64

PREMIERE

Arnold Rennsalaer told the Beaver Dam police that Perry Lee had contacted him, and offered him an ounce of coke to "take care of his ex-girlfriend." He also told Rennsalaer about the rare primo Firebird, and offered to hook him up with a chop shop in Milwaukee that would pay ten thousand dollars for it. The chop shop shipped automobiles to the Middle East where collectors paid top dollar.

The Dane County District Attorney issued a warrant for Lee's arrest.

Josh went back to delivering summonses, hanging out with Ray, watching her rehearse the troupe. Twenty-four actors were in *Kung Fu Musical*, which was due to open on November 19. *Isthmus* gave it a big write-up. Nelson came by for the dress rehearsal on November 17. Vanessa the Motorcycle Cop rode a Honda Grom with red and blue flashing lights. The show stopper, in the third act, involved a gang fight on skateboards on ramps, ledges, and banisters.

The skating kung fu fighters belonged to the Chop Sock-eys. Facing off against Russel for the first time, they sang, "Who do you think you are, boy? To put yourself on a par, boy? Do you even have a scar, boy? Do you even know how to spar, boy? Have you got the moves that make the grooves, to send the bad guys packing? Do you have the arts to upset carts, or are you sorely lacking?"

Defiant, Russel, played by Nelson's twenty-four-year-old student Art, flips his board up and grabs it overhead, leaps high in the air, placing the board beneath him, lands on it, and sings, "I've been training in the woods, killing my own foods, slabbin' and stabbin', I built my own cabin. I learn from the forest and the owls and the squirrels. Doing lots of squats and using rocks for curls."

Tommy Girl, played by Ray's student Yolanda, takes on four Chop Sockeys while singing "Girl Power." At the end, Russel sails offstage on his board followed by a cacophony of breaking glass, clanging pots and whistles. Josh sat with the Lowrys for the premier. There were multiple standing ovations, people lowering their masks to whistle, and three curtain calls. Josh went backstage for the after-party, found Ray laughing with the woman who played Vanessa, wearing her cute little cop outfit with blue shorts, a short-sleeved blouse, and Wild One hat.

"Josh, this is Kim."

"You were great! Do you ride?"

"No! I never rode a motorcycle until I had to ride that

little thing for the play! Now I love it. I'm thinking of getting one."

"Where'd you get the Grom?"

"I bought it," Ray said. "Four hundred, at Blake's Power Center. Kim, you can have it when we're done."

"You're sure?"

"What the hell. It's not like I pay you anything!"

A balding man with a beard and wire-rimmed glasses approached. "Ray? Marty Garmin from *Isthmus*. Got a few minutes?"

Ray winked at Josh. "Sure, Marty."

Josh walked around backstage. Everyone but he was wearing a mask. Kim handed him a khaki-colored mask that said FRONT TOWARDS ENEMY.

"Here. Figured you'd wear this."

Josh put it on. "How do I look?"

"Like a psycho."

Nelson sat on a bench wearing an XXXL Packers hoodie with a couple of his students who'd been in the play. Josh went over.

"Whadja think?"

"Had everything but a Lion dance. I told Ray that if she did it again next year, we'd be happy to throw it in."

Josh pulled the mask below his chin to quaff beer, then put it up again. Across the backstage area, Ray was now talking to a man in a blue sports jacket, white shirt, and jeans. He caught her eye. She held up a finger.

Fifteen minutes later, she worked her way through the

crowd, hooked her hand in his arm and pulled him toward the back. "Let's blow this popsicle stand."

"Who was the guy in the suit?"

"An agent. Used to work for Ken Adamany. He thinks a studio might be interested. Wouldn't that be great?"

"Interested in what?"

"A movie, silly! He thinks it would be a perfect vehicle for Capucine."

"Who dat?"

"I forget you only watch *Jay Leno's Garage* and that motorcycle show. She's the new hot young thing! She'd be perfect for Vanessa, and Mo knows her agent."

"Mo?"

"Mo Harding, the agent." She handed him a card. They went out the back door, where her Prius was parked.

"Leave your car. I'll bring you back in the morning."

"Okay."

As they walked down the alley toward East Wilson, Josh's phone chimed. Unlisted number.

"Pratt."

"My man, my man."

"Ninja. Where the hell are you?"

"At an undisclosed location. We'll get to that later. I found Perry Lee."

Josh turned away and spoke very softly. "Where is he?"

"He's driving a white Rogue, license plate FLP 20. He just left the Sinclair gas station at East Wash and Fifty-One heading for the capital. I used face recognition tech and he showed up on a security camera. Just wanted to give you a heads up."

"He doesn't know where I live."

"He knows where Ray lives."

"How do you know that?"

"A hunch. He found out from Kayla. He'd want to know."

Ray stood with hands on hips. "What?"

"Ninja thinks Perry's headed to your place."

Ray went white. "Oh my god. What do we do?"

Josh phoned Calloway.

"What's up, Josh?"

Josh told him. "Can you do something?"

"I'll see what I can do, but we're ridiculously short-handed. I was supposed to retire last week and they begged me to stay on until the end of the year."

Josh turned to Ray. "They don't have any men to spare."

"We have to go."

"What? Why?"

"Because he'll break in and kill Sid Vicious. You know he will."

"Are you serious?"

"Please, Josh. You know what it's like. You have Fig."

"I'll go. But you have to stay here. Better yet, go to my place. You know the garage door code."

"I'm coming with you."

"Like hell. How's that gonna help?"

Ray sank into a stance with arm extended, fore and middle fingers straight up, the others curled.

"This isn't a kung fu movie."

"Take Nelson."

Josh grinned. He found the sifu on the same bench. Josh stood behind and whispered into Nelson's ear.

"Hey, would you come with me while I rescue Ray's cat from a scumbag?"

Nelson looked at his watch. It featured a Chinese dragon. "Let me phone my wife."

CHAPTER

65

VACUUMS

Josh parked in the condo parking lot. No white Rogue. Perry wasn't that stupid. He used Ray's security code to enter the building. They took the stairs to the fourth floor. A vertical window looked out from the landing.

"Why don't you wait here and I'll wait in the condo," Josh said.

"What do you want me to do?"

"I guess we'll just hold him for the police."

"But what if the police don't come? You said they were short-handed."

"We'll take him to the police station."

"What if he has a gun?"

"You know, this is probably a stupid idea."

"Maybe we should go."

Josh sighed. "I can't let him kill that fucking cat. I should tell him to just take the cat and we'll call it quits. Do what you gotta. He's not gonna mess with a complete stranger. Act like you live here."

Josh slipped out of the stairwell and let himself into Ray's place with his key. Sid Vicious came up mewing, twining between his legs.

"Oh sure. Now you're all lovey-dovey. C'mere, you little shit."

Josh stooped, picked the cat up and sat on the sofa in the living room with Sid purring in his lap. He'd never spent any time in the living room. A thirty-six-inch flat screen crouched above a cable box with a DVD player on a low wooden cabinet, beneath a framed poster of Mikhail Barishnikov in mid-flight. Another wall held several framed photos of Ray with her troupe, the newest a publicity photo from *Kiss Me Kate*. A small Bose stereo occupied a shelf on a floor to ceiling rig jammed with books, CDs, and DVDs. *White Nights* and *Kiss Me Kate* faced out.

There was a stack of books on the end table next to a lava lamp. Josh picked up *Spark of Hope* by Kathleen Kelly. The cover showed a lissome babe seated behind a bearded, leather-jacketed biker. He laughed. Beneath it was *Ink's Temptation* by Samantha McCoy, *Devil's Henchmen MC Next Generation Book 4*, with a bare-chested tatted bully boy.

"Looks like I came just in time," he said to the purring cat.

There was a key in the door. Josh leaped up, sending Sid squalling. Josh stood behind the door as the key fumbled around. The door swung open, two hands gripping a revolver. Josh grabbed the barrel in his left hand and smashed down on the wrists with his right elbow. He grabbed Perry by the wrist and swung him into the room, tripping him. Perry went down, banging his head on the TV table. As he turned, Josh kicked him under the chin.

Perry sat up and bared his fangs. Nelson filled the door.

"Is there a problem?"

"Not anymore. Let's take this shitbird to the police station." Perry waved his hands. "Wait a minute! Wait a minute. Listen. I know a big score.   How'd you guys like to make a whole lot of money?"

Josh barked. Nelson held his hand out to Perry, who looked at it.

"Come on. Get up."

Perry got to his feet, looked around wildly, ran into the bedroom and locked the door. Josh and Nelson stood outside wondering what to do.

"Man, I hate to smash in her door," Nelson said.

"Where's the fucking cat?"

They looked around. Josh called the cat. A startled squall came from inside the bedroom.

"Fuck! Break it down."

Nelson lunged, planted his size fourteen sneaker in the middle of the door and it popped open. Perry stood on the balcony dangling Sid Vicious by the scruff of his neck.

"Stay back or I drop the cat."

Josh laughed. Perry held the cat over the balcony. "I warned you."

Sid Vicious chomped down on the webbing between thumb and forefinger and clawed up Perry's arm like a ro-to-rooter, painting a red groove from Perry's right eye to his chin, leaped to the balcony and ran into the apartment between Josh's legs.

Nelson grabbed Perry by the neck and got him in a wrist lock. "Come on."

Sid Vicious went behind the sofa and yowled.

"Sid! I take it all back."

They closed Ray's unit, marched Perry to the elevator and put him in the trunk. They drove to the Monona Police Department at 5211 Schluter Road, pulled Perry out and went inside. The desk sergeant, a middle-aged black woman with Adams on her chest looked up.

"What's this?"

"Perry Lee. He's wanted for questioning in the death of Kayla Bissel in Madison."

"And you are?"

"Josh Pratt."

"Nelson Ferreira."

She turned to her computer. A minute later she turned back. "All right. We'll take Mr. Lee. Do you mind telling me how you came to apprehend him?"

"I knew Kayla through my friend Ray McRaney. She runs the Rise Up Dance Studio. I had gone to Ray's apartment to look in on her cat for her, and that's where I encountered Mr. Lee, trying to break into her apartment. Although Lee is not directly responsible for Kayla's death, he contacted Arnold Rennsalaer, a career criminal who served four years in prison for armed robbery. They were prison buddies."

Two Monona PDs came out of the back and took Lee into custody.

Adams looked at Nelson. "What's your involvement?"

"I was just along for the ride. We're old friends."

"I see. May I see some identification?"

An officer Marquesa, dark-complected with a hairline mustache, interviewed them in a conference room. Josh walked him through it, from Ray's appeal, his first encounter with Perry Lee, the black Firebird, the murder, Beaver Dam, and the capture.

Josh's phone buzzed. Ray. He held up a finger. "I have to take this."

"What's going on?"

"Be back in about an hour, babe. We got him."

"Thank heavens! I was so worried."

"Nothing to it. Can't talk right now. Talking to the Monona cops."

"Can't wait to see you! Do you know anything about these signs?"

"My yard signs?"

"Yes. They were sitting on the stoop when I got here."

"Yeah, I ordered them."

"I put them out in the yard. Is that all right?"

"That's great, babe. See you soon."

Ray made kissing noises. They finished the interview.

Josh and Nelson stood.

"Try to stay out of trouble, would you Mr. Pratt?" Marquesa said.

Josh dropped Nelson off at his car at one in the morning. It was one forty-five by the time he pulled into his own driveway next to Ray's Prius. Fig barked. Ray squealed.

Three yard signs stuck up from his front lawn.

The first one read: "FIG PRATT SAYS NO TO VACU-UMS. They're loud and they freak him out."

The second: "FIG PRATT WANTS YOU TO KNOW, someone rang the doorbell. And he is prepared to bite them if you need, especially if they are wearing a hat."

The third: "FIG PRATT HATES SQUIRRELS. Those thieving punks are everywhere."

The door opened. He spread his arms for his dog and his woman.

A LOOK AT: FLORIDA MAN BY MIKE BARON

MIKE BARON DELIVERS A RIOTOUS, HEART-FELT AND ULTIMATELY UPLIFITING STORY IN FLORIDA MAN.

Gary Duba's having a bad day. There's a snake in his toilet, a rabid raccoon in the yard, and his girl Krystal's in jail for getting naked at a Waffle House and licking the manager.

Gary's a redneck living in a trailer by the swamp. But he's got dreams, big dreams. Every time he tries to get ahead, fate deals him a low blow. But then he gets lucky…

With his best friend, Floyd, Gary sets out to sell his prized Barry Bonds rookie card to raise the five hundred needed for bail. But things always find a way of getting out of hand.

"Florida Man will make you laugh out loud. It's sui generis."

AVAILABLE NOW

ABOUT THE AUTHOR

Mike Baron is the creator of Nexus (with artist Steve Rude) and Badger two of the longest lasting independent superhero comics. Nexus is about a cosmic avenger 500 years in the future. Badger, about a multiple personality one of whom is a costumed crime fighter. First/Devils Due is publishing all new Badger stories. Baron has won two Eisners and an Inkpot award and written The Punisher, Flash, Deadman and Star Wars among many other titles.

Baron has published ten novels that span a variety of topics. They have satanic rock bands, biker zombies, spontaneous human combustion, ghosts, and overall hard-boiled crimes.

Mike Baron has written for The Boston Phoenix, Boston Globe, Oui, Fusion, Creem, Isthmus, Front Page Mag, and Ellery Queen's Mystery Magazine.